Also by Cathy O'Neill

The Princess Revolt

Unraveled

the Tapestry of Tales

By Cathy O'Neill

Aladdin

New York   London   Toronto   Sydney   New Delhi

ALADDIN
An imprint of Simon & Schuster Children's Publishing Division
1230 Avenue of the Americas, New York, New York 10020
First Aladdin hardcover edition March 2023
Text copyright © 2023 by Cathy O'Neill
Jacket illustration copyright © 2023 by Sarah Mensinga
All rights reserved, including the right of reproduction in whole or in part in any form.
ALADDIN and related logo are registered trademarks of Simon & Schuster, Inc.
For information about special discounts for bulk purchases, please contact Simon & Schuster Special Sales at 1-866-506-1949 or business@simonandschuster.com.
The Simon & Schuster Speakers Bureau can bring authors to your live event.
For more information or to book an event contact the Simon & Schuster Speakers Bureau at 1-866-248-3049 or visit our website at www.simonspeakers.com.
Jacket designed by Karin Paprocki
Interior designed by Mike Rosamilia
The text of this book was set in Bodoni Egyptian Pro.
Manufactured in the United States of America 0123 FFG
2 4 6 8 10 9 7 5 3 1
CIP data for this book is available from the Library of Congress.
ISBN 9781534497771 (hc)
ISBN 9781534497788 (pbk)
ISBN 9781534497795 (ebook)

For Rose

the Tapestry of Tales

Chapter 1

I N THE DAYS WHEN WISHING WAS STILL OF SOME use, a king's son was enchanted by an old witch and shut up in an iron stove in a forest. There he passed many years, and no one could deliver him. Then a king's daughter who was lost herself came into the forest, and after she wandered about for nine days . . ."

Romy looked up from the Brothers Grimm book and made a face. She was lying on my bed, elbows bent, with her chin resting on the palms of her hands.

"What is wrong with the girls in this book?" she asked, tapping a finger on the page and swinging her

legs behind her. "They're always getting lost in forests."

"Maybe this one's actually going to rescue the prince? And it's just taking a while?" I suggested, though I knew it was a long shot. Romy and I were halfway through the 203 stories in the Brothers Grimm book, and so far, the most exciting thing a girl had done was shear a sheep.

I sighed and stared at the pile of clothes I was sorting through, wondering what to wear for the first day of eighth grade. It felt nice to think about something other than the fact that I'd read hundreds of pages of fairy tales over the summer and still hadn't found what I was looking for.

I spotted the putrid-green T-shirt Romy had brought back from Italy for me in the jumble of fabrics and, grinning, threw it at her.

"I'm never going to wear this. I said I wanted to wear brighter colors this year, not look radioactive!"

"Radioactive would be a great look for you," said Romy, laughing as she caught the T-shirt and threw it back to me.

We both jumped when Mom knocked on my bedroom door. "CIA! ROMY! It's seven thirty!"

"The book," I hissed at Romy, a bubble of panic rising inside me. "Hide it!"

Romy shoved the book under a pillow just as my mom opened the door a fraction and peeked in.

"Come on, you two. Don't be late on your first day back."

Mom looked at the makeshift bed Romy had put together on the floor and winced. "Did you sleep okay on that?" she asked.

"Totally fine, Mrs. Anderson," said Romy, stifling a yawn. Actually, we'd stayed up most of the night talking, so neither I nor Romy had slept much. She'd come over right after getting back from a three-week European cruise with her family—which sounded like it had been amazing—and I'd been away at camp since the beginning of the month, which had been awful. The camp hadn't allowed phones, so Romy and I had a lot to catch up on.

"We'll be right down," I said, reaching under my bed for my sneakers. I hoped Mom wouldn't notice the squeak in my voice or the way Romy kept checking that no part of the book was poking out from under the pillow.

"I made chocolate chip pancakes. Back-to-school

eighth-grade special," said Mom, still standing in the doorway. She didn't like cooking and hardly ever made breakfast, but when she did it was pancakes, and they were always really good. She finally closed the door and shouted "Get them while they're hot!" as she went down the stairs.

Romy waited a moment, then reached under the pillow and pulled out the Brothers Grimm book.

"I still can't believe your mom would freak out if she saw you reading this," she said, frowning as she stared at the navy-and-gold cover. In the middle of the illustration, there was a castle perched on a hill, and in the corners, there were fairies, each one carrying a wand and trailing fairy dust. The picture was way off, as there weren't a lot of fairies in the book, and we'd yet to find any mention of fairy dust. "You'd think it was a pack of cigarettes or something."

Romy shrugged and put the book in her backpack. "I just don't get it, Cia," she continued. "Why won't she just talk to you? She knows that you know fairy tales are real."

"Shhh," I said, wanting Romy to lower her voice. My little brother, Riley, was probably downstairs devouring pancakes, but he might still be in the bedroom next door, and I didn't want him to hear what we were talking about.

"I don't know what her problem is," I admitted, feeling frustrated. "She just keeps telling me it's too 'dangerous.' That I need to focus on school and forget about magic and fairy tales."

"Yeah, right!" sputtered Romy, stopping midway through brushing her hair, as if the eye roll she was giving me required all her energy.

I couldn't blame her—I felt like rolling my eyes too. After everything that had happened, there was no way we could just forget about fairy tales. Before the end of seventh grade, I'd stopped needing to sleep, been kidnapped by Snow White (and she'd been just *one* of the fairy-tale characters who had been out to get me), and turned John Lee, the boy I liked, into a beast. All thanks to a spell gone wrong, cast by a rogue fortune-teller/fairy godmother—I still wasn't completely sure who, or what, Madame Fredepia was. We'd managed to break the spell, and my mom, who I learned knew all about magic and fairy tales being real, had told me that everything would go back to normal.

And things had gone back to normal. Which had felt fantastic after having to worry about fairy-tale characters trying to kill me, maim me, or turn me into a mermaid. The first month of summer vacation had been great. I'd been lazy, played board games with Riley, taken family trips to the beach, and read. But then I'd gone to camp for two weeks. . . .

As I tied my sneakers, I thought about what had happened at Camp Killary. It was a place that—according to its brochure—"shows girls how to strive to be their best selves." I hadn't cared about the striving part—it had only been a couple of months since I'd escaped from two fairy-tale villains, negotiated with a third, and saved Riley's life, so I'd been feeling pretty good about myself—but the camp had looked really pretty, on the shores of a lake in Maine, and the swimming, archery, pottery, dance, and climbing had all sounded like a lot of fun. So when Mom had suggested that I go, I'd said yes.

The first night, we were all sitting around the firepit roasting marshmallows when Brianna, one of the camp counselors, told us we'd be having an icebreaking session. Then she'd asked me the first question.

"What's the latest you've ever stayed up at night?"

My heart had started racing. The marshmallow I'd just eaten felt like it was turning into a lump of lead in my stomach.

What was the latest I had ever stayed up at night?

All the girls turned to look at me, and most of them started giving me friendly smiles, like they knew how uncomfortable it felt to be the first to have to speak up in a group. They didn't know that the reason I was blushing, the reason I was staring into the fire, the reason I couldn't speak, was because my answer to that question—a question that every other girl around that firepit could have answered easily—was that the latest I had ever stayed up at night was fourteen days. How could I tell everyone that I'd once stayed awake for 336 hours?

Brianna saved me by moving on to the next girl, who said that she'd once stayed up all night watching movies. As soon as I heard her answer, I felt annoyed with myself. Why hadn't I just said something like that? I got ready for Brianna's next question, determined that, this time, I was going to act like everyone else. A normal thirteen-year-old girl.

But then she asked me this:

"What's something you don't have in common with anyone else?"

What's something I don't have in common with anyone else?

Before I knew what I was doing, I had let out a loud snort. I pressed my lips shut to hold back the laughter that I could feel fluttering in my chest. I was starting to feel hysterical. What's something I don't have in common with anyone else? I've been spelled. I've met fairy-tale characters. I've had tea with Cinderella's stepmother and stepsister. I turned the only boy I ever had a crush on into a beast, went to visit him in the hospital, and told him he was disgusting. I traded ten years of youth for a spell-breaking candy that was eaten by a sea lion in the middle of a storm whipped up by the Sea Witch.

All the girls were staring at me. A few of them were still giving me sympathetic smiles, but most of them looked confused. I noticed a girl who had complimented the mug I'd made in pottery class lean over and mutter to the girl sitting beside her. I couldn't hear what she said, but in my imagination it was *What's wrong with her?* or, *I'm glad she's not in our cabin.*

I had the urge to blurt out the truth, but I knew that if I started talking about my close encounters with fairy-tale characters, everyone would think I was just trying to get attention or acting like a jerk. I tried to come up with an answer that would make me sound normal, but my brain seemed to have stopped working. So, I mumbled something about having a stomachache and ran back to the cabin.

Then for the next two weeks, Brianna made a big show of saying hi whenever she saw me, as if I had a flashing sign above my head that read NEEDS HELP. SOCIALLY AWKWARD.

It. Was. Horrible.

"Come on, Cia. I'm starving," said Romy, cutting through my thoughts. "I want breakfast."

"You go on," I said. "I'll be there in a minute."

I had an icky, uneasy feeling, and all of a sudden the idea of pancakes made my stomach turn. The feeling that I'd had at camp, that I just didn't fit in anymore, washed over me. And the thought that I'd been trying to ignore ever since that first night in Maine came rushing into my head. What if being spelled and crossing paths with fairy-tale characters made me weird, and not, as Romy kept telling me, cool? What if the reason Mom kept refusing to answer my questions about fairy tales was because she knew that what had happened to me was weird, and the danger she kept telling me about was the danger of me being discovered as . . . as what?

The reason I kept asking Mom about magic and fairy tales, the reason I was reading the Brothers Grimm book and whatever other fairy-tale-related material I could get my hands on, was because I wanted to understand what had happened to me. Why it had happened to me. And whether it might happen again. And part of me—I hadn't even told Romy about this—part of me was hoping that I'd read about someone else who had been spelled and dragged into the lives of fairy-tale characters. I wanted to read about someone like me.

I wanted to know that I wasn't alone.

Chapter 2

AFTER BREAKFAST, DURING WHICH RILEY gave a detailed description of the new monkey bars and swing set he'd seen at his elementary school (I missed the days when I'd get excited about a playground makeover), Romy and I went to the garage to get our bikes.

Romy immediately rode out onto the street, but I took a minute to look over my bike. Just to make sure nothing magicky was going on. My bike had been turned into a pumpkin around the same time the effects of Madame Fredepia's spell had kicked in; the frame was still a deep orange color, and every time I added air to the tires, I got

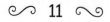

sprayed with pumpkin seeds. But it looked like the pedals and wheels and everything worked fine, and I couldn't see any new changes, so I threw my backpack into the basket and hopped on.

By the time Romy and I pushed our bikes into the stands at school, I was starting to feel better, minus the normal first-day-back nervousness. No one at Hill Country Middle School knew anything about my fairy-tale adventure, after all. Well, almost no one. Romy knew everything, but she wasn't going to tell anyone, and there was John Lee, who didn't know all the details but still knew that I had been responsible for turning him into a beast at the end of seventh grade.

I felt pretty sure, though, that the last thing John wanted to do was talk about me. A week before I'd left for camp, I'd been behind him in line at Yo-Yo Swirl—the frozen yogurt place near school—and when he'd seen me, he'd jumped, spilled raspberry Froyo down his T-shirt, and run off like I'd just tried to electrocute him.

"Hi, guys!" Raul Sheldon had appeared in front of us and was grinning and looking like he was dying to tell us something.

While Romy and I locked our bikes, I smiled and said, "What's going on, Raul?" Raul always knew—or at least, always acted like he knew—what was going on.

"So, we're getting a new science teacher . . . ," he began, leaning in closely and glancing around as if he wanted to make sure no one else could hear. Even though he'd probably already told half the eighth graders. "She used to be in some kind of a cult. . . ."

"A cult?" I repeated, picturing people wearing robes and standing in a circle chanting.

"That's the rumor anyway," said Raul knowingly.

"That you probably started," said Romy, raising her eyebrows and grinning at Raul. Whenever a new teacher came to Hill Country Middle School, Raul would throw out some wild theory about what'd they been up to before they started teaching. Spying for the CIA. Landscape gardening for the queen of England. Working as a stunt double.

"Just wait till you see her," said Raul, giving Romy a significant look and putting up his palms. "Then you'll know what I'm talking about. I'm telling you she's strange." He drew out the last word so that it came out as "straaaaaaange."

The bell rang.

"That's class in five minutes," announced Raul, picking up his pace as the three of us walked toward the school entrance.

"Oh, I left my water bottle by the bike stand," said Romy. "I'll catch up with you inside." She took off running.

"Hey." Raul stopped midstride and turned to face me. "I almost forgot. You're entering the competition, right?"

Competition?

"I don't really care about meeting that Elvira Queen lady, but it would be so cool to go to Paris."

Raul was so excited and spoke so fast that I was sure I had misunderstood what I'd just heard. He couldn't be talking about *the* Elvira Queen, could he?

"Elvira Queen?" I said, my heart starting to pound in my chest. "The woman who owns that company Forever Young? She's running a competition?"

"Yeah," said Raul, holding the door to the school entrance open. "Her. And she's looking for kids with empathy and courage and that kind of stuff. . . ."

I walked away from Raul, stepping into the crowd of students looking for their lockers and high-fiving friends. I didn't want him to see how worried I was.

I'd met Elvira Queen. I knew that she wasn't just the CEO of an international skin care company; she was *the* Evil Queen. She was Snow White's power-hungry, looks-obsessed stepmother. Why was she trying to get kids to Paris? What did she want with a bunch of middle schoolers?

What was going on?

At my first class of the day—English—I grabbed a seat beside Mia Johnson. If Elvira Queen was running a competition, Mia would know all about it. She loved makeup, bought all the newest eye shadow palettes as soon as they came out, and knew the names and products of skin care companies the way other girls knew the names and music of their favorite bands.

"Hey, Mia, did you have a good summer?" I asked. I hoped I sounded casual and that she didn't notice that I was clenching my fists.

"Pretty good," she said. Her eyelashes were blue, green, and pink—I never knew mascara came in different colors. It looked really pretty and made me wonder if I should have worn the green T-shirt after all, instead of the gray one I'd chosen. "How about you?"

"Good," I said, crossing my arms and leaning my elbows on the desk. I had to focus. Get right to the point. "So, have you heard anything about a competition that Elvira Queen is running?"

"Yeah," said Mia excitedly. Seeing her reaction, the hope I'd had that Raul hadn't really known what he was talking about disappeared. Mia gave me a sympathetic smile. She must have thought that the look on my face was from disappointment, not fear.

"It's okay," she said. "The deadline isn't until five o'clock tomorrow—you just send in a video about your talent. You can still enter."

Mrs. Greene, our teacher for the period, walked into the classroom. She'd taught most of us English in sixth grade, so she didn't waste any time on introductions. Instead she got right to it, turning her back to us and writing on the board.

"Have you," I whispered, trying to get the words out before Mrs. Greene turned around, "entered?"

"You bet I have," said Mia, grinning. "I sent in a submission for creativity and another one for working under pressure."

I nodded. I'd seen Mia curl eyelashes, conceal zits, and find just the right shade of lipstick in the time it took to walk from one classroom to another. She was definitely creative and knew how to work under pressure.

Would Elvira Queen select Mia? I didn't want any of my classmates near that horrible woman. None of them, other than Romy, knew that she was Snow White's step-mother. None of them knew that before she had recreated herself as the CEO of a skin care empire, she had ordered a huntsman to kill her stepdaughter and that the hunts-man had returned and tricked her with the lungs and liver of a deer, which she had eaten. That was the worst part of the "Snow White" story, a detail that had been on my mind the whole time I was in Elvira Queen's office. It still made me feel sick.

"She's just so beautiful," gushed Mia, sounding star-struck. "And so smart . . . she won the Nobel Prize. And she's stylish. . . . Have you seen her clothes?"

"Mmm . . . ," I said, wondering how beautiful and stylish Mia would think Elvira Queen was if she knew about the liver/lung-eating. I shuddered and looked around the classroom, wondering who else had entered the competition.

I accidentally caught John Lee's eye from where he was sitting three desks over. I'd been so focused on talking to Mia that I hadn't even noticed we were in the same class. That would never have happened last year. For all of seventh grade, I'd had a John Lee detector in my head—if he'd been within a hundred feet of me, I would have known it. My heart would start racing, my mouth would go dry, and I'd start blushing. It was so embarrassing, but maybe embarrassment was better than the guilt and fear I was feeling now. What if John still had side effects from being a beast? My bike was orange now and spat out pumpkin seeds, so what if John still had huge hairy feet and gross toenails? (He was wearing sneakers, so I couldn't see what was going on under his socks.) And what if he started telling people at school that I'd turned him into a beast? What if Raul found out? My close encounters with fairy-tale characters would be all anyone would be talking about. It would be horrible. And not just for me. What if people started calling John a freak?

John looked away quickly, his eyes locked on Mrs.

Greene as if her explanation of Shakespeare's rhyming couplets was the most fascinating thing he'd ever heard.

I looked down at my notebook for a moment, and when I peeked back over at him, he was staring straight ahead and clenching his jaw so tightly that a vein in the side of his neck was bulging out. He looked terrified. Was he terrified because I was sitting three desks away from him? Was John Lee that scared of me? My stomach twisted with—shock? Anger? Disappointment? I couldn't tell. For a moment I wondered if John being scared of me made it more or less likely that he would tell people about what I had done, then I immediately felt guilty for thinking that John being terrified of me might be a good thing.

"Cia," snapped Mrs. Greene, rapping her knuckles on my desk. "Pay attention . . . or do you already know everything there is to know about William Shakespeare?"

"Sorry," I muttered, sitting up straight and looking at the whiteboard. I sighed. It was going to be a long day.

Although John wasn't in my next two classes, I still couldn't focus on what the teachers were talking about. Was it going to be like this for all of eighth grade? John acting terrified just because I was in the same room as him? John refusing to look at me, like I was that Greek woman Medusa, whose stare turned men into stone?

I wondered what John would do if I just went up and started talking to him. That's what Romy had suggested I do, after I'd told her about him running out of Yo-Yo Swirl. She'd also suggested that I explain to him exactly how, and why, he'd been turned into a beast. Just share all the details about Madame Fredepia and being spelled and crossing paths with fairy-tale characters. The way Romy saw it, John needed an explanation. Part of me knew that she was right, but just the thought of having that conversation made me feel sweaty and uncomfortable. I'd have to tell him about the crush I had on him. A crush that was so huge, it was powerful enough to turn him into a beast. How would I explain that?

Occasionally I took a break from thinking about John and wondered why the Evil Queen was holding a talent competition. My mind kept pinballing between intense guilt—was it my fault that John was acting like a nervous wreck? (It totally was.)—and stomach-churning anxiety: what was the Evil Queen up to?

By the time lunch arrived, I was exhausted and jumpy and starving.

Romy and I filled up our trays, then grabbed a table in the quiet corner of the cafeteria. It was close to where the teachers usually sat, so most students avoided it.

"I finished that 'Iron Stove' story," said Romy, tearing a bread roll in half. "At the beginning of history. Mr. Gossett was late," she added, answering the question I was about to ask. "It was really good. The princess actually rescues the prince for a change. She goes over a glass mountain and a lake and disguises herself as a maid—"

"Mmm," I said absently, scanning the cafeteria for John. An awful thought popped into my head. What if, in an effort to avoid seeing me, John wouldn't even come into the cafeteria? I pushed away an image of him sitting on the toilet in a restroom stall, eating a sandwich. I needed to focus on something else anyway. Something that was more important than me feeling guilty and John feeling terrified.

"This thing with Elvira Queen, do you think a lot of students have entered it?" I asked Romy, assuming that someone had already told her about it. "Mia told me she's entered for creativity and working under pressure."

"Yeah," said Romy, nodding. "That figures. The categories are pretty cool, actually. Gavin just told me that his submission is for bravery."

Gavin had rescued me from a pigeon attack last semester. Everyone else, including the teacher, had panicked and either hidden under tables or run out of the classroom, but Gavin ran straight into the birds and saved me. I guessed that counted for bravery.

"He is really brave," said Romy, nodding and biting her lower lip.

"What do you mean?" I asked. Romy looked so serious; she couldn't just be talking about Gavin rescuing me with the fire extinguisher last year.

"His mom is really sick," she said softly. "Mia told me. Her mom and Gavin's mom are friends. So, she's, like, really sick. . . . She's been in the hospital since the middle of the summer. She might . . ." Romy trailed off. She wouldn't finish the sentence, but I could guess what she was going to say.

"That's horrible," I said, scanning the cafeteria for Gavin. He was sitting with a group of boys, laughing at something someone had said. Romy was right—he was brave. It would be so hard to come to school and just act like everything was okay, when really you were terrified that your mom might be dying. "Poor Gavin."

For a moment Romy and I sat in silence.

"Anyway, I found the rules," said Romy, looking down at her phone. "Only thirteen-year-olds can apply. There's a list of special skills that"—she glanced up at me and raised an eyebrow—"Elvira Queen wants to showcase, like . . . focus, loving to read, persistence . . ."

"So, none of the usual talent-show stuff then?" I asked, pushing away my mac and cheese. I wasn't hungry anymore.

"Oh, she's looking for that too," continued Romy. "Singing and dancing and performing magic tricks—"

"And what's the prize? A lifetime supply of face cream?" I asked, thinking of Willy Wonka.

"Let's see," muttered Romy, creasing her forehead. "Elvira Queen will pick ten submissions. Those ten kids get a private tour of her European headquarters and get to fly to Paris on her private plane." She paused and looked up at me. "That's cool."

I nodded. That would be cool, minus the whole evil fairy-tale character thing. Although less so for Romy, as her family actually had a private plane. Most of the time I forgot about how rich Romy's family was, but then something like private planes would come up in conversation and I'd remember that they had about a gazillion dollars.

"What do you think is going on?" I asked Romy. "Why is she doing this?"

"I don't know," said Romy, putting her elbows on the table and resting her chin on the palms of her hands. "Maybe it's all part of some advertising thing for her company. . . ."

"So, more people are going to buy her five-hundred-dollars-an-ounce creams because she runs a talent competition for middle schoolers?" I shook my head. "That doesn't make any sense."

"What do you think though, Cia?" Romy said, giving me a big grin. "Let's enter this thing. I could submit something for optimism, and you can enter for creative problem-solving. You're so good at that. Come on! We'd totally make the cut. Imagine the two of us in Paris!"

"No way," I said firmly. "There is no way we're

entering." I lowered my voice. "She's the EVIL QUEEN."
I glanced around the cafeteria, noticing that everyone
seemed extra excited today, even for the first day of
school. Vikram Rawie was slapping spoons against the
sides of his legs, and a seventh-grade girl was trying to
juggle plastic plates. I felt like I was watching the opening
scene of a horror movie. What if someone ended up going
to Paris? What would happen to them? What would the
Evil Queen *do* to them?

"Yeah," said Romy, nodding. "But we can—you can—
totally handle whatever the Evil Queen throws at us, Cia."

I shook my head. Romy was always doing this.
Overestimating how good I was at something and under-
estimating how scary something could be. "No way,
Romy."

The one and only time I'd met the Evil Queen, I'd been
terrified. I'd barely managed to string a sentence together.
There was no way I wanted to see her ever again. And I
didn't want Romy to meet her either. Looking around the
cafeteria, I realized I didn't want *any* of my classmates to
meet her. Just the thought of it made me queasy.

I sighed.

"You have any classes with John?" asked Romy, taking a sip of water.

I sighed again and groaned. "English."

I filled her in on how panicked he'd looked, which wasn't fun to think about, but I was happy to get a break from worrying about the Evil Queen and thinking about Gavin. He had a loud laugh, and every time the sound reached our table, my heart dropped as the thought of his mom being so sick popped back into my head.

"Do you still like him?" asked Romy. The expression on her face—she was wrinkling her nose—made me think that she thought I couldn't possibly still like John.

"No," I began. "I mean, I don't know. I don't think I like him anymore. I just feel guilty whenever I see him. You can't like someone if just seeing them makes you feel bad."

Romy nodded and took a bite of her sandwich. "You need to tell him what actually happened, Cia," she said. She gave me a firm look. "All he knows is that he ended up in the hospital because he was . . ." She flared her nostrils, puckered her lips, and beat her chest.

"He didn't turn into a gorilla," I hissed.

"You know what I mean," continued Romy, shrugging her shoulders. "He ended up in the hospital, then he was fine, then he came with me to get you at Snow White's house . . . but"—she paused to take a bite of her apple—"he didn't know that it was Snow White's house. . . . Then there was the kissing thing." She chewed and swallowed. "And then he turned into a beast again. . . ."

"I know all this," I interrupted, wincing at the memory of kissing John in the basement of Snow White's cottage. That had been excruciatingly embarrassing. Romy didn't need to give me a detailed recap of what had happened, especially not at school where someone might overhear.

"Yeah, *you* do," said Romy. "But John doesn't know *why* that stuff happened to him. So he's still freaking out. You have to explain it to him, Cia."

We sat in uncomfortable silence for a moment, Romy finishing off her apple and me staring at the table.

"What are you so worried about?" asked Romy softly. "He's going to believe you. The guy was turned into a beast."

Was I worried that John wouldn't believe me?

No, it wasn't that.

I was worried that John would think I was weird. I was worried that John would think there was something wrong with me. I was worried that John would think that if I'd been spelled once, I might be spelled again.

Because I was worried about all those things too.

The bell rang. Afternoon classes were about to start.

"Hey, we've got science," said Romy, picking up our trays. "Let's see what Raul was talking about."

Chapter 3

FOR ONCE RAUL HAD NOT BEEN EXAGGERATING.

I'd never seen anyone who looked quite like our new teacher.

She was sitting on a stool in the science lab, smiling at all the students as we entered. Everyone did a quick double take as they passed her, because she was wearing an unbelievable amount of clothes. It looked like she had pulled every single thing she owned out of her closet and decided to wear everything at once.

I looked around the class, and Gavin motioned at me to go join him. Ever since he'd rescued me from that

pigeon attack, he had insisted on sitting next to me when-ever we had class together, like I needed a bodyguard. It was a little bit annoying, but also sort of sweet.

"Hey, Gavin," I said, sitting down beside him. I almost started to ask how his summer was—because that was the way every conversation with my classmates had started today—but then I stopped myself. Gavin's summer must have been terrible. Should I say, *Sorry to hear about your mom*? Or would that be the worst thing to say? Maybe he just wanted to be at school and not think about his mom. . . .

"Hi, Cia," he said, pulling his notebook toward him to make room for my stuff. Maybe I was imagining it, but he seemed thinner, even smaller, than he'd looked at the end of seventh grade. "Thanks for saving me a seat," I said, wondering—and feeling a stab of shame—if I'd ever actually thanked him for all the times he'd saved me a seat before. "That's really nice of you."

"Sure."

He gave me a small smile and shrugged.

Romy sat down on the other side of me, saying hi to Gavin as she pulled in her chair.

Gavin gestured at our new teacher. "What's going on with her? Isn't she hot in all those clothes?"

I looked up at the woman sitting on the stool and wondered the same thing as Gavin. How was she not sweating? She was wearing a pencil skirt that stopped a few inches short of her ankles, which meant that we could all see the jeans she was wearing underneath, and the huge red basketball shoes that looked way too big for her. There were three belts, all cinched across her rib cage like an old-timey corset. Underneath all the belts was a tweed vest, and there were about four scarves wrapped around her neck as well as a velvet headband on her head.

A hum of conversation buzzed all around us—everyone seemed to be talking about our new teacher's outfit. I glanced around, looking for Mia. Mia knew a lot about fashion. Maybe what the teacher was wearing was actually amazingly stylish? It's not like I knew what was cool.

"Good afternoon, everyone," she said, clapping her hands. I noticed how pretty her pink lacy gloves were and what a nice voice and smile she had. "I'm your new science teacher. I'm—" She paused, and her face fell. Reaching into one of the pockets on her vest, she pulled out a scrap of paper and read it.

"I'm Miss Pesky," she said, waving the piece of paper at us.

I exchanged a glance with Romy. Did our new teacher not know her own name?

"What's your first name, Miss Pesky?" shouted Roger Wu from the back of the class. Usually Roger Wu's questions were annoying, pointless, and/or rude, but this time he had a point. Did Miss Pesky even know her first name? It got so quiet in the lab that I could hear Mr. Wilder teaching in the classroom next door.

"It's . . . mmm . . . ," she said, glancing at the piece of paper, as gasps and laughs broke out around the classroom. She *didn't* know her name.

"Leonora," she announced. "It's Leonora." She put the paper back into her pocket. "Now, let's start the class."

But it was too late for that.

"Is Leonora Pesky even your real name?" said Roger, leaning over his desk.

"Of course it's my real name," said Miss Pesky nervously. She straightened out her vest and looked at Roger

Wu. "I just have a lot to keep track of today. Now, tell me your name?"

"..."

Every head turned toward Roger, who was sitting with his mouth slightly open, staring at Miss Pesky.

"I ... I ...," he stammered. His eyes squinted from the effort of thinking.

"See," said Miss Pesky, throwing a kind look at Roger. "Happens to all of us. Names can be tricky. Now, let's get started on photosynthesis."

"What was that all about?" I whispered to Romy and Gavin.

"I think she's from Europe ...," said Gavin. "Maybe she's in witness protection...."

"No," I said to Gavin. "I mean, what did she do to Roger?"

"See, if she was in witness protection, she'd have been given a different identity and maybe she'd forget her new name sometimes. ... And all the clothes? Possible disguise ...," whispered Gavin, a slightly awestruck tone in his voice. "I wonder how she helped the police. Maybe Interpol's involved?"

I ignored Gavin, leaning across him to whisper to Romy.

"She made Roger forget his name."

I glanced at Roger, who had his head down as he was copying the chart from the board. I'd never seen him so focused on schoolwork.

"I know," said Romy, eyes blazing with excitement. "Do you think she's a . . . " She lowered her voice so much that I almost didn't hear her. "A witch?"

Ever since last year, Romy and I had been on the lookout for fairy-tale characters, because if Snow White, Rapunzel, Cinderella's stepmother and stepsisters, the Evil Queen, and the Sea Witch were all in New York City, who else might be here? It was one of the reasons we were reading through the Brothers Grimm book. We wanted to know what, or who, was out there.

I looked toward the front of the classroom. Miss Pesky was facing the class and smiling, looking so happy and kind that it was hard to imagine that she had a witchy bone in her body. I thought about all the fairy tales Romy and I had read, but there wasn't one about an overdressed woman/witch who made people forget their names.

"If she was a special agent, she'd have special skills," whispered Gavin out of the side of his mouth. "Martial arts, mind reading . . . Hypnotism would be no problem."

"You think she hypnotized Roger?" I asked. Maybe that was a more logical explanation than the one Romy and I were leaning toward. Miss Pesky wasn't a witch; she was a highly trained special agent? Working as a teacher at Hill Country Middle School? No, that didn't make any sense either. (Though Raul would probably love it.)

I tuned in to what Miss Pesky was saying. She was much more interesting than the substitute teacher we'd had after our seventh-grade science teacher, Mrs. Taylor, had had to take an early retirement after her lab had been attacked by pigeons. And it looked like Miss Pesky had a sense of humor. She'd put a silly picture on the screen behind her—a cartoon of a drooping flower with the caption IF A PLANT IS SAD, DO OTHER PLANTS PHOTOSYMPATHIZE WITH IT?—but she hadn't pointed it out to the class yet.

Miss Pesky started walking around the classroom, weaving her way through the desks, pausing to compliment students' handwriting or correct their spelling.

"Have you ever lived in Europe, Miss Pesky?" asked Gavin when she got to our table.

"No," said Miss Pesky, looking surprised by Gavin's question. "But I'd love to visit."

Miss Pesky was standing right beside our workstation. She lifted up her arm to adjust her velvet headband. I saw that she had a tiny tattoo on the inside of her wrist. Just four letters in black. FFTC.

FFTC?

I wondered what it stood for. I glanced at Romy to see if she'd noticed the tattoo. It didn't look like she had, as she was busy pointing out the cartoon at the front of the classroom to Gavin. I felt myself smiling. If Gavin spotted the letters on Miss Pesky's wrist, he'd probably think they stood for "Finds Felons and Tracks Crooks," and he'd volunteer to help her do both.

When the bell rang for the next class, Roger was the first one to stand up.

"It's Roger Wu!" he yelled, banging on his desk as if he'd just figured out how to split an atom. "My name is Roger Wu!"

Chapter 4

THE REST OF THE SCHOOL DAY WAS PRETTY normal, other than everyone talking about Miss Pesky and what she'd done to Roger Wu. Gavin's theory became the most popular, and there was a general agreement that no one should look her directly in the eyes. Romy and I only managed to exchange a few words about it as we went off to our separate classes. We both wondered if Miss Pesky might be another fairy-tale character, but if so, why would she want to be a science teacher at our middle school?

The one person who might know why was Mom. Mom, who wouldn't talk to me about fairy tales.

As I cycled home, I felt a surge of frustration. Why wouldn't Mom answer my questions? Parents and teachers were always telling us to "think critically" and be "intellectually curious," but Mom just wanted me to accept everything she said. And she was acting weirdly. A couple days ago, when I'd sat beside her at the kitchen counter, she'd almost fallen off her stool when I'd asked her who she was texting. The contact name on her screen said SISTER NUMBER 2, but Mom didn't have a sister. She was an only child. So, who was Sister Number 2? She'd turned off her phone and told me who she was texting was none of my business. Nothing made any sense.

When I got home, I found Dad in the kitchen chopping onions at the counter.

"Is Mom here?"

"Yep," he answered, wiping his eyes with the back of his hand. "Getting ready for her flight. Off to Istanbul in a bit."

"Okay," I said, grabbing a banana from the fruit bowl and running upstairs.

I opened the door of my parents' bedroom.

"Hey, Mom, do you have a minute?"

"Of course, love," she said, smiling at me. "Happy to get a break from this." She motioned at the pile of clothes on her bed and the shoes scattered across the carpet.

Mom traveled so much for work—she was always going to universities all over the world, giving lectures on fairy tales and folklore—she should have been a packing expert, but she still got frazzled every time she had to catch a flight.

"How was the first day back?" she asked, picking up a red sandal from the floor, considering it for a moment, and then putting it back down.

"Okay, but a bit strange," I began. I was about to tell Mom about Miss Pesky but stopped. There was something—someone—more important that I needed to talk to Mom about.

"Mom, I know you don't want me to talk to you about fairy tales," I said, speaking quickly so she wouldn't get a chance to interrupt me. "But something's happened that you need to know about."

Mom took a deep breath. She closed her eyes as if bracing herself for bad news.

"What's going on, Cia?"

"So, Elvira Queen, the Evil Queen—" I paused. "Snow White's stepmother."

"I know who Elvira Queen is, Cia," said Mom, opening her eyes. She smiled and seemed relieved. Had she been worried I was going to ask her about something else? "She's running that big skin care company and making a fortune."

"Well, she's putting on this competition—it's like a talent show, and there are students in my school who are applying, and I think maybe she's up to something evil . . . and—"

"Or maybe she's just being a smart businesswoman and getting everyone to talk about her company," interrupted Mom, lifting up the green silk scarf she always wore when she was traveling. It had an outline of a tree on it. She shook it out and then wrapped it around her neck.

"Yeah," I answered dismissively. "Mom, I don't think that's what's going on. . . . Like, what do empathy and bravery and songwriting have to do with skin care? What if she's planning something bad?"

Mom knew that the Evil Queen was not just a smart businesswoman. She knew that she'd taken ten years of my youth. And she didn't just know about the Evil Queen; she knew that the Sea Witch had locked me up and would have forced me to be a performing mermaid if I hadn't broken Madame Fredepia's spell. Mom knew that Cinderella's stepmother was cruel and abusive to her own daughters. Fairy-tale villains were *villains*. And some of the supposedly good people, like Cinderella and Snow White, had some villainous tendencies too. Mom knew that. What was wrong with her? Why was she still packing instead of trying to figure out what the Evil Queen was up to?

Mom didn't answer me. She just kept fixing her scarf.

"Mom!" I shouted, losing my patience. "Will you just listen to me? She's called the EVIL Queen for a reason...."

"She's called the Evil Queen because—" Mom began, but then she stopped midsentence. She took a sweater off the bed, threw it in her bag, and zipped it closed. "Look, Cia, you need to stay away from fairy-tale characters." She paused and looked like she was thinking about what to say next. "There is great danger in those tales. And I'm so sorry about what happened when I was away last year, but all of that's over. You broke the curse. You have nothing to worry about."

Her expression was the same one she used when she told Riley to stop picking his nose or to sit up straight. And now she was looking at me that way? Like I was a six-year-old?

"Mom," I snapped, glaring at her. I hadn't felt this mad since a girl at camp had told me I'd be really pretty if it weren't for all my freckles. "What if one of those fairy-tale characters is going to hurt people? What if the Evil Queen hurts someone and we're the only people who know? We have to do something."

"Cia, shhh," said Mom, putting a finger to her lips. I hadn't realized I was being so loud. "Riley and your dad are downstairs—they don't need to know about any of this." She paused, took a deep breath, and sat on the bed, pushing aside the clothes. She patted the empty spot beside her.

I stayed standing, feeling too upset to sit down. I folded my arms across my chest and glared at Mom. I wanted her to know how mad I was.

"I wish you didn't know about any of it either," Mom continued, shaking her head. She spoke so softly that I could hear Dad downstairs whistling. "Cia, I'm so sorry that you do. Sweetheart, the thing is that there are forces that you don't understand . . . that you need to stay away from . . ."

"But that's just it," I interrupted. "I want to understand. I want you to tell me everything. I know fairy-tale characters are real. I know magic is real. What else is there to know?"

"Just stop it!" said Mom, the harsh tone of her voice shocking me. Mom hardly ever got mad, and she never shouted at me. I felt like I'd just been slapped.

Mom got up from the bed and stood in front of me. She reached out and gripped my shoulders, giving them a gentle squeeze, before looking at me directly in the eyes.

"Cia, promise me you will not interfere with fairy tales. Promise me you will just go to school and be a normal teenager and leave the fairy tales alone."

"I-I promise," I muttered. The way Mom was looking at me—like she was about to start crying or shouting again—was freaking me out. I was so confused. I felt like I should be mad at Mom—it wasn't right that she wouldn't explain things to me, and it wasn't right that she didn't accept that the Evil Queen might be planning something terrible—but I also felt really bad for making her upset.

"Okay," she said, sighing and wrapping her arms around me in a hug. I leaned in and hugged her back, but I still felt hurt and confused. What was she trying to keep from me?

"Hey, what's with the big goodbye?"

It was Dad, coming into the bedroom.

"It's only a three-day trip! Don't look so sad!" he continued, reaching across us to get Mom's bag. "Have you got bricks in this, Helena?" He winced as he held up the bag. "It weighs a ton."

Mom stepped back and adjusted her scarf so that the tree pattern was draped across her chest. It looked nice.

"Love you, Cia," she said, wrapping an arm around my shoulder and giving me another hug. She whispered in my ear just loudly enough for me to hear, but so softly that Dad probably couldn't. "Just leave the worrying to me."

"Time to go," said Dad. He looked at me. "I'll be right back after I drop off your mom. Dinner's on the stove, and Riley's watching TV. Don't let him stay up too late."

"Love you, Cia," said Mom again as she followed Dad out the door.

"Bye," I said, now alone in the room. I fought back frustrated tears. Why couldn't Mom just talk to me? I wasn't a little kid. If I was old enough to take care of Riley, I was old enough to know about whatever those forces were, and why Mom thought I needed to stay away from them. What was she not telling me?

Chapter 5

"IT HAS COME TO MY ATTENTION THAT—" MRS. Everley, the principal, adjusted her jacket, paused, and looked out at all of us. It was the first school assembly of the year. She'd already officially welcomed and introduced Miss Pesky as "a dedicated scientist who has spent the last five years studying plants in the Amazon." A ripple of excited chatter had spread through the crowd, and Gavin had commented—loudly enough for everyone to hear—that it "might be where she'd learned hypnotism." Mrs. Everley pretended not to hear him, but Miss Pesky smiled at Gavin and pressed two fingers to her lips like she was trying not to laugh.

"It has come to my attention," repeated Mrs. Everley, "that some of our eighth graders have entered a certain competition."

I sat up straight in my chair. I'd tuned out when Mrs. Everley had started talking about line-jumping and improperly stacked trays in the cafeteria, but this was interesting. I nudged Romy, but she was already paying attention, her eyes locked on Mrs. Everley.

"The Elvira Queen Awards promoting excellence in youthful endeavors . . . ," she continued, reading off a notecard.

I listened intently, hoping she was about to tell us that we weren't allowed to enter the competition or that if a student was selected, they wouldn't be allowed the days off school. This was good; maybe I didn't have to worry about Gavin or Mia or Vikram or any of my classmates coming face-to-face with the Evil Queen.

"Present a wonderful opportunity for many of you to display your talents . . ."

My heart slammed against my chest. Mrs. Everley wasn't forbidding anyone from entering; she was encouraging it.

"And I'm delighted to announce that Gavin Shortt's entry for"—she looked down at another notecard—"bravery . . ." She gazed out at the audience and pointed in Gavin's direction. Everyone turned to look at him. He was staring at the floor but grinning from ear to ear. My heart dropped.

". . . has been selected, and Gavin will be traveling to Paris tomorrow."

Loud applause erupted, and there were whoops and shouts of congratulations for Gavin. I could barely hear what Mrs. Everley was saying about the awards ceremony and meeting with Elvira Queen. But while everyone was celebrating, I felt like screaming.

"I found out something about her," said Romy, leaning over to me. She was clapping her hands in a half-hearted way. She looked as happy as I did about Gavin's win. "The Evil Queen," she mouthed.

The bell rang, interrupting the celebration. "Let's go to lunch. You can tell me there," I said, getting up from my seat.

Weaving through the crowd of students who were heading toward Gavin, Romy and I went the opposite way. I followed her out of the gym, into the cafeteria, and to the quiet table. Romy was reaching into her backpack when Raul grabbed a chair and sat in front of us.

"Awesome news about Gavin!" he began, but then he stopped, narrowed his eyes, and looked back and forth from me to Romy. "Hey, what's going on with you two? You just ran out of assembly. . . ."

Someday Raul was going to make a brilliant detective or CIA operative or investigative journalist, but right now, his ability to sense that something was going on was just annoying. I looked around the cafeteria for something to distract him.

"Oh look, I think Miss Pesky needs help," I said, pointing at the nearby teacher's table.

Miss Pesky was carrying a tray piled with plates and drinks. Her face was shining with sweat—possibly from the effort of holding an overloaded tray, or because she was overheated from wearing so many clothes—and it looked like either the plates or Miss Pesky herself were about to topple over.

"I'm on it," shouted Raul, jumping up and running over to her.

"Quick," I said to Romy, not knowing how much time we'd have before Raul came back. "What did you find out?"

"So, Noah's making a documentary about the tenants who live in this cool old building. . . . Most of them are really, really old . . . ," began Romy.

Romy's brother Noah was in film school and was always doing fun projects. Usually I loved getting all the details, but Romy needed to hurry up. Raul would be heading back our way soon.

"And he found out something about the Evil Queen?" I offered.

"Well, he and Mom and Dad were fighting last night," Romy continued, looking down at the table. "They want Noah to quit film school and go into business with them." She sighed and paused. I could tell Romy had a lot to say about the fight, and I made a note to ask her about it later. She pulled her eyes away from the table and looked at me. "Mom grabbed a file that had some stuff the tenants had given Noah, and this fell out of it."

She reached into her backpack, took out a folded piece of paper, and very carefully—I could see it was old and fragile—unfolded it before handing it to me. It was a page from a newspaper, the *Coney Island Gazette*, dated July 7, 1942. Half the page was a black-and-white photograph of a pretty woman in a bathing suit with a sash that said MISS CONEY ISLAND 1942. She was being crowned by a dark-haired woman who looked familiar. For a moment I wondered if she was an old movie star, but then I realized who it was.

"That's the Evil Queen," I whispered, staring at the photo. "She looks exactly the same now. But this is . . . eighty years ago . . ." Even though I knew fairy-tale characters didn't age, I was still surprised. Seeing her looking just like she did now was so creepy.

"I know," said Romy quickly and dismissively. "She judged the beauty competition. I asked Noah about this lady. . . ." Romy tapped her finger on the newspaper cutting. "The one who was Miss Coney Island in 1942. She's almost a hundred, and she lives in the building that he's making the documentary about. She told him that the night she won, her eyebrows and her eyelashes fell out, and she started growing hair on the soles of her feet and out of her ears. . . . And she told Noah that the same thing happened to every one of the contestants."

I knew what Romy was thinking. "You think the Evil Queen did that?"

"For sure," said Romy firmly. "Though Noah said that Miss Coney Island thinks it had something to do with all the free hot dogs they ate." She shook her head. "Anyway, I researched beauty competitions last night"— she wrinkled her nose and puckered her lips as if she were eating something sour—"and back in the seventies and eighties when they were a thing, Elvira Queen was a judge in a *lot* of them. And whenever she was on the judging panel, bad stuff happened to the contestants. At one of them, a light fixture fell and killed the winner and the runner-up. In another, a fire broke out in a dressing room, and ten women were burned." Romy went pale as she remembered whatever she had read or seen. "Like really badly burned, Cia."

Romy stared at me. For a moment neither of us said anything.

"You were right, Cia," said Romy. "Elvira Queen is evil. Bad things happen when she's involved. . . . We have to stop her."

Part of me was relieved that I wasn't overreacting, that

I was *right*, even if Mom didn't believe me. But a bigger part of me was scared. What could we possibly do to stop the awards ceremony from happening? I looked around the cafeteria, wishing that I could just be like the other students, eating lunch and not worrying about how to stop a fairy-tale villain. I was so mad at Mom. If she'd just taken my questions seriously, then I'd have some idea about what to do next. Now, I'd just have to do what I'd done all summer—look for answers in books. But there was barely any time for that.

I pointed at Romy's backpack and said, "Have you got the book?" It had been a while since I'd read the original "Snow White" story. Maybe there was something in it that would help us figure out what to do.

"Yeah," she said. She reached into her bag, pulled out the Brothers Grimm book, and handed it to me.

I found the story and skimmed through it, quickly finding the first description of the Evil Queen.

"'She was a beautiful woman, but she was proud and arrogant, and she could not stand it if anyone might surpass her in beauty,'" I read aloud.

"'She could not stand it if anyone might surpass her

in beauty,'" repeated Romy slowly, leaning back in her chair. "And she thought those women in the beauty contests surpassed her"—she moved closer to the table and tapped her finger on the page—"so she had them killed or disfigured."

"Yeah," I said. "But this time it's not a beauty contest; it's a talent contest. So why does she care if people are better singers and dancers? Why would she care about Gavin being brave?" I looked out at the cafeteria, wondering where Gavin was, finally spotting him sitting with a group of boys. He looked happy. He was getting to fly on a private plane, go to Europe, and get an award. Who *wouldn't* be excited about that? If you didn't know that the organizer of the competition had a history of maiming, and possibly murdering, the contestants, that is.

"I don't know why she's doing it," said Romy, her eyes squinting from concentrating so hard. "But she's up to something." She looked around her and scowled. I noticed Mia Johnson heading toward our table, but she glanced at Romy and then made a sharp turn left. I wouldn't want to sit with us either. Romy looked intense, like she was ready to hit someone.

Finally relaxing her face and sighing, Romy pointed at the pages in front of me. "What else does it say?"

I scanned the page, my eyes skipping over the bits about the dwarves and the queen disguising herself as a witch and poisoning the apple. I remembered all those parts. But then I came to the last paragraph.

"Ugh, I forgot about this bit," I said, lowering my voice. "It's how the queen was defeated. It's pretty . . . gross."

"Go on," whispered Romy. "Read it."

"It says she went to Snow White's wedding." I paused, wondering why the Evil Queen would have wanted to go to that. "And," I continued, reading the last couple of lines of the story, "'they put a pair of iron shoes into burning coals. They were brought forth with tongs and placed before her. She was forced to step into the red-hot shoes and dance until she fell down dead.'"

"That's what we need to do!" said Romy, folding her arms. "Stick a pair of red-hot shoes on her."

"How are we going to do that?" I asked, rolling my eyes, but I felt like laughing too. Romy was smiling at me, as if we now had a solid plan.

"Oh, you'll just figure it out," said Romy. She waved

her hand like she was swatting away a fly. "Just do your thing—"

"My thing?"

"You know, your thing." Romy dropped her voice. "Like how you used a flower to get into the hospital. . . . You know, magic—"

I groaned. The hospital where John Lee had been quarantined had been enchanted; I'd just figured out how to get into it. I hadn't used magic.

"Romy, I can't do magic."

"Mmmm," muttered Romy, raising an eyebrow in a way that said, *Yeah, right. You so do.*

"Why are you reading that?"

It was Raul. I'd been so distracted that I hadn't noticed him heading back toward our table. He looked at the Brothers Grimm book as if he couldn't imagine a worse choice of reading material.

"Isn't that just for little kids?"

Just for little kids.

I wished that I still believed that. I wished that I'd never learned the truth; because if I thought—like Raul did—that "Cinderella" and "Snow White" and "Rapunzel" and all the other fairy tales were just stories, then I wouldn't have to figure out how to stop the Evil Queen. I'd be thinking about what outfit to wear to school tomorrow or how much homework we were getting and not wondering about how I was going to find a pair of iron shoes and get a fairy-tale villain to wear them.

"Yeah," I muttered, grabbing the book and getting up from the table, relieved that the bell was ringing. I didn't want to talk to Raul. Or Romy. What she had said about me being able to do magic . . . Romy probably thought she was giving me a compliment, but I felt like I'd just been called a witch.

Chapter 6

THE REST OF THE SCHOOL DAY WAS AWFUL. Whenever anyone mentioned—which they did a lot, because it was all anyone wanted to talk about—that Gavin was going to Paris, my stomach clenched and I started sweating. I ended up with really bad armpit sweat stains, and trying to hide them by keeping my arms crossed or straight by my sides just made it worse. By the time school ended, I was a sweaty, exhausted mess.

It wasn't my fault that Gavin had entered and gotten a winning spot in the competition. It wasn't my fault that Elvira Queen was actually the Evil Queen and that she had a history of hurting people in everything she was involved in. None of that was my fault; but it didn't matter. I felt so guilty. I felt responsible for Gavin. Other than Romy, I was the only person who knew he was in danger.

I had to do something.

I got home from school and flung my backpack on the kitchen counter. Maybe it was because of the Brothers Grimm book I'd put in it, but the whole cycle home I'd felt like I was carrying bricks on my back.

"Hi, Cia," said Dad, putting a plate with a grilled cheese on the counter. "I made this for Riley, but he's not hungry. You want it?"

"Thanks, Dad," I said, pulling the plate toward me. I sat on a stool.

"He's been too busy," said Dad. He laughed and gestured at Riley, who was building a fort underneath the kitchen table. He'd made a wall with the backs of the chairs—his teddy bear was sitting on top of one of them with a fork wedged under its arm. Riley was hauling in two flowery sofa cushions from the living room.

"He hasn't stopped since he got home," said Dad proudly. "If I could bottle that kid's energy, I'd make a fortune."

"Mmm," I murmured in agreement as I took a bite of the gooey sandwich. But as I chewed, his words sank in. "Wait, what?" I said, putting the grilled cheese back on the plate. "What did you say?"

"It's just a phrase, Cia," said Dad, taken aback by whatever expression (my guess would be terror) was on my face. "It's just something people say. It means that if you could capture energy like the kind Riley has and put it in a bottle, people would pay a lot of money for it—"

"I know what it means," I said, my heart starting to hammer in my chest.

And I knew what the Evil Queen wanted. I knew why she was running a talent competition. She was going to "bottle" the contestants' talents. . . . Gavin's bravery and someone else's persistence and another's violin playing, and on and on until she had shelves full of bottles filled to the tops with other people's skills. And she'd use those bottles to—what? Make a fortune? The Evil Queen had told me that she wanted to be the richest person in the world. How much would people pay for a liquid or a pill that would make them confident or creative or just punctual? Probably even more than the five hundred dollars an ounce some were paying for Forever Young's skin cream. Or maybe the Evil Queen would just keep all the skills for herself? They'd be ingredients for whatever potions she needed to magic up? And what about Gavin and the other "winners"? They'd go to Paris, and they wouldn't even notice that the very talent that had earned them a winning spot was being taken away from them.

I thought about what the Evil Queen had done to me. I'd just stood in front of one of her mirrors, and she'd extracted what she wanted. I'd had no idea what had happened—I hadn't felt anything—until she'd told me what she'd done.

Gavin would have his bravery taken from him. Bravery that he needed. His mom was dying.

"I'm not hungry anymore," I muttered, grabbing my backpack. I ran up the stairs and into my bedroom.

My hands were shaking as I texted Romy, filling her in on what I had just realized.

She texted me back immediately.

I'm coming over.

* * *

It usually took Romy twenty minutes to bike to my house, but it was an hour by the time I heard the doorbell ring. I ran downstairs and opened the front door.

"What took you so long?" I asked. I'd been trying to keep myself from panicking by helping Riley with his fort. We'd brought pillows from the bedrooms, built a moat, and put his stuffed crocodile in it. Riley had been thrilled, but it hadn't really stopped me from worrying.

"Had to figure something out with Noah," said Romy, pulling off her bike helmet. She took a step back, motioning at me to come outside. She seemed to be a bit out of breath and slightly giddy. What was going on?

"We're going to Paris," she said matter-of-factly. "I asked Noah, and he said we can take our plane. Mom and Dad are in India, so they don't need to know about it."

"What?" I said, taking a step back. I'd spent the last hour thinking about how I could—without revealing my encounter with the Evil Queen or any other part of my history with fairy-tale characters—persuade Gavin not to go to Paris. Meanwhile Romy had been arranging for us to fly there?

"Romy," I began, shaking my head. I couldn't believe

what she was saying. "I'm just going to tell Gavin not to go. I'm going to show him that newspaper article and the stuff you found about what happens when Elvira Queen is judging a competition—"

"But it's not just about Gavin, Cia," said Romy, cutting me off. "What about the other kids who are going to show up thinking they've won a competition, but actually they're getting whatever it is that makes them special sucked out of them? What about them?"

My stomach dropped. Romy was right. We weren't just responsible for Gavin. We were responsible for all the other kids who didn't know what Elvira Queen was up to.

"But we can't just go to Paris," I said. Right? Was that even legal? Thirteen-year-olds couldn't just fly on their own to a different continent.

"We can fly out tonight . . . like in a couple of hours. . . . Noah said the plane is ready. And—"

"Noah's really okay with all this?" I interrupted Romy. Noah was the nicest guy and a great big brother, but great big brothers didn't usually help their little sisters skip school and run off to foreign countries.

"Well, he has some conditions," said Romy,

shrugging. "But basically, he's fine with it."

"Okay," I said, beginning to wrap my mind around what Romy was suggesting. If Noah said it was okay for us to take their plane and fly to Paris, then I guessed it was okay. He wouldn't let us do something illegal—I remembered that he'd once warned Romy and me not to pull a fire alarm because we could end up in prison—and he loved Romy; he wouldn't let her do something he thought was dangerous.

Plus, these weren't normal circumstances. Gavin's life—all of the winners' lives—would be changed forever if the Evil Queen had her way. If there was ever a good time for drastic measures, it was now.

I was about to ask Romy what Noah's conditions were, but she started talking again.

"So, with the different time zones, we'll be in Paris by eight a.m. tomorrow." She grinned at me. "We'll land in the morning. Confront the Evil Queen. Stop her before the awards ceremony even starts."

My heart dropped. Getting to Paris was now possible, but how would we confront the Evil Queen? I wasn't worried about getting in to see her. That part would be easy.

She'd drop everything to pose with an adoring fan, and Romy could pretend to be one of those; but how would we stop her from being evil? If Romy mentioned hot iron shoes one more time, I'd hit her.

"We'll be back here on Thursday morning," Romy said. "We'll just miss one day of school."

"Okay," I said, making myself speak slowly. I was feeling light-headed, like I was on a really fast roller coaster. "So, we're just away tonight, and we fly back tomorrow night."

I could tell Dad that I was staying with Romy for a couple of nights—which was technically true. Then I thought about Mom. I didn't want to break my promise to her, and if I went to Paris and confronted the Evil Queen, I'd be breaking my promise. Then again, Mom had ignored me when I'd told her the Evil Queen was up to something. She'd said that Elvira Queen was just a smart businesswoman getting publicity, but I'd been right. I'd been right and Mom had been wrong. Ten kids *were* in danger. Anger flooded me, drowning out the guilt I felt about breaking my promise. "Okay," I repeated. "Let's do it."

"Get your stuff and come to my house," said Romy,

putting her helmet back on. "Noah will drive us to the airport."

She swung her leg over her bike. "We have an evil queen to thwart."

I went back inside. Dad was on his laptop and said sure when I told him I'd be staying over with Romy for a couple of nights. It was almost too easy.

I ran upstairs wondering what I should pack. Did I need to wear something fancy to go on a private plane? I wished I'd asked Romy. And what about when we were confronting Elvira Queen? The last time I'd met her, I'd had on a sweat-stained, dirty T-shirt and a battered baseball cap. Maybe looking better would make me more confident? But the queen was so elegant and perfect and superior, she'd make me feel badly dressed no matter what I had on.

I went into my parents' bedroom and took my passport out of the drawer in their closet where they kept important papers. I felt guilty about doing it, even though I told myself that it was *my* passport I was taking. Then I ran into my room, where Riley was pulling a blanket off my bed.

"It's for the fort," he explained. His little face was all scrunched up, either from the effort of dragging the blanket or from thinking so hard about what he was going to do with it. He looked so cute and so serious that it made me smile.

"It could be the roof?" I suggested. I put my passport into the back pocket of my jeans. I didn't want Riley seeing it. "And hang on—" I got down on my hands and knees and looked under my bed for the blue rug I'd made in fourth grade. It had a goldfish pattern. I found it and held it out to Riley. "You could use this as a pond or even a swimming pool."

Riley dropped the blanket and grabbed the rug.

"You have the best ideas, Cia!" he said, smiling at me like I was the world's most awesome sister. I knew it wasn't hard to impress a six-year-old, but it still felt amazing when Riley said things like that. It did make me feel kind of awesome.

"You put the swimming pool in it," he said, holding the rug back out to me.

"Oh, Ri," I said, hating that I was going to make him disappointed. I was feeling disappointed too. I wished I could stay and play with him instead of having to skip school and confront a fairy-tale villain. "I'm going to Romy's house. I'll be back the day after tomorrow."

"The day after tomorrow?" whined Riley, his eyes widening. "That's forever."

"You can take anything from my room while I'm gone. You can build stuff in here too if you'd like," I said, desperate to make Riley feel better—I couldn't stand it when he was sad. But then as I saw him looking at my closet, I started regretting my offer. When I'd been away at camp, he'd made a "home" for a bunch of bugs he'd found in our backyard. He said he'd used my closet instead of his because it was nicer for the bugs. I was still finding dead insects in there.

Riley turned and, surprising me—because Riley wasn't a big hugger—threw his arms around me. I hugged him back and thought about how much I loved him. I wondered if I'd ever be able to tell him about all the unbelievable fairy-tale stuff that had happened to me. When he turned thirteen—the age I was now—I'd be nineteen. It was so weird to think about Riley as a teenager, but at the same time it was sort of comforting. One day I *would* tell him about all the things that had happened to me. I wouldn't be like Mom, who thought thirteen years old was still too young to be trusted with anything. I wouldn't treat Riley that way.

He pulled away from our hug and headed back downstairs, carrying the rug and dragging the blanket behind him.

I grabbed my backpack. I didn't have time now to think about what clothes to bring, so I just started throwing the first things I found into my bag. Then, when it was almost full, I shoved the Brothers Grimm book in on top of everything. I'd have another look at the "Snow White" story while I was on the plane.

As ready as I could be, I raced downstairs, got my bike from the garage, and started cycling to Romy's house. As I rode, doubt began creeping in again. Maybe going to Paris was a terrible plan? What if we couldn't stop the Evil Queen? Then I thought about what Riley had said, and as I pedaled, I made myself repeat those words over and over again. *You have the best ideas, Cia. You have the best ideas, Cia.*

Maybe everything would be okay.

Chapter 7

I LEFT MY BIKE IN ROMY'S GARAGE AND WALKED into the kitchen, where Noah was at the counter drinking a soda.

He looked up when I came in and he smiled. Noah had a really nice smile. You just felt happy whenever he smiled at you. But I was too anxious to feel the effect this time.

"Hey, Cia," he said. "Romy's nearly ready; then we'll get out of here. There're some nachos if you're hungry." He pointed at the plate in front of him.

"Thanks, Noah," I said. "These look good." I stared at the nachos and realized I didn't actually want anything to eat. And I didn't particularly want to chat with Noah—I didn't know what Romy had told him about our trip to Paris, and I didn't want to say anything that might make him change his mind. I still couldn't believe that he was going to let us do it.

"This is pretty wild, you know," said Noah, getting up and putting his glass in the sink. "You two going to Paris for a night." He raked his hand through his hair. "But you gotta build up that muscle when you're young. So that you have the strength to rebel when you have to."

I nodded, even though I had no idea what Noah was talking about. I reached for a nacho just to have something to do. I wished Romy would hurry up and come downstairs.

Noah continued, "You have to follow a dream . . . do what you want. I wish I'd built up that muscle when I was younger . . . so that I'd be able to follow my dreams now. You know what I mean?"

I just kept nodding, even though Romy and I weren't actually following a dream; up until about an hour ago, I'd never even thought about going to Paris. I was starting to understand, though, why Noah had agreed to help us.

I remembered what Romy had said about how their parents were putting pressure on Noah to quit film school. He was helping his sister because he knew what it felt like when your family didn't support what you wanted to do.

Noah's phone beeped. He picked it up from the counter, glanced at it, and grimaced. I felt a spasm of guilt. Was Hildee texting him? I'd set Cinderella's stepsister up on a "date" with Noah a few months ago, and Romy had told me she'd been messaging him ever since. Hildee was very sweet and friendly, but she thought that going for a coffee with someone meant it was time to start printing wedding invitations.

Noah put the phone down without typing out a reply, and I felt a pang of concern for Hildee. Would she be upset when he didn't answer her? But I didn't even know if it was Hildee who was texting him; if it was her, it might be her millionth message of the day, and maybe Noah *should* ignore it?

"Ready!" shouted Romy, running into the kitchen. She was holding her backpack in front of her and had a beige beret on her head. She threw a navy one at me.

"Do people in Paris really wear these?" I asked,

catching the pancake-shaped hat and putting it on my head.

"We gotta go," said Noah, rubbing his hands together. "The plane leaves in less than an hour."

We all headed outside and followed Noah to his blue Jeep that was parked at the curb. It was getting late, and the street felt busy with people walking dogs or heading home from work or out to dinner. Noah's phone beeped again. He pulled it out of his pocket, rolled his eyes—I bet it *was* Hildee—and said, "I gotta take this. . . . I'll be right back. Go put your stuff in the trunk."

He turned back toward the house while Romy and I walked to the back of the Jeep. As we approached it, I saw someone speeding toward us on a bike with their head down; they were crouched over the handlebars like they were training for the Tour de France. As the bike got closer, I saw that it was John Lee, dripping with sweat.

My heart did a little jump. Romy and I were about to skip school, and here was one of our classmates literally catching us in the act. Though once he saw me, John would probably keep cycling. There was no way he'd want to talk to me.

"Hey, Romy!" he shouted, stopping his bike inches from where Romy and I were standing. He braked so suddenly that he almost went flying over the handlebars.

"Hey, John," said Romy, looking surprised. "I didn't know you lived around here. . . ."

"I don't," panted John. He looked terrible. His face was white, and he had dark circles under his eyes.

"Are you okay?" I asked.

"I just—" gulped John, not looking at me and keeping his eyes fixed on Romy. "I just . . . ehh . . . wanted to talk to you about something." He gripped the handlebars of his bike so tightly that his knuckles were turning white. He kept looking from Romy to the ground and then back at Romy, completely ignoring me. Not so much as a glance in my direction. I turned away in case my face was giving away how I felt—maybe he didn't want to talk to me, but John could at least acknowledge that I was standing right in front of him. I wasn't invisible.

"Oh sorry, John. We're actually going on a trip. . . . Just leaving now," said Romy, pointing at the Jeep.

"But . . . ," said John. I peeked over and saw his face fall, a look of desperation filling his eyes. "I just really need to talk to you. About something. It's—like—urgent."

"Well, okay . . . ," said Romy, throwing me a questioning look. I shook my head. I had no idea what was going on.

"You can just tell me now," continued Romy, closing the trunk. She gave John an encouraging smile. "What's up?"

"I . . . ummm . . . need to speak to you . . . like in private," stammered John, glancing at me for a fraction of a second and then yanking his eyes back to Romy as if it hurt to look at me. I felt like I'd been punched in the stomach. Because the "something" that John wanted to talk about was obviously me.

"Guys," said Noah, joining us at the back of the car. "We gotta go."

He did a double take when he saw John.

"Hey, dude—you need a glass of water or something?"

"I just need to talk to Romy," pleaded John. The word came out like a croak. His hands were trembling, and sweat was dripping from his forehead. He hoisted one leg over his bike and almost fell onto the trunk of the Jeep.

"This is John Lee," explained Romy to Noah. "He's in our grade. . . . John, this is my brother, Noah."

"Hey, John," said Noah softly, obviously worried about the sweating, shaking boy in front of him.

"I just need to talk to Romy," repeated John, throwing a desperate look at Noah.

"Okay, dude," said Noah. He stepped back onto the curb and motioned for me and Romy to join him. We followed him over to the sidewalk.

"That guy's having a panic attack," Noah whispered. "He's a wreck. We can't just leave him." He paused, and the three of us looked back over at John. He was now buckled over as if he had a stomach cramp. "Look, he can ride to the airport with us, and then I'll drop him off wherever he lives—you two okay with that?"

"Sure," said Romy, shrugging.

"Fine," I said. Noah was right; we couldn't just leave John. He looked like he wouldn't be able to get back on his bike, let alone make it home.

The three of us walked back over to John. I wasn't looking forward to spending time in the car with someone who was terrified of me, but we needed to get on that plane and to Paris on time.

"Hey," said Noah. "You want to ride with us to the

airport? It's, like, twenty minutes away, and then I'll bring you home or wherever you want? You can talk to Romy on the way."

John's face sagged with relief. "Th-thanks. . . ." He gulped as if he were gasping for air.

"We'll just throw your bike in here," said Noah. He opened the trunk, lifted John's bike, and put it in.

"You should sit down, dude," said Noah, reaching along the side of the car and opening a back door. "Hop in."

"Thanks," muttered John, walking over—I noticed his legs were wobbling—and getting into the back seat.

"Cia, you sit up front with me," said Noah, making sure that Romy took the back seat with John. That was fine with me. It didn't matter where I sat. I'd still be able to hear whatever John said.

"So," said Romy as Noah pulled out of the parking spot, "what's going on?"

Chapter 8

THINGS ARE HAPPENING AGAIN," JOHN WHIS-
pered. "Like last time."

"What?!" I said, whipping around so I was facing them both. My heart started pounding. Was John
becoming a beast again? How could that happen? It had
been months since the spell had been broken. I stared at
him. He looked totally normal. I couldn't see his head,
though; he was still wearing his bicycle helmet. Were
there horns growing under there?

"I'm getting bigger," he stammered. "And my hands . . .
they're huge." He held his hands up in front of his face.

They did look big, but not freakishly so. I glanced at Noah's hands on the steering wheel. John's were about the same size. "And my feet . . . She—she's doing something to my feet. . . ."

She? He didn't look at me, but I knew he meant me. I looked down at John's sneakers. He was still wearing them, which I took as a good sign. When he'd been a beast, his feet had gotten so big that they had burst through his sneakers. I felt myself calm down. Maybe John's hands and feet were getting bigger, but that didn't mean he was becoming a monster.

"You look fine," I offered. *And I haven't done anything to your feet.*

But John wouldn't look at me. He kept his attention on Romy, who did look concerned, but not panicked like John did.

"You do look fine, you know," she added.

"I'm hungry all the time. . . . And my voice," said John, patting his throat. "It croaks and squeaks. . . . It's just weird. It's not like normal. . . ."

"And you think this is all happening because of something *I've* done?" I asked, trying not to sound annoyed.

John really was upset. And I was sorry he was upset, but why was he blaming me? Didn't everyone get big hands and feet at our age (I'd heard that that happened just before growth spurts), and didn't most boys' voices get squeaky and croaky? Just today Raul's voice had dropped an octave midsentence while we were talking, but he didn't start accusing me of doing it.

"It sounds normal," said Romy gently. "You know, like normal stuff is happening . . ."

"How can you be sure?" whined John, finally untying the straps of his bicycle helmet. His hands trembled as he took it off. I was happy to see everything looked normal underneath. He wiped the sweat from his forehead with the edge of his sweatshirt. "What if this is just the beginning, and more stuff is going to start happening . . . like . . ."

Like before, I thought.

Normal teenage stuff was happening to him, and he thought it all meant that he was transforming into a beast. He was worrying himself sick over it. What had happened to him was awful, but it was over now.

I should have explained everything to him.

"I'm really, really sorry, John," I said.

"You did something," he whimpered. He finally looked at me for just a moment, and then he snapped his head back down to look at the floor.

"No, no, I haven't," I said, angling myself away from my seat and leaning closer to him, but John pushed himself back as if trying to get away from me, so I gave up. "I promise. I just mean I'm sorry for what happened before and how it's making you worry now. But I promise I haven't done anything to you."

"Sounds like puberty, buddy," said Noah, raising his eyebrows at John in the rearview mirror. "It can be a real pain. . . . A lot of changes, you know. . . . But you look fine. . . . Nothing to worry about. . . ."

"You are fine," said Romy reassuringly.

"I grew five inches in, like, three months when I was your age," added Noah. "I'd eat about three burgers for lunch . . . and drink a gallon of milk."

"And Cia's not doing that stuff anymore . . . ," said Romy encouragingly.

I glared at Romy. Why did she say that? I hadn't actually ever done *that stuff*. John's transformation into a beast had been caused by a spell that had been cast by Madame Fredepia. Not me.

"Okay." He sighed, looking at Romy. Her comment— and maybe what Noah had said—seemed to be making him feel better. I could see his shoulders relax, and his breathing was slowing down. "So, you're sure she's not going to do anything?"

"I'm still right here," I muttered. Did John actually think that just looking at me was dangerous? Or that saying my name would summon a curse? Was I so terrifying that he couldn't just ask me a question directly? It wasn't my fault that he was going through puberty!

I folded my arms, turned away from John and Romy, and looked out the front window. Nothing I said seemed to help, so I decided to leave them to it. We had to be almost at the airport by now anyway. I felt a bubble of excitement balloon inside me. I still couldn't believe I was going to fly to Paris. With my best friend. On a private plane. Then I remembered why we were going and who we had to meet. The Evil Queen. That part wasn't exciting. It was terrifying.

I heard John and Romy chatting behind me. It felt like

the atmosphere inside the car had changed. Romy was laughing about something, John had lightened up, and Noah, who had started whistling, seemed happy too. He swung the Jeep to the right, and we drove down a road that opened onto a big area where there were—I counted them—five planes. They were smaller than any plane I'd ever flown on, but they also seemed a lot cooler. Like a plane that a spy or a movie star would use.

"Whoa," said John. "You guys are flying on one of those?"

"The one with the red stripe," said Noah, pulling up alongside one of the planes. It had eight windows that gleamed gold in the early evening light.

"You're going on a private plane," gushed John. He sounded completely awestruck and not at all anxious. The sight of the plane seemed to have wiped out whatever was left of his panic attack.

"John, do not," said Romy firmly, "tell anyone about this."

"I won't," said John. "It's just so cool, you know. . . ."

"Yeah," said Romy, her voice softening. "I know. Do you want to see the inside?"

"Yeah!" said John. "That'd be awesome!"

"Let's get you guys on board," said Noah, turning off the ignition. As he opened his door, Romy, John, and I opened ours and stepped outside. I looked at the little set of steps coming down onto the tarmac from the door of the plane. We could just walk right on. No security. No standing in line. This was amazing. There was even a glamorous-looking woman—she had a silk scarf wrapped around her head and enormous sunglasses, even though it was getting dark—walking toward us and waving, like she was about to welcome us on board. Was she the flight attendant? As she got closer, I realized that I recognized her. Long blond hair, big toothy smile.

It couldn't be, could it?

Chapter 9

I T COULD.

"Why is Hildee here?" gasped Romy, wheeling around to face Noah.

"Because she's going with you," said Noah, pulling my and Romy's backpacks from the trunk.

"Oh, come on," whined Romy.

"I told you. You have to have a chaperone, Romy. You're thirteen. You're not going to Paris on your own," said Noah firmly.

"But I thought when you said chaperone . . . you meant *you* were coming . . . ," pouted Romy.

"Well, I'm not," said Noah, placing the backpacks on the ground. "And if you two want to go, then Hildee has to go with you."

Romy threw me a questioning look. I shrugged back at her. It was fine with me if Hildee came along. It might even be better to have an adult with us. Not that I'd ever really thought of Hildee as an adult, but she was definitely older than me and Romy. And we didn't have a choice. Noah could veto the whole trip if we said no. Hildee could be a bit annoying when she started complaining about Cinderella and not being able to find a prince, but other than that, she was really nice.

"It's fine with me," I said. "I like Hildee."

"Romy, Hildee is nice," continued Noah, narrowing his eyes at his sister. "She's been to Paris before, so she knows the city, and she'll keep an eye on you guys."

"Hi," squealed Hildee, running over to us. She grabbed my arm—possibly to stop herself from falling; she was wearing sandals with heels that were at least four inches high—and planted a kiss on both my cheeks. Then she did the same with Romy. Noah ducked out of the way just before she made contact, but Hildee kept going and kissed John instead.

"That's how they do it in France," she said to John, who was blushing a deep red.

"You still want to take a look inside?" said Romy to John as she grabbed her backpack.

John looked up longingly at the plane.

"Yeah, I'll just take a quick look," he said, turning to Romy. "I bet it's awesome. . . ."

The two of them started walking up the steps.

"Do you want help with all that?" I asked Hildee. A porter had walked over and dropped off luggage on the ground beside her. There were three suitcases, a garment bag, and a cylindrical container that could have—based on its size and shape—contained either a hat or a cake. (I hoped it was a cake; I was starving. I should have had more nachos when I had the chance.)

"Just need to say goodbye to my sweetie pie," she said, taking off her sunglasses and smiling at Noah, who was looking uncomfortable.

"I'm not your sweetie pie, Hildee," said Noah, looking her firmly in the eyes. "You know that."

"Oh, you'll miss me," she said, fluttering her long eyelashes and touching his shoulder. "I'll text you every hour . . . just like I always do . . ."

"Don't." Noah sighed. "Maybe don't even think about me at all." He stuffed his hands into his pockets. "Just go and have a good time. And don't think about me. And don't text. There's a time difference, you know. . . ." He trailed off and suddenly looked very tired.

I felt a stab of guilt again. I'd introduced Hildee to Noah. He'd thought it was because she was thinking about going to the same college as him, but Hildee had just been excited to meet Noah, because according to the internet, he was one of New York's most eligible bachelors. It was my fault that she was calling him her "sweetie pie" and texting him every hour. But maybe some other guy would make her forget about Noah? It didn't seem to take much for her to think she was in love. I'd remind Hildee that there was actual royalty in Europe.

"I'll just take this one," I said, grabbing a suitcase from the top of the pile.

"Have a great time, Cia," said Noah, handing me my

backpack. "Let John know that I'll wait for him in the car. I have to make some calls anyway."

"Bon voyage!" shouted Hildee happily to Noah's back. She didn't seem to be at all upset that he wasn't responding to her gushy goodbyes.

I followed Hildee up the six steps that led into the plane. It was even better inside and surprisingly big. It had looked small from the outside. It looked like the inside of a fancy train, not an airplane.

"You put the bags in there," said Romy, pointing at a compartment in the wall of the plane. So that's why it was so roomy. There were no overhead bins for the luggage like in a regular plane.

I bent down and put the bag I'd carried for Hildee away. As I set my backpack on one of the tables, she brushed past me and positioned herself in front of a window.

"I wish he was coming too," Hildee said dreamily, placing her palm on the window. "Paris is supposed to be the world's most romantic city. Perfect place for a proposal." She sighed again, then turned around and looked at Romy. "Unless . . . ," she said, brightening. "Noah wants you and me to spend some time together because"—she broke into a huge smile—"we're going to be sisters!"

Romy let out an explosive groan and got busy looking in her backpack.

"We could look at wedding dresses...," gushed Hildee giddily. "Paris is the fashion capital of the world. . . ."

A loud frustrated snort came from Romy's backpack.

I hoped Hildee didn't hear it. Yes, she sounded ridiculous, but Hildee had grown up with a horrible mother who'd made her feel like she was worthless because she couldn't get a rich husband. Hildee was just trying to prove her mother wrong. You couldn't blame her for trying to turn a couple of encounters with Noah into an epic romance.

"Do you want a cookie, Hildee?" I asked, grabbing a platter of fancy-looking wafers from a table.

"Oh no," said Hildee, shaking her head and patting her stomach. "Need to stay trim for the dress fittings."

"You'd look beautiful in any dress," I said. It was true. Hildee was beautiful. And as her face lit up, it made my heart sore to see how happy my comment made her. She probably never got any compliments from her mom or sister.

I turned to John, who was trying out the recline function on one of the cream leather chairs.

"Do you want a cookie?" I asked, taking a step back as his legs shot out toward me.

"This is amazing," he said, spinning around in the chair. "Way better than the one we have at home. I didn't know planes could even have seats like this." He reached over and grabbed three cookies. "Thanks, Cia."

John looked right at me as he spoke. It seemed like he had finally realized that talking to me wouldn't make him sprout extra hair and horns. I couldn't remember the last time he'd acted normally around me, and it felt really nice. Maybe we could actually have a real conversation?

I sat down on a chair opposite him. He was right. It was amazingly comfy.

"So, you guys are going to Paris?" said John. "That's awesome. I'd love to go to France."

"Bye-bye, sweetie pie," shouted Hildee as she gazed out the window.

"Hang on," gasped John, getting to his feet. "Are we moving? Is the plane moving?"

I looked out a window. The plane was definitely

moving. I saw us pass by another airplane on the tarmac. Then another one.

"I gotta get out!" yelled John, running to the door of the plane. I hadn't noticed it being closed. Who had closed it?

"I'll ask the pilot to stop," said Romy. She held her phone up. "Noah's not answering." She ran past John, who was grabbing the handle of the door.

Romy returned thirty seconds later. "So, here's the thing," she said slowly. She looked at John and then at me. "The pilot says we're in line for takeoff. . . ."

"So?" gasped John. "I've got to get off. . . . He has to stop the plane!"

"Well," continued Romy, chewing her bottom lip. "He said he doesn't know how to turn it around—"

"WHAT?" spluttered John, charging past Romy into the cockpit.

The plane started moving faster. Had Romy just said that the pilot didn't know how to turn the plane around? Was that normal? I leaned forward, straining against my seat belt, and looked down the aisle. I could see into the cockpit, but I couldn't see the pilot. John's back was to me. He was waving his arms around.

"I've got football practice!" John's voice carried all the way down to where I was sitting.

He turned and stumbled down the aisle, looking like he'd just been hit in the head.

"He won't let me off," he gasped.

"John, you need to sit down and buckle up," said Hildee, sounding surprisingly calm and bossy. "You too, Romy." She directed Romy to sit in the chair opposite her. "Buckle up."

John looked around him. His mouth was hanging open.

The plane was moving faster. The engines revved. I felt myself being pushed back in my seat as the nose of the plane lifted off the ground. We were taking off.

John collapsed into a seat.

Other than the roar of the engines, the plane was silent. Then John let out a yell.

"I don't even have a passport!"

Romy leaned over to him.

"Don't worry," she said. "Cia can stun the customs officials."

* * *

Once the plane had leveled out and it was clear that the pilot was definitely not going to be turning around to let John get off, I glanced over at him. He was scowling and muttering to himself, gripping the sides of his seat. I caught the word "idiot." Was he calling himself an idiot? Or did he mean the pilot? Then I heard him say "kidnapping." My stomach dropped. Were we kidnapping John?

Hildee was sitting next to him, leafing through a magazine called *Sophisticated Weddings*. She caught my eye and then pointed at my seat belt. "You can unbuckle now, if you'd like."

"Oh, okay," I answered, opening my seat belt. I felt relieved that Hildee was taking her role as the only adult passenger on the flight seriously. Maybe she'd know what to say to French customs so it wouldn't be a big deal that John didn't have a passport?

The seat in front of John was empty. I walked over and sat down on it.

"So, we're just going to Paris for one day," I began. "We're flying back tomorrow night. You'll only miss one practice—"

"What?" said John. "You're flying to Paris for a day

to look at dresses?" He pointed at Hildee's magazine. He looked disgusted.

"No, not shopping," snapped Romy. "This is not a shopping trip. It's a . . ." She paused and leaned forward in her seat. "Rescue mission."

"What?" said John, looking from Romy to me and then at Hildee, who looked surprised, but not—I was happy to see—disappointed. (She'd seemed really excited about the dress shopping.) "Who are you rescuing?"

"Gavin and the other kids who've won that competition that Elvira Queen is running," said Romy matter-of-factly. "She's actually the Evil Queen."

"What?" said John, pushing himself back farther into his seat and staring at Romy as if she'd grown an extra head. I felt annoyed at Romy. I was already annoyed at her for telling John I could just *stun the customs officials.* What was that supposed to mean? Shouldn't the two of us have talked about how to explain all this to John instead of her just charging ahead and dropping a bomb in his lap? He looked totally confused.

"The Evil Queen is Snow White's stepmother," clarified Romy.

John let out a nervous laugh.

"And I suppose Hildee is Cinderella?"

He gestured at Hildee, who, for just a fraction of a second, looked taken aback, and then absolutely delighted.

"Do you think so?" she said, beaming at John and twirling a strand of her hair. "Do you think I look like Cinderella?"

"No, I just . . . ," began John, staring at Hildee for a moment and then looking back at Romy. He shook his head as if he were trying to clear it.

"Anyway," said Romy. "We think that the Evil Queen is planning on siphoning off Gavin's bravery—and taking whatever talents the other winners have—because she's done that sort of thing before. Right, Cia?"

"Yeah," I said. Romy was moving too fast. John looked like his head was spinning. We needed to back up a bit. "The thing is," I continued, addressing John, "fairy tales are actually real."

I let that hang in the air for a moment.

"Magic, too," added Romy.

"No way," said John, shaking his head. "Fairy tales and magic . . . that's just in stories. That stuff's not real."

John had actually met some fairy-tale characters last year, though he'd probably never realized it. And he'd been turned into a beast—how did he think that had happened?

"But at the end of seventh grade, you were turned into a—" I began.

"That's got nothing to do with fairy tales," said John, his voice choking with emotion. "You did that to me." He looked down at the floor of the plane. "You poisoned me or cursed me or something—"

"So, you think Cia's a witch, but you don't believe in magic?" said Romy, rolling her eyes.

John turned his body so far away from me that it looked like he was trying to crawl out the window.

"I am not a witch," I said firmly. I couldn't believe I had to say that. I scowled at Romy. Putting my name and "witch" in the same sentence was not helping this situation. At all.

"How about we all get something to eat?" said Hildee, getting up from her seat. She went to the back of the plane and returned with a platter of croissant sandwiches. She offered the plate to John, who took a sandwich, muttered a thank-you, and turned his face to the window.

She passed the plate to me. I took a sandwich and went back to my seat.

Out of the corner of my eye, I saw Hildee showing John the personal screen that was hidden in the console beside his seat.

Romy came and sat down beside me.

"Stop looking at him," she whispered, staring at her screen and selecting a movie that seemed to have a lot of car crashes and exploding buildings. "He's *fine*." She handed me some earbuds. "Why don't you watch something? If he wants to sulk, that's not your problem."

But maybe it was my problem. John wouldn't have shown up at Romy's in the grip of a panic attack if I hadn't turned him into a beast last year. I'd been denying that it was my fault, but deep down I worried that it was true. It was the curse on *me* that had affected him, and if I hadn't had a crush on him, he wouldn't have been turned into a beast or stuck on this plane with us.

"This is not your fault," continued Romy. Sometimes it felt like Romy could actually hear what I was thinking. "It's not like you dragged him onto the plane." She threw a dark look at John. "I don't know what he's complaining about.

He's flying to Paris! He'll only miss one football practice, and he's getting to miss school. Anyone else would be thrilled." She put in her earbuds and started watching her movie.

Across the aisle, John had pulled out his phone and was frowning down at the screen.

"Do your parents know *why* you're going to Paris?" he asked, looking over at me. I guessed I was his only option since Romy was occupied watching a movie. "What am I supposed to tell mine?" He shook his head and looked down at his phone as if he didn't know how to use it. "They'll be worried sick if I say I'm on a plane. They think I'm at football practice."

"Mine don't actually know I'm going to Paris," I said. I let out a nervous laugh. I'd been trying not to think about what I'd told my dad. I'd lied for a really good reason, but not telling your parents that you were leaving the country—that was a big deal. I felt like I needed to explain myself to John. "I told them I was staying with Romy for a couple nights. . . . And I *am* staying with her . . . so . . . ."

"Right," said John slowly, pulling his eyes away from me and focusing on his phone. He tapped out something on the screen, obviously figuring out what he needed to tell his parents.

I turned on a movie, but I couldn't concentrate on it. I kept glancing over at John, wondering what he'd told his parents. I got up to get out the Brothers Grimm book and opened it to "Snow White" when I got back to my seat. We'd be in Paris in the morning, and I still didn't know how we were going to stop the Evil Queen. The way to beat her had to be in the story.

There must have been something that I'd missed.

Chapter 10

C IA, WAKE UP."

I opened my eyes. For a moment I had that weird feeling of not knowing where I was; then it all came back to me. I was on my way to Paris. Beside me Romy was yawning. She rubbed her eyes and stretched out her legs. As I sat forward and swiped at my face for any embarrassing drool, I felt pressure in my ears and the plane pitching forward slightly. We were getting ready to land.

"Seat belts on," ordered Hildee, standing over me. She had gotten changed at some point during the flight and was now wearing a navy blazer, jeans, and white sneakers. A blue-and-red silk scarf was tied around her neck. Hildee looked nice and a lot more comfortable than she'd seemed in her suit and sky-high heels.

"What?" grumbled John, pulling out his earbuds and looking over at Hildee. I was happy to see that he'd been watching TV, so he probably hadn't spent the whole flight thinking about how awful I was. "We're there already?"

I looked out the window next to me and saw that it was pitch-black outside. Squinting, I tried to make out the skyline of the city, but all I could see were a few lights on the ground below. Wasn't Paris a massive place? Where were all the lights and buildings? Maybe the airport was outside the city limits?

This was it. We'd be landing in a few minutes.

A terrifying thought popped into my head. What if John—when asked why he didn't have a passport—told immigration officials that he had been *abducted*? What if I got arrested? What if Romy, Hildee, and I all got thrown in jail?

I glanced over at John, who was looking out his window.

"Can we see the Eiffel Tower from up here?" he asked excitedly.

I felt myself relax. If John was able to get excited about the possibility of spotting the Eiffel Tower from the air, then maybe he was excited about seeing Paris. . . . And maybe he'd forgiven me.

"You can't miss it. It glows gold at night," said Hildee, who had obviously been learning more about Paris than the names and locations of bridal shops. "It's lit up with five thousand lamps."

I peered out my window, searching for the gold lights. I felt a flutter of excitement. This was so cool. I'd seen the Eiffel Tower in pictures and in a couple of movies—and now I was going to see it for real.

"This isn't . . . ," said John, sounding so confused that I turned away from the window and glanced over at him again. He stared back at me, looking shocked. His expression reminded me of the way Roger had looked during science when he couldn't remember his name. "This isn't . . ." He turned back to his window.

What was wrong with John? What had he seen outside? I whipped my head back to look out my window. It was still almost totally black. No sign of those five thousand lamps, even as the plane was dropping fast. We'd be on the ground in seconds. Below me I saw fields. I didn't know there were fields in Paris. Then I squinted, not sure what I was seeing. Were those cows? There were cows beside the runway that we were rapidly approaching.

I felt myself being pushed back into the seat as the plane landed.

Then I realized why John had looked so surprised.

There was a cactus outside my window.

"This isn't Paris," I gasped.

Chapter 11

BUT IT *WAS* PARIS.

Paris, Texas.

From my window I saw a sign that said WELCOME TO PARIS in front of a single building that made up the entire airport. The *A* in the sign was shaped like the Eiffel Tower and had a red cowboy hat perched on the pointy bit at the very top.

The plane came to a stop.

"This isn't Paris!" yelped Romy, unbuckling her seat belt and leaning over me to get a better look out the window.

Hildee got to her feet too.

"Oh, we're going to Paris, Texas?" she asked, as if that had been the plan all along.

"No," snapped Romy. "We're going to Paris, France . . . where they speak French . . . and"—she motioned at the sign outside the window—"don't wear cowboy hats."

I looked over at John. He was holding his head in his hands, and I hoped he wasn't having another panic attack. I was feeling a bit panicky myself. This was awful. We'd just flown from New York to Texas, and I wasn't great at geography, but I was pretty sure that we were now even farther from Paris, France, than we had been when we left New York. For the past—I checked the time on my phone; it was 10:00 p.m.—three hours, we'd been flying in the opposite direction from our destination. We'd been flying away from, not toward, France. Away from the Evil Queen and whatever she was planning to do to all those "winners."

"There's a Paris, Texas," groaned John, still holding his head in his hands. "There's a Paris, Texas." His shoulders shook, and his head bopped up and down. He wasn't crying, was he?

No.

He was laughing.

"Two bridal salons in Paris, Texas," announced Hildee, looking up from her phone. "We can make that work. . . ."

"We are not staying here," grumbled Romy. "What is wrong with that pilot?" She got up and walked toward the cockpit just as the pilot came out, smiling and rubbing his hands in a satisfied way. His name tag said CAPTAIN ARGUS.

"Ten minutes ahead of schedule," he said, beaming at us. "Shall I help with your bags?" He reached forward to open the luggage compartment, and I noticed that he had a tiny tattoo on the crook of his elbow.

"We're about four hours *behind* schedule," said Romy, leaning back on the armrest of one of the chairs. "This is the wrong Paris. You're supposed to be taking us to Paris, FRANCE."

Captain Argus looked at her blankly.

"The wrong Paris?" he repeated. "There's more than one?"

"Well, yeah," said Romy. She stared at Captain Argus for a moment, looking completely confused.

I was confused too. If Captain Argus thought there

was only one Paris—which, up until a few moments ago, was what I had always thought—why would he think that Paris was in Texas? Had he never heard of Paris, France? How could a pilot never have heard of Paris, France? (I was fairly certain that even Riley would say "France" if I asked him where Paris was.)

"Well, I just put it in the system: *P-A-R-I-S*," he explained, miming out pressing buttons. "And here we are."

"Okay, well, let's just go to the other Paris now, then?" said Romy. "Because that's where we need to get to. . . ."

"Well, I don't," said John, staring pointedly at Romy. "I don't need to get to Paris. I don't want to go to Paris. . . . I want to go back to New York. . . ." So he hadn't been that excited about seeing the Eiffel Tower.

"No," said Captain Argus, shaking his head. He looked at John. "You can't do that. There are no more planes coming in or leaving here tonight."

"But—" began John.

"You need to stay with the group, John," interrupted Hildee. She sounded like a teacher scolding a student who was wandering away from the class on a field trip. "We have to stick together."

"But I never signed up for this group," groaned John.

"That doesn't matter," said Hildee, adjusting her navy blazer. "You can't just stay here waiting for a plane. I won't allow it." Hildee sounded like she was channeling Mrs. Everley. "I'm the chaperone. I've been tasked with escorting you all to Paris and then getting you home safely. And that's what I'm going to do. I'm a protectress."

A protectress?

There was a stunned silence as everyone—even Captain Argus, who looked taken aback—let that word sink in. Hildee was our protectress?

"Noah gave me a job to do," she added. "And I am not going to disappoint him."

"Oh, for goodness' sake," muttered Romy under her breath. "She thinks she's trying out for the role of Noah's girlfriend or"—she made a face—"bride."

"Well . . . ," I said, ignoring Romy's comment. Even if Hildee's motivation was a bit strange, it was still nice that she cared so much about being a good chaperone. Noah had actually done a really good job picking Hildee to come with us to Paris. "I guess we can still all go to Paris then?"

I directed my question at Captain Argus but looked at John out of the corner of my eye. He seemed to be resigning himself to sticking with us. He was slumped down in his chair with his arms folded.

"Out of the question," replied Captain Argus. "No, no, no. There's not enough fuel left."

"Can't you just put more fuel in?" I asked, the panicky feeling in me beginning to get bigger. This was an airport. There had to be fuel for the airplanes.

"No fuel tank operators at this time of night. We'll have to wait until the morning," said Captain Argus. He looked really sorry.

If we didn't fly until the morning, we'd arrive in Paris tomorrow night, and the awards ceremony and the Evil Queen's extractions would already have happened. There was no point going to Paris if we didn't go *right now*.

I was dimly aware of Hildee, Romy, and Captain Argus talking. The words "fuel," "time zones," and "Houston" drifted toward me, but I was too agitated to focus on what was being said. My heart was racing, and I felt like I couldn't quite catch my breath, even though I was sitting down.

"This might help."

I looked up. John had gotten out of his seat and was standing beside me holding out a brown paper bag.

"You know, with breathing," he explained, looking a bit embarrassed, like he was the one who was hyperventilating. "You hold it up to your nose and mouth. . . ." He lifted it up to his face to demonstrate. "And then you just breathe into it . . . like . . . about six times."

"Oh, thanks," I said, taking the bag from him. I was feeling surprised and grateful.

"No problem," he said, not quite meeting my eyes as he sat back down.

As I breathed into the bag, I realized how ridiculous it was that John, who had just been panicking hours earlier, was now helping me—who was sort of the reason for his panic—with anxiety.

I let out a groan.

"Water helps too."

Out of the corner of my eye, I saw him holding out a bottle of water.

I shook my head. John was being so nice, and the guilt I was feeling was almost worse than the anxiety.

I glanced over at Hildee, Romy, and Captain Argus.

Captain Argus was adjusting his cap. I stared at that small tattoo in the crook of his elbow, visible as he lifted his arm to his head. I recognized it. I had seen it somewhere before. Where had I seen it?

"Miss Pesky!" I shouted.

Everyone turned to look at me.

"Your tattoo," I said, crumpling up the paper bag. I pointed at Captain Argus's arm. "It says 'FFTC.'"

Captain Argus, looking alarmed, quickly put his jacket back on.

"FFTC," I continued. It didn't matter how many layers of clothes Captain Argus put on. I knew what I had seen. The same letters had been on Miss Pesky's wrist. Miss Pesky, who hadn't been able to remember her own name and had made Roger Wu forget his.

What did "FFTC" mean?

"Do you know Miss Pesky? At Hill Country Middle School," I asked, my mind scrambling to figure out how our new science teacher and this polite but geographically challenged pilot might be connected. I'd never seen an FFTC tattoo before yesterday, and now I was seeing another one?

"Are you . . ." Captain Argus's voice dropped to a whisper, and he gestured excitedly at me, Hildee, Romy, and John. "Are you all FFTCs?"

"FFTCs?" asked Romy.

"Former Fairy-Tale Characters," said Captain Argus proudly.

Chapter 12

AFTER A MOMENT OF STUNNED SILENCE, everyone started talking at once.

"Were you . . . ," gasped Hildee excitedly, narrowing her eyes at Captain Argus as if she were seeing him for the first time. "Are you . . . a prince?"

"He flew . . . he flew the plane . . . ," exclaimed John, gesturing at Captain Argus and looking at me. "He thinks he's a fairy-tale character! How is he a pilot?"

"You can just magic us to France!" announced Romy, looking like she was about to hug Captain Argus. "You don't need fuel!"

Captain Argus looked at each of us, his expression growing more and more confused.

"Which fairy tale are you from?" asked Hildee.

"I don't know what it's called," answered Captain Argus. "It's not one of the big ones . . . might not even have a name. . . . I was just a woodcutter." He looked apologetically at Hildee as he said this. I wondered if this was because he'd realized that she was from "one of the big ones," or if he was just letting her know that he wasn't a prince.

"A woodcutter flew the plane," muttered John. "A woodcutter . . ."

"Who cares?" said Romy impatiently. "So"—she looked pointedly at Captain Argus—"you can get us to Paris, right?"

How was Romy moving on so quickly? This was huge. Our pilot was a former fairy-tale character? What did it mean to be a *former* fairy-tale character? So, Captain Argus used to be a fairy-tale character, but now he wasn't. How had he gone from being a woodcutter to a pilot? How had he learned to fly a plane? And what about Miss Pesky? She had to be one too. Why else would she have that tattoo? How many former fairy-tale characters were there?

"Cia," snapped Romy, cutting through my thoughts. "We have to get out of here."

She was right. We had to get to Paris.

"Captain Argus," said Romy firmly. "We're ready whenever you are."

He looked at her blankly.

"Magic," said Romy, waving her fingers. "However you want to do it . . . flying creature, magic carpet. . . . Whatever you've got. . . ." She glanced at me, John, and Hildee, as if looking for more ideas.

"A spell," suggested Hildee. "A spell would be fine."

"A spell would be good," agreed Romy.

I heard John let out a strangled whimper. Was he beginning to accept that fairy tales were real? I glanced at him. No. He wasn't. He was looking at Hildee, Romy, and Captain Argus as if they were speaking gibberish.

"I can't do magic," said Captain Argus, taking off his cap and scratching his head. "I told you I was a woodcutter. . . ."

I thought about all the fairy tales I'd read. Captain

Argus was right that usually the characters known only by their jobs—like woodcutters and millers and bakers—didn't have any magic powers, but there was often someone else in the fairy tale who did.

"Was there—is there someone else in your fairy tale who does know magic? Maybe they could help us?" I offered, trying to ignore the grumbling that was coming from John.

Captain Argus looked thoughtful for a moment.

"Well, there were the goblins . . . and one of them, Tragus, he left too. . . ."

"And what is he now?" sputtered John sarcastically. "A computer engineer? A nuclear physicist? A brain surgeon?"

"No," answered Captain Argus, looking taken aback. "He runs a little jewelry and antiques store. . . . Tragus's Treasures."

"That sounds lovely," said Hildee, giving John a reassuring look.

"And very appropriate," added Romy. "Sounds like this guy is still in the goblin business." She looked at me. "I'd say he knows enough magic. Will you call him?" she asked, turning to Captain Argus. "Tell him we need to know how to get to Paris. Fast."

"Well, he's not—" began Captain Argus, frowning and looking like he was trying to decide something. He turned to me and sighed. "But, well . . . he might . . ." He trailed off as he pulled his phone from his pocket, scrolled through it, and called Tragus. The rest of us were silent as the phone rang, and then we heard a mumbled "hello" as Tragus picked up.

Captain Argus quickly explained our situation, then held out his phone to us. A very old bald man looked out at us from the screen. His face was wrinkly; he had wide-set, smiley green eyes under wire spectacles and a neat, white beard.

"He looks nice," whispered Romy to me, nodding approvingly.

He did look nice in a twinkly, smiley way. He wouldn't look out of place in Santa's workshop.

"You're lucky that it's high tide. . . . I can get you to Dieppe on the coast . . . like that," he said, snapping his fingers. Tragus had big, jeweled rings on every finger, which made me think of treasure hunters—which was what it seemed he was. On the shelves behind him there were silver candlesticks and ornate mirrors and shiny goblets. "Hundred miles from Paris. That's the closest I can get you."

"Do you have any iron shoes?" asked Romy, pointing at the shelves.

"I'm a goblin, not an elf," said Tragus gruffly, narrowing his eyes at Romy.

"We're very grateful for your help," I said quickly, shooing Romy away—but she'd already moved on. She was asking Captain Argus if he knew any elves. "A hundred miles is great," I continued, turning to Hildee. "That's okay, right? We can catch a train or . . ."

"Train, car, bus, horses . . . ," said Hildee, listing them out on her fingers. "A chaperone is prepared for all transportation options."

Horses? Hildee had planned for the possibility of us having to ride horses? Was that why she had so much luggage?

Pushing past that thought, I nodded at the phone screen. I just wanted to get this done as quickly as possible. If I thought too much about it—getting help from a goblin, who, the more I looked at him, the less likely it seemed that Santa Claus would ever hire him—I might change my mind.

"High tide tonight," repeated Tragus. "It'll pull you in." He adjusted his glasses and leaned closer to the screen. "Now, listen well. . . .

> *A smear of fish behind the ears*
> *A sprinkle of salt upon the chin*
> *Three turns clockwise as you say*
> *'Groac'h, Groac'h, pull me in.'"*

"Groac'h?" I asked. "What's Groac'h?"

"Gotta go," said Tragus, cocking his head to the side like a dog picking up a scent. "Customer."

The phone screen went black.

"What's pulling us in?" I said again, even though I knew no one—other than possibly Captain Argus, but he was shrugging his shoulders and looking confused—would know what "Groac'h" meant.

"It's French for a hot alcoholic drink," said Hildee, waving her phone at me. "I just looked it up. *Grrow* . . . *och* . . . like a brandy or a whiskey. . . ."

"How?" I asked. "Is a brandy going to pull us in? You're saying a drink is going to pull us thousands of miles across the Atlantic?"

"It's magic, Cia," said Romy impatiently. "Magic." She waved her fingers in front of her face. "That's how it works. And it's not just the drink. . . . We have to use salt and fish." She paused and chewed her bottom lip for a fraction of a second. "I guess we could go find a store and get a tin of tuna?"

"What about these?" asked Hildee, producing a bag of fish-shaped crackers from her purse and holding them out triumphantly.

"Yes! Those will work!" said Romy. She took off running to the back of the plane and returned clutching tiny packets of salt. She threw them on the table. "And we can use these!"

"Everyone ready, then?" said Hildee in her bossy chaperone voice. "Now, grab your luggage and stand up. . . . I'll smear and sprinkle, and then we have to turn three times."

"This is ridiculous." John sighed.

I was glad that John wasn't freaking out, but after

everything that had happened last year, I also knew that even if this seemed ridiculous, there was a possibility—a possibility that I was hoping for—that it would work and we would all get magicked across the ocean.

"You don't have to do this, you know," I said to John. "You can stay here with Captain Argus. . . . He seems nice. . . . I bet he'd fly you back to New York tomorrow. . . ."

"We're all going to be staying here with Captain Argus," said John, running a hand through his hair. "Because salt and crackers and spinning clockwise is not"—he got to his feet—"it's just not going to work."

"But that Tragus guy . . . he's a goblin," I said, wishing that John would accept the possibility that magic was real. If he thought it was possible for me to curse him, why couldn't he think it was possible that a spell might magic us to France? "He might know what he's talking about. . . ."

"Look," said John slowly, as if he were suddenly very tired of the conversation. "I'll do it first. That way you'll all see that this is"—he paused and looked at Hildee, Romy, and Captain Argus—"just stupid."

He approached Hildee, who had opened a packet of

salt and the bag of crackers while John was talking.

"Rub that behind your ears," she instructed as she handed him a cracker.

As John applied the cracker, he tilted his head back, and Romy stood on her tippy-toes to sprinkle salt on his chin.

"Now turn clockwise three times," she said. "And—"

"Say 'Groac'h, Groac'h, pull me in,'" said John wearily as he finished the first turn.

I watched him turn again, a bad feeling growing inside me. John shouldn't be trying this first. He didn't need to go to Paris. He didn't even *want* to go to Paris. I stepped toward him and yelled "Stop!" just as he completed the third turn and disappeared.

Chapter 13

WELL, IT WORKS," SAID ROMY MATTER-of-factly.

"We need to go after him," I shouted. The spell had worked, which was good for Romy and me, but John would be completely freaked out. I hoisted my backpack onto my shoulders and stepped in front of Hildee. I smeared, she sprinkled, and I turned, chanting "Groac'h. Groac'h . . . pull me in. . . ."

In a flash, the airplane disappeared, and I was standing on a beautiful beach. The sun was just visible over the horizon, lighting up the early morning sky.

"Wow, this is amazing," said Romy breathlessly, appearing alongside me.

"Fabulous," agreed Hildee, inhaling deeply. She was standing a little in front of me with her luggage arranged neatly in a tower at her feet. She still had the salt packages and cracker bag in her hand. Hildee crumpled them up, put them in her purse, and pulled out a tube of lip gloss. She applied it and smacked her lips together.

Some part of my brain—the part that wasn't freaking out—told me that something incredible had just happened. We'd used magic—and not even very complicated magic (spinning and crackers and a rhyme)—to travel thousands of miles. A moment ago, I'd been on an airplane on a runway in Texas, and now I was on a beach in France.

"Where's John?" said Hildee, looking around her.

My stomach dropped. Where *was* John?

I scanned the long, wide beach. It stretched for miles, and other than a few seagulls diving in and out of the water, it was completely empty.

Where was John? I had arrived on the beach less than ten seconds after him. He couldn't have gotten very far in that time, right? Behind where Hildee, Romy, and I were standing, there were soaring cliffs topped with grass. I gazed up at them, wondering if John could possibly have climbed them. No, they were too steep—and even if he'd wanted to climb them, he'd still be almost at the bottom. Where was he? An awful thought popped into my head: What if he had landed on a different beach?

"JOHN!" shouted Hildee, cupping her hands around her mouth and walking away from us along the beach.

"Maybe he landed in the water?" said Romy, squinting out at the sea and holding her hand over her eyes. "He can swim, can't he?"

"Yeah," I said, but then fear gripped me. Could John swim? I'd assumed he could, but maybe he didn't know how. I ran toward the water and stopped suddenly when I saw something—sleek brown shapes—moving from the sea toward the edge of the beach. At first I thought they were seals, but then, as they emerged from the water and got gracefully to their feet, I saw that they were people. Women who all had long brown hair and tanned skin. They were wearing brown fabric draped over one shoulder and wrapped around in the style of a Roman toga. The fabric was mottled with flecks of gray and white.

"They're selkies," said Romy excitedly.

"What?" I said. I'd never heard the word before.

"Selkies . . . shape-shifters," explained Romy. "I read about them in a book on Celtic fairy tales." She raised her eyebrows and widened her eyes. "They're seals in the sea"—she dropped her voice; the selkies were just a few feet away from us—"and women on land."

"Are they nice?" I asked through gritted teeth, hoping that they hadn't tied John to a rock or something.

"Hopefully," said Romy, looking straight ahead and smiling at the approaching group. I counted five women, and there seemed to be at least another five coming out of the water.

"Good morning," I said, not knowing what else to say to the selkie who had stopped in front of me. If I hadn't seen it with my own eyes, I'd never have believed that she—just moments ago—had been a blubbery, whiskered sea animal. Other than her big brown eyes, she didn't look like a seal at all. She wasn't even wet.

"The Groac'h," she said, shaking her head. She spoke with a French accent, rolling out the *r* and the *o*, making it more likely that we were actually in France. Until the selkie had spoken, I hadn't realized that I'd been worried we might have ended up in the wrong place. Again.

"The Groac'h," she repeated sadly, pointing over my shoulder, "has taken the boy."

The boy? My heart skipped a beat. She had to mean John. I turned my head around to look at where she was pointing, toward the base of the cliffs.

"What do you mean, it took him?" I asked frantically, half expecting to see some awful sea creature in the distance scuttling around with John in its mouth. Why had we listened to Hildee? Groac'h must be some kind of monster . . . and we'd asked it to pull us in. Why had we taken advice from a goblin?

"Where did it take him?" said Romy, whipping around to look in the direction the selkie was pointing.

"To its home," said another one of the seal ladies, gesturing at the cliffs. I turned and squinted, and this time I saw a dark opening at the base of the cliffs. It looked like a cave.

"Let's go!" I shouted at Romy, throwing off my backpack and starting to run toward the cave.

Hildee ran back toward us.

"Where are you going?" she asked.

"To find John," I said, rushing past her. "Ask them"—I jerked my head back toward the selkies—"what they know about the Groac'h . . . then follow us."

"And it's not a hot drink," yelled Romy over her shoulder as she sprinted beside me.

We reached the cave entrance. It was much bigger than it had looked from where we'd been standing on the seashore. The opening was as high as a house and wide enough to drive a car through. I peered inside, but it was too dark to see anything.

"Ugh," exhaled Romy. "This looks like the kind of place a dragon would live."

"Yeah." I shuddered. I'd been thinking the same thing. And "Groac'h" sounded like a very dragon-y name.

"What have you read about dragons?" I asked Romy.

"They breathe fire and like gold," she said, shrugging.

I glanced back at the seashore where Hildee was chatting excitedly with the selkies. Hopefully she was getting the information we needed to—what? Persuade a dragon to give us back John? To fight it? I shook my head, not wanting to think about what was inside the cave. It didn't matter what was in there, though. We—I—had to go in.

I stepped inside.

I shivered. It was cold. I wished I had my sweatshirt on. Romy came alongside me and took my hand.

"Can you see anything?" she whispered, holding her phone out in front of her. The little bit of light it gave off didn't help at all.

I squinted and scanned the area around us. My eyes started to adjust to the gloom, and I spotted a glow of light in the distance. I squeezed Romy's hand and pulled up both our arms to point toward the glow.

"I see it," she said. "Let's go."

We took a few tentative steps forward, still gripping each other's hands. I felt like I was back in the House of Terror, a maze/escape room place where Romy had her last birthday party. I'd hated it. We'd wandered around in the dark for what felt like hours, with fake bats whizzing around and plastic spiders dropping from the ceiling and skeletons appearing out of nowhere. Even though none of it had been real, I'd screamed my head off. I could feel a scream inside me now, just waiting to burst out. My foot crunched on something, and my heart jumped.

"It's just shells," I muttered, not looking down. "Lots of seashells in here. . . ."

"No, it's not," gasped Romy, pointing the flashlight from her phone down at my feet. "It's . . ."

Why couldn't Romy finish her sentence? I looked down.

Bones.

"Just bird bones, probably," sputtered Romy. "Or fish. . . ."

"Birds and fish don't . . ." I gulped; I was having a hard time breathing. "Have . . ." One of the bones was long and knobby. "Fingers . . ."

I pulled Romy's hand. We needed to move fast before John got—no, I couldn't even think it. I looked over my shoulder. It was completely dark behind us. The entrance of the cave was no longer visible.

"We have to run," I said, letting go of Romy's hand.

I went first, sprinting toward the light, trying to ignore the crunching sounds that my feet made when they hit the ground. The light seemed to be getting bigger and brighter. The path we were on started to rise into an incline and got so steep that I slowed to a jog. I could hear Romy behind me breathing hard. The trail dead-ended abruptly on a ledge. I stopped and looked down.

"What the—" said Romy, standing beside me and looking down.

There was a living room laid out below us, tucked into another cave. It was a cave within a cave. And there was John, sitting in the middle of the assorted lamps and sofas and tables piled high with plates, glasses, and candlesticks. I exhaled with relief. He was alive. But he was tied to a red velvet chair, gagged, and—I could see it clearly, even from twenty feet above—absolutely terrified.

John's body was covered with long lacy seaweed that was wrapped so tightly around him, it looked like he was wearing a slimy green sweater. I could tell that he was hyperventilating underneath his seaweed straitjacket, his chest rising and falling rapidly. He was sweating, and his eyes, wide with terror, were glued to a figure bent over a blazing fire. Romy and I could only see its back, but judging by the fear on John's face and the fact that there was a black pot bubbling over the fire, I felt pretty sure that we were dealing with a witch.

"So, that's the Groac'h," whispered Romy. "She doesn't look too bad. . . ."

Didn't she? Sure, she wasn't a dragon or a many-headed, tentacle-y sea monster, but she'd tied up John and was going to—to what? What was she going to do to him? The pot on the fire was tiny. It would be hard to boil an egg in it, let alone a person. I stared around the living room, looking for clues. There was a big piece of flat rock jutting out of the cave wall that was being used as a mantelpiece. Every bit of it was covered with decorative figurines, necklaces, clocks, and other knickknacks. It looked like a display in a shop. There was a candlestick that looked exactly like the one that had been on a shelf behind Tragus. Was the Groac'h in business with him? I can't believe we'd trusted him. When we got back home, I'd find Tragus and . . . I didn't know what I'd do. . . . I'd—

I heard Romy stifling a gasp.

I pulled my eyes away from the candlestick and saw what had made her shudder. The figure had turned so that now we were looking at her profile. I had been right.

She was a witch. She had warts on her nose and chin, long gnarly fingers grasping a big wooden spoon, and—this was a detail I had never seen or heard about any witch having before—two walrus-style teeth that extended from her mouth almost to the ground. She was hideous. I couldn't help but feel a pang of sympathy for her. No wonder she lived in a cave. The other witches—the ones with normal, black witchy teeth—must have made fun of her.

The Groac'h walked over to John, and he tried to get away from her, but all he could do was jerk his head about from side to side and make strangled noises. She pinched his stomach.

"This doesn't look good," I whispered, my sympathy for the Groac'h and her terrible teeth disappearing. Pinching . . . it was straight out of the "Hansel and Gretel" playbook. The witch in that was always poking the brother and sister to see if they were fat enough to eat.

"Ah, no," muttered Romy. "She's not going to eat him. . . . The pot's too small. . . ."

"I don't think that matters," I whimpered, thinking of the way the ground had crunched underneath me when we'd run through the cave. "She might not need to cook him. . . ."

I stared at the scene below. The Groac'h's walrus tusks were moving, and John was squirming in front of her. She was saying something to him, but we were too far away to hear it. We needed to get closer. There was another path to the right of where we were standing that led down to the cave. If we stayed close to the rock wall, we'd be able to get down without being seen.

I nudged Romy and pointed at the path. Carefully, we made our way down and hid ourselves behind a boulder. By peeking around the side of it, we had a clear view of the Groac'h.

"Lovely bit of man-fish!" said the Groac'h.

"She *is* going to eat him," I said, feeling sick.

"We'll bring her some other fish," said Romy eagerly. "I bet those seal ladies would get us some. . . . We'll just trade them with her for John."

"She wants a man-fish," I whispered. "Not a *fish*-fish."

There was a gentle tap on my shoulder. It was Hildee. I'd never been so happy to see her.

"Did you find out anything about her?" I jerked my head toward the Groac'h.

"Yeah," said Hildee, positioning herself between me

and Romy. "She turns young men into fish and then she eats them."

"Already figured that bit out," I said. "Any idea of how to . . . like . . . defeat her . . . ?"

Hildee shook her head. Her eyes were fixed on John. "We've got to save him," she muttered.

"What about powers?" I asked as loudly as I dared. "What can the Groac'h do?"

"The seal ladies didn't say," said Hildee, adjusting the strap of the purse that was on her shoulder. "Maybe she just turns men into fish. . . ."

"She doesn't have a wand," said Romy hopefully. "She can't do much without a wand. . . ."

"She's got a wooden spoon though," I said, watching the Groac'h. She was striding back and forth from John to the fire, swinging the spoon above her head before she dipped it into the pot. Maybe it was a cooking utensil *and* a wand? Whatever was in that tiny pot was going to turn John into a fish. I felt sure of it.

"I think we can take her down," whispered Romy. "She's not that big, and there are three of us. . . ."

The Groac'h was tiny. She looked like she wasn't even

five feet tall. But she'd managed to tie up John, and he was way bigger than her. We couldn't underestimate her just because she was small.

"What's in your bag?" I asked Hildee. She'd come through with those crackers when we were on the plane. What else did she have in there?

"Makeup. Manicure set," began Hildee as she looked in her bag. She took out a tube of lip gloss and applied it. "Eyelash curler, loofah, nail polish . . ."

"Okay," I said with a sigh. Unless we could dazzle the Groac'h with the promise of a makeover, Hildee's bag was useless.

"How about I just throw this at her?" said Hildee, removing an enormous hair dryer from her purse.

"That could work," I said. The hair dryer looked heavy. If it hit the Groac'h, we'd have a few moments to untie John and then just run for it.

"It's the best plan we've got." I gulped. "Let's do this."

The Groac'h was polishing a knife and fork with a fold of her black cape and smacking her lips together. We needed to move fast.

"Romy, we'll untie John," I said, as Hildee handed me

a nail file. "Hildee, you throw the hair dryer. . . ."

"Aim for the head," added Romy in a steely voice. "Knock her out."

"And then . . ." I took a deep breath. "We run for it."

I waited a moment for the Groac'h to turn and face the fire so her back was to us; then I whispered, "Go."

We scrambled out from our hiding place and rushed into the living room/cave. Romy and I headed straight for John. For a fraction of a second, his eyes widened with surprise and then filled with fear. Out of the corner of my eye I saw Hildee swinging her hair dryer over her head like a cowboy getting ready to lasso something. The Groac'h came barreling toward us, her wooden spoon held out in front of her like a sword. I heard a cackle and a shriek as the hair dryer that Hildee had sent flying exploded into pieces.

"You want my man-fish!" screamed the Groac'h, pointing her wooden spoon at the mantelpiece and sending candlesticks, cups, and vases at us like they were missiles. A candlestick hit me in the stomach, and I fell over. Beside me Romy screamed and scrambled to the ground, narrowly missing having a plate smash into her face. The Groac'h grabbed me and Romy by our hair and pulled us over to the fire. She yanked us into a kneeling position, her feet slamming down onto the backs of our legs and pinning us to the ground. I felt the heat of the fire blaze on my face. My eyes teared with the pain of the hair-pulling, the pressure of the witch's foot on my calf, and the horrible realization that we had failed. We couldn't take down the Groac'h. We couldn't stop her from eating John. We were probably going to be eaten too. And Gavin would lose his bravery, but at least he'd still be alive. . . .

I felt a vicious pull on my neck as the Groac'h twisted my head around. I could see that John was still tied up, and now Hildee was tied up beside him too.

"I'll have my man-fish," hissed the Groac'h, stepping away from me and stirring whatever was in the tiny black pot. "Lovely, tasty bit of man-fish."

I tried to move, but I was still rooted to the spot, like I was held down with invisible ropes. Romy too was straining and grunting with the effort of trying to free herself from whatever magic the Groac'h was using to stop us from escaping.

"LET US GO!" yelled Romy.

The Groac'h ignored her and kept stirring.

I had to do something. We couldn't give up now. I stared at the tiny black pot. What kind of potion was in it that would turn a person into a fish? The Groac'h was tending to it so carefully, dipping her spoon in and out of it, taking tiny sips and sprinkling grains of salt or herbs—I couldn't really tell what—that she took from inside her robes. If I could stand up, I could kick it over into the fire. No potion. No man-fish for the Groac'h. If I could stand up. But I couldn't move. Instead I had to watch this revolting witch make her revolting potion. I felt a flash of disgust for the Groac'h, and then a flash of something else popped into my brain.

A flash of revolting brilliance.

I let my mouth fill with saliva, and then I leaned my head back. I snapped my head forward and blew out my mouth, aiming right at the center of the pot, just the way Mom and Dad had shown me and Riley when we spent an afternoon over the summer spitting watermelon seeds in the backyard. My spit landed in the pot, sending up a sizzle.

"NO!" wailed the Groac'h, the distress in her voice

confirming what I'd hoped. If you wanted to sabotage a potion, a big glob of spit would do nicely.

The shock of having her potion ruined seemed to break whatever spell the Groac'h was using to root me and Romy to the spot. We jumped up and ran to Hildee and John. I pulled out the nail file that Hildee had given me and slashed at the seaweed, freeing them both.

"Look out!" yelled Hildee.

The Groac'h was charging toward us. Hildee swung her purse and whacked the Groac'h in the stomach.

"RUN!" I shouted, scrambling up the steps we'd come down to get into her cave.

Romy ran alongside me. "John and Hildee, they're right behind us . . . ," she panted. "Keep running."

I raced up the steps, wondering if we had bought ourselves enough time to outrun the witch. Maybe the walrus teeth would slow her down. A piece of rock came crashing onto the step in front of me, blocking my path. I clambered over it as more rocks started falling from the cave roof.

"She's trying to bury us alive!" yelled Romy.

I looked over my shoulder. John and Hildee were one step behind me, heads down, panting heavily as they pushed on. And at the bottom of the steps was the Groac'h, using her wooden spoon to zap the walls of the cave, sending chunks of rock hurtling down on top of us. The path we'd taken on the way in was blocked.

I spotted some light up ahead, pivoted to the side, and ran toward it. In a few steps I was out of the cave. I kept running.

Chapter 14

T HIS IS FAR ENOUGH," PANTED HILDEE, PUT-
ting her hands on her hips. "The seal ladies said that
the Groac'h can't leave the ocean. . . ." She leaned
over to catch her breath. "She has to be close enough to
smell the salt. . . ."

I stopped running and fell onto the grass. My heart
felt like it was going to burst out of my chest, and my legs
were shaking. I felt sick. I'd never run so fast in my life.

"All I can smell is cow poop," sniffed Romy, throwing
herself down beside me.

I sat up and looked around. We were in a field

surrounded by other fields. The fields were separated by hedges, and in the distance there was a road. It was so quiet that I could hear the cows in the next field chewing and a car driving by on the faraway road. At least we knew these were French cows this time.

John was bent over with his back to me. His shoulders were heaving up and down. I hoped he wasn't about to throw up. I looked around for my backpack; I had some gum in there that I could offer him.

"Oh no! Our stuff!" I shouted, realizing that my and Romy's backpacks were still on the beach.

"Aargh," groaned Romy. She hit her forehead with the palm of her hand. "I just got that phone. . . ."

I wondered if we should try to get back to the beach and get our bags, but then I immediately pushed away the thought. It was too dangerous—if we got anywhere close to the beach, the Groac'h would be able to grab John again.

"I bought eight pairs of shoes for this trip," pouted Hildee. "A different pair for every occasion . . ."

"But you've still got that," I said, pointing at the purse she was holding.

"Oh, I never let this baby out of my sight," said Hildee, giving her bag an affectionate pat like it was a pet. She pulled a hairbrush out of it and started brushing her hair. I hoped she had her wallet in there too, and a phone. Makeup wasn't going to get us to Paris.

"Maybe the seal ladies will like my shoes . . . ," she mused, hairbrush raised midway to her head. "They can wear them, so they won't go to waste. . . ."

"Shoes," sputtered John, like the word was caught in his throat. "Why are you talking about shoes?"

He knelt for a moment and then got to his feet, swiping at the tentacles of seaweed that were still attached to his sweater. "She was going to eat me," he whimpered.

"But she didn't," said Romy encouragingly, smiling at John as she waved away Hildee's offer of her hairbrush, even though she had a bit of moss stuck to her head. "And we're miles away from her now."

"SHE WAS GOING TO TURN ME INTO A FISH AND EAT ME!"

John roared so loudly that a cluster of cows grazing in a corner of the next field raised their heads and looked in our direction.

"It wasn't that bad," scolded Romy. "She didn't even get to the fish bit. . . ."

"I don't think that's really the point, Romy," I said softly, glancing over at John. "John's allowed to be . . . you know . . . upset. . . ."

"Oh, I am, am I?" shouted John, whipping around to face me. "I'M ALLOWED TO BE UPSET? Well, thank you very much for that!" I took a step back, surprised at how much John's words hurt me. He pulled the last of the seaweed fronds off his shoulders and flung them onto the grass.

"Sorry," I said, feeling the heat of a blush growing on my face. "I mean . . . I just mean . . ."

I didn't know what I meant. What were you supposed to say to someone who had been almost eaten by a witch?

"Cia's the one who saved you," said Romy, folding her arms and glaring at John. "She took off and ran into that cave, and even when we stepped on human bones"— John's face fell, and he took a step back—"she just kept going. And if she hadn't spat in that pot . . ." Romy paused and looked at me. "That was awesome, by the way." She turned back to John. "We'd still be stuck in that cave, and you *would* be a fish."

"This is not making things better," I whispered to Romy. John was sweating and shaking. He looked awful, the way he had when he'd turned up at Romy's on his bike.

"I'm done with all of you," said John. His voice shook, and he had that pinched, tense look people get just before they burst into tears. "I get it, okay? I get it! Fairy tales are real." He put his hands up like he was surrendering. "That . . . that thing was a witch . . . and she had real magic . . . and she was going to turn me into a fish."

"But she didn't," said Romy under her breath.

"Magic is real," stuttered John. "And it stinks."

He brushed away a tear, wheeled around, and started walking away from us.

"Where are you going?" shouted Romy.

"I'm getting out of here," John shouted without turning around. He picked up his pace and strode across the field.

I got up. I needed to go after him.

"Leave him alone for a bit," said Hildee, taking a mirror and a blush brush out of her bag. She pointed the brush at me. "He just needs to calm down." She looked in her mirror and applied a sweep of pink to her cheeks. "I feel a bit like that whenever the prince picks Cinderella . . . like nothing's ever going to go my way. . . ."

"That's not really the point," I began, wanting to explain that being almost eaten by a witch was hardly the same thing as not being picked by a prince, but Hildee looked so sad that I stopped talking.

I sat back down on the grass but kept looking at John, who had made it to the middle of the field. He was walking in a zigzag pattern, obviously trying to keep as far away as possible from the cows that were scattered all over the field.

He stopped in his tracks, turned, and yelled back at us.

"Are these even actually cows?"

"What's he talking about?" asked Romy. "Of course they're cows."

"And not people," John yelled, "who've been turned into cows?"

"What is wrong with him?" snapped Romy, getting to her feet. She waved her arms above her head and shouted across the field. "THEY'RE JUST COWS!"

But I knew what was "wrong" with John. I remembered how strange it had felt when I'd realized that fairy tales were real and that the characters that I'd always thought of as make-believe were as real as—well—real, actual people. It had felt horrible. Like I didn't know what to believe anymore. Sure, I'd gotten used to the idea, and knowing fairy tales were real didn't freak me out now, but I understood what John was feeling. It was different for Romy. She'd never been spelled or had fairy-tale characters hate her or been worried about being turned into a fish entrée. Romy could just enjoy how cool it was that magic was real, but John and I knew that it was dangerous.

"THEY'RE JUST COWS!" she repeated.

John turned away again and continued toward the road. What was he going to do when he got there? Hitchhike back to America? Hang on, how were we going to get back to America?

"If the plane is in Texas, how are we going to get home?" I asked Romy. She was sitting on the grass and leaning back on her hands. "And our passports are on the beach."

I was surprised about how calm I felt over losing my passport and possibly getting stuck in Paris. Maybe almost getting killed by a man-eating witch made everything else seem like a small problem?

"Noah can organize another plane to bring us back from the airport in Paris," said Romy, closing her eyes and lifting her head up toward the sun. It was starting to get warm. "I don't know about passports though—"

"Let me call that snuggle bunny," said Hildee, smiling. Romy glanced at Hildee and let out a tiny groan. I was just relieved that Hildee was with us—Noah was right; she was a good chaperone—and that we had at least one phone among the four of us. Hildee tapped on her phone and then held it to her ear. I noticed she'd done something to her eyelashes; they were now so long that they touched her eyebrows. She looked like she was on her way to a fancy party.

"Voicemail," she mouthed at us. "Sweetie . . . we'll be in Paris in an hour or so. . . . We're going to need a flight back at . . ." She paused and looked at me and Romy.

"Tell him nine o'clock tonight," said Romy. She turned to me. "That gives us all day to stop the Evil Queen."

I nodded and looked down at the grass. Romy mentioning the Evil Queen made me feel instantly nauseous. Stopping the Evil Queen wasn't just an idea anymore. We were hours from actually doing it. It had to happen today.

"Nine o'clock tonight," repeated Hildee into the phone. "And Cia and Romy have lost their passports, so I'll contact the embassy about that. Missing you *soooooooo* much." She made kissing noises into the phone before hanging up.

"Now, I'll get us a ride to Paris," said Hildee. It was amazing how quickly she could switch from lovesick teenager to take-charge chaperone.

"Just a car, please," I said. "Nothing, you know . . . magicky . . . or fairy-tale-ish. . . ."

John might pass out if a horse and carriage showed up. We were going to have enough trouble even getting him into a car with us.

"I don't know any magic," said Hildee matter-of-factly. "Anyway, Belle will just send Claude to pick us up. He can figure out the passport stuff too. He's good at all that." She waved her phone at me. "I'll call her now."

"Do you mean THE Belle?" I asked.

Hildee nodded as she tapped on her phone.

"The one in 'Beauty and the Beast'?" I whispered, worried that John might overhear, even though he'd almost reached the other side of the field. If there was one fairy tale likely to really freak him out, it would be that one. "You two are friends?"

Hildee nodded again.

"That's so cool," grinned Romy. "We're gonna meet Belle! Nice!"

Hildee was chatting away happily on her phone, presumably to Belle, explaining how we'd landed on a beach. So, they really were friends. I hadn't thought Hildee would like any of the princesses. She'd once referred to Snow White as "the competition," and she hated Cinderella. What was different about Belle? When I'd met the Evil Queen, she'd told me that, out of all the princesses, Belle was the only one doing anything "remotely interesting" and that she wasn't obsessed with finding a husband. Maybe that was why she and Hildee were friends? I wondered what Belle was like. If she was Hildee's friend, then I figured she'd have to be nice—but then again, almost every single fairy-tale character I'd met so far other than Hildee (and possibly the selkies) had been evil.

"All set," said Hildee, putting her phone away and getting to her feet. "Claude will meet us at the crossroads over there." She pointed behind my head. "We just go through that gate there. . . ."

"Claude?" asked Romy.

"He's a butler, handyman, driver . . . ," said Hildee, smiling and smoothing down her ponytail. "Belle's right-hand man. He's amazing."

She put her hands on her hips and surveyed the fields around us. "Oh dear, look at John. . . ."

John had crossed the field we were sitting in and was trying to get to the next one by climbing over a hedge. It wasn't going well. His leg was stuck, and he was swatting furiously at something—probably the same type of flies that were swarming around the cows—on his head.

"I'll go get him," said Hildee, straightening her blazer.

Hildee walked toward John, waving her hand at him and calling out, "You're going the wrong way!" John whipped his head around and fell off the hedge. Hildee leaned over and pulled him to his feet. She pointed back at us and to the road beyond. She looked tiny standing beside John; without her massive heels on, she was at least six inches shorter than him.

"Wonder what she's saying to him," I said, turning to

look at Romy, who was leaning back with her eyes closed and face angled toward the sun.

"Mmm," she said, looking lazily over her shoulder. "Whatever it is, it's working."

Hildee and John were walking back toward us. As they got closer, I saw that John looked better. His face didn't have the scowl it had had when he'd stormed off. He didn't look happy, exactly, but he didn't look angry anymore, so that was something.

"I guess we're all still going to Paris," he said, taking a deep breath and shrugging his shoulders. He broke into a big smile and pointed behind me. "Check out our car!"

How had a car gotten here so quickly? It couldn't have been more than five minutes since Hildee had finished her conversation with Belle.

I turned around and saw the car coming to a stop alongside the field. It was beautiful. It looked like it belonged in an old movie. I didn't know much about cars, but I knew what this one was. It was a Rolls-Royce. It had the little silver statue of a woman on the hood, looking like she was about to fly off, and two *R*s interlocking beneath her, all glinting in the morning sunlight. A man wearing a uniform that was the exact same shade of gray as the car got out. The jacket had a high collar and two rows of shiny silver buttons running from top to bottom. His gray pants were tucked into knee-high black boots, and he also wore jet-black leather gloves.

"Nice car," said Romy, taking a deep breath as she stood up. "That must be Claude."

We followed Hildee, who was waving excitedly at Claude.

"Mademoiselles . . . monsieur," said Claude, tipping his chauffeur cap at us with one gloved hand and opening the back door of the car with the other. "Paris awaits."

Chapter 15

WHATEVER MAGIC CLAUDE HAD USED TO pick us up, he wasn't using it to get us to Paris. Once we were all settled in the car—Hildee in the front seat beside Claude, Romy and me on one side of the back seats facing John, who had taken the other—he announced that the drive to Paris would be ninety minutes. Claude invited us to use the blankets that were draped over the seats and help ourselves to the picnic basket on the table between the seats in the back.

Hildee took off her shoes and draped a blanket over herself, looking like she was getting ready for a nap. Beside me Romy let out a long yawn. I looked over at John. His eyes were still a little red, but he must have been feeling better, because he started looking through the picnic basket. It was stuffed with bottles of lemonade, sandwiches wrapped in red-and-white-checked paper, and tiny boxes tied with a green ribbon, each one just big enough for a single chocolate or piece of candy. My stomach was in knots, and just looking at the food made me feel nauseous.

I wondered if I should pretend to sleep. I wasn't tired at all; I felt wide-awake, almost hyper, but maybe closing my eyes would be better than sitting in an uncomfortable silence with John for the next ninety minutes. I didn't know what to say to him.

John sat back in his seat, wincing as he massaged one of his shoulders.

He must have been aching from being tied up. My neck still hurt from the Groac'h yanking my head back.

"That was so scary. I'm really, really sorry about what happened," I said, rubbing my neck. I felt like I was apologizing to John every couple of hours now, and every time I did it, I just felt more and more guilty, but it seemed like it was the only thing I was able to say to him.

"Yeah," muttered John, turning his attention back to the hamper and pulling out a baguette.

"Don't you know how to accept an apology?" said Romy, reaching over and grabbing the blanket that was next to John, even though she had already put one on her lap. She folded it into the shape of a pillow and propped it against the window. Then she pulled the other blanket up to her chin, leaned her head against the pillow, and said as she closed her eyes, "Stop acting like a jerk. None of this is Cia's fault."

I bit my lip. I wished that Romy would stop speaking for me, but at the same time, I didn't seem to be able to tell John how his words were making me feel. My guilt was way bigger than my anger and my hurt.

"I figured that out," said John, staring at the baguette he was holding and speaking so softly I almost didn't hear him. "I know that it wasn't Cia's fault."

My eyes started stinging, and I felt like I might cry. Did John mean that he wasn't blaming me anymore? I sank into my seat, feeling myself relax and the knot in my stomach loosening. John unwrapped the baguette, took a bite, and chewed it slowly. He glanced at me and looked away quickly. Did he want me to speak? I didn't know what to say. Tell him he wasn't a jerk? Offer a thank-you because he'd just said that everything wasn't my fault?

For a few moments John just ate his sandwich and I sipped lemonade. Other than the sounds of chewing and the fizz of the lemonade bubbles, the car was quiet. I stared out the window. The countryside we were driving through was very pretty: lots of green fields with bursts of purple and red and yellow flowers. There were church steeples and slanted rooftops just visible in the distance. Romy seemed to have fallen asleep. I fought the urge to nudge her and wake her up so that I wasn't sitting "alone" with John. Claude had turned on the radio, and romantic classical music was playing; the sound of cellos and violins were creating a sort of bubble around the two of us. The music and the lovely basket of delicious food on the table between us made me feel like we were on a date. A really uncomfortable date. (Not that I'd ever actually been on any sort of date, but I knew how they went.)

"What do you think he's like?" whispered John.

I pulled my gaze away from the window. John put his elbows on the table and looked me straight in the eyes.

"Who?" I asked, leaning forward so that I could hear John better. He was squinting and looked like he might be holding his breath. Why did he look so serious? Who was he talking about? He couldn't mean Claude, could he?

"You know," said John, breaking away from looking at me and staring at his hands. He pulled at his fingers. "The Beast. We're going to meet him too." He looked up at me again. "Right?"

The Beast.

So, that was why John had agreed to get in the car with us and keep going to Paris! He wanted to meet the Beast. It made sense. Of course John would want to meet someone who'd had the same weird and scary experience as him. I knew what that felt like. The thought that I might be the only person who'd been spelled and gotten mixed up with fairy-tale characters had made me feel lonely and scared and different (but not in a good way). John must have been feeling those things too.

"Yeah," I said slowly, enjoying the sense of connection that I suddenly felt. "We're going to meet Belle, and he's part of her story, so I guess the Beast will be there. . . ."

I paused, realizing that I wasn't absolutely sure that

the Beast would be there. I didn't know what part of Belle's story we'd be stepping into. What if she was still living at home with her father?

I turned away from John and looked over my shoulder at Claude. He'd put on a pair of sunglasses and had both hands on the steering wheel. I noticed that his gloves were embroidered with an outline of a tiny rose, making me feel more confident that we were headed to the right place. "Are we going to a castle?"

"Indeed, mademoiselle," he said, not taking his eyes off the road.

"Thanks," I said, turning around so that I was facing John again. I felt ridiculously happy to be able to give him some good news. "Yeah, looks like we'll meet him."

"Great," said John, nodding and letting out a huge breath. He glanced out the window and then looked back at me. "And thanks," he said, tilting his head at Claude. He stretched his arms above his head and then reached into the hamper, giving me a questioning look. "The sandwich is really good, you know. Do you want one?"

I nodded and took the sandwich that he handed to me. Suddenly I was really hungry. I carefully tore off the checkered paper wrapper from the baguette so that the noise wouldn't wake up Romy. Then I took a tiny bite. John was right. The sandwich was delicious. Chicken, with some type of soft cheese and grapes. The bread was soft on the inside and crispy on the outside. Some crumbs fell as I took a bigger bite. John handed me a napkin.

"Thanks," I said, speaking with my mouth full and putting the napkin on my lap. I finished the sandwich in a couple of bites and a feeling of okay-ness came over me. Maybe it was the food, or John sort of apologizing to me, or him wanting to meet the Beast, but talking to him didn't seem like such a big deal anymore.

"John, you said you knew all this wasn't my fault." I looked down at my hands and started crumpling up the checked paper that had wrapped my sandwich. I glanced over at John; he was leaning forward in his seat again. "What did you mean?"

"Well," he said, sitting back and running a hand through his hair. "You were freaking out on the plane, just like I was. You didn't know what was going on either. And it's not your fault that I got pulled into all this." He gave me a small smile. "It's not like you dragged me onto the plane."

I swallowed back a laugh. John was saying the exact same thing that Romy had said.

"So, the Evil Queen is in Paris," continued John. "And Beauty and the Beast too. . . . What about other fairy tale characters?"

"Well, there's Hildee." I gestured at Hildee, who was sleeping so deeply that her head was thrown back onto the headrest and her mouth was hanging open. "She's Cinderella's stepsister. If you haven't figured that out already."

John obviously hadn't. He stared at Hildee as if seeing her for the first time.

Then I filled him in quickly on the other fairy-tale characters I'd met or heard about, like Rapunzel, who was running a hair salon in Brooklyn, and the Sea Witch, who was in prison for race fixing.

"And what about the Groac'h—do you think she's a fairy-tale character?"

"I don't know," I said, shrugging. "I mean, there are thousands of fairy tales. . . . Maybe tens of thousands, so she's probably in one of them."

"Tens of thousands?" said John, his eyes widening.

"There are tens of thousands of fairy tales? I thought it was just 'Sleeping Beauty' and 'Snow White' and a few others. . . ."

"No," I said, shaking my head. "They're just the big Disney ones. There're loads more. And—"

I paused to take a drink. John was furrowing his eyebrows. He looked like he was as surprised as I'd been when I'd realized that there were tens of thousands of fairy tales. He was sitting up straight and still looking right at me like he couldn't wait to hear what I was about to say next. It felt really nice. "No one knows who wrote them—"

"Wasn't it those Brothers Grimm guys?" interrupted John.

"No. They just collected them from old grandmas, who heard them from their old grandmas, and so on. It's like the stories have just always been there. There's a 'Sleeping Beauty' story from Iceland that's more than fifteen hundred years old."

"Whoa," said John, sitting back into his seat. He stretched his legs out. "That's so cool."

I nodded. It *was* cool. I was really enjoying talking to

John. I wondered how much longer we had before we got to Belle's. Glancing out the window, I saw that we were driving by buildings and there were lots of other cars on the road. It wouldn't be long now. I took a deep breath. I might not have a chance like this again to tell John what I should have told him at the end of seventh grade. I looked at Romy. She seemed to be fast asleep. Good. I didn't want her to hear what I was going to say.

"John." I lowered my voice, and he leaned in closer to the table. "You know what you said earlier, that none of the bad stuff that happened was my fault?" I looked down at the blanket on my lap. I pulled at it, rubbing a bit of the fabric between my thumb and index finger. I snuck a peek at John. He was nodding and keeping his eyes fixed on me. "Some of the stuff that happened to you *was* my fault. The reason you got turned into a beast is because . . ." I glanced at John. He was still staring at me. "Well, a woman put a spell on me, and it made the opposite of certain fairy tales happen to me. So, like, you know how Belle turned the Beast into a man because she liked him? And I . . ." Why hadn't I put a note in John's locker when I'd had the chance? I thought I was ready to tell him. But maybe it would be too embarrassing?

"Just do it," muttered Romy softly, putting her head on my shoulder as if she'd rolled over in her sleep. Had she been pretending to be asleep the whole time?

"Well, I did the opposite of that," I said, speaking fast so I wouldn't lose my nerve or give Romy a chance to interrupt me. "Because I liked you . . . and that meant I turned you into a beast."

Part of me felt relieved. It felt good to say the words that I'd been holding back for months. And part of me felt scared. I'd just told a boy I liked him. What would John do now?

He didn't say anything.

I glanced over at John. He was staring blankly at his sneakers. I couldn't read the expression on his face. I couldn't tell what he was thinking. Shouldn't he say something? I'd just told him I'd liked him. If someone told me that they liked me, I wouldn't ignore them and keep looking at my feet. I'd say something. And if I liked them too, I'd say it.

"Thanks for telling me," said John, shifting his position. "I kind of figured that you had a crush. . . . It's okay."

It's okay? What did that mean?

"What happened to me . . . that beast thing." He ran a hand through his hair again and looked at me. "That wasn't your fault. You didn't do it on purpose. It's okay."

I waited for him to say something else, to maybe even say that he'd liked me too. Instead, he reached into the picnic basket and pulled out another bottle of lemonade.

"You want one?" he asked, holding out the bottle to me.

"No thanks," I said.

John opened the bottle and took a long drink; then he grabbed another sandwich. He looked out the window and alternated between big bites of the baguette and sips of the lemonade. I'd just told John that I'd liked him, and all he'd said was *okay,* and now he was munching on a sandwich. The relief I'd felt about telling him everything disappeared, and disappointment and embarrassment flooded me. Sure, it could have been worse. He might have said *I didn't like you,* but just saying *okay*? That was almost as bad.

"I don't like you now, though," I blurted out, and then immediately felt sorry for saying it. I snuck a peek at John. His eyebrows were knitted together, and he swallowed hard. He looked upset. I cleared my throat. "I just mean that the crush I had, that's gone now."

"Any food left in there for me? That sandwich looks delicious!" said Romy loudly, making a big show of looking in the hamper. She pulled out a napkin, shook it out, and positioned it under her chin. "What's the filling?" she asked, directing the question at John.

"Chicken," John answered in a flat voice, looking down at his feet.

"I just mean . . . ," I continued. I didn't know what I meant. I just wanted to say something to make John feel better. "I don't like—"

Romy put her hand on my knee and threw me a look that said, *Shut up, Cia.*

For a few minutes, the only sound in the car was Romy making *mmmm* noises as she ate a sandwich.

The car slowed down and stopped.

Romy grabbed one of the tiny boxes and opened it.

"Looks like it's time to meet Belle," she said, popping a chocolate in her mouth.

Chapter 16

WELCOME TO PARIS."

Claude, with Hildee by his side, held open the back door of the car, and Romy, John, and I stepped out.

We were outside an old-timey bookshop. The building looked like it was at least two hundred years old—it was redbrick and had pillars on either side of the front doors, and from what I could see from the huge front window, the books inside were old too. An antique-looking sign swung from the side of the building; it had the words LA BELLE LIBRAIRIE written on it in a curvy script. We followed Hildee, who seemed to know where she was going, onto a porch in front of the store. Claude had said we were going to a castle, but that wasn't what this place was. Maybe we were just making a quick stop here?

"Here we are," said Hildee, pulling on the solid brass bell that was attached to the wall and ignoring the sign that said (in English and French), ENTRY BY APPOINTMENT ONLY. DO NOT RING BELL.

Through the glass door I saw a woman approaching from inside the bookshop. She was about the same age as Hildee and had a really cool haircut, shaved at the sides with a messy bun on the top of her head. Actually, all of her looked really cool. She was dressed from head to toe in black—black turtleneck, black cropped pants, and flat black shoes. One of her ears had a line of tiny gold studs in it. That was the only jewelry she had on, other than a gold chain around her neck with glasses dangling from the end. If this was Belle, she didn't look at all how I'd expected. But what had I expected? A swishy ball gown and a tiara?

"'Ildee!" she shouted, opening the door wide and smiling. "*Entrez . . . entrez.*" She stood back to give the four of us space, and we stepped over the threshold into the bookshop.

"Wow," gasped John and Romy at the same time as they looked around them.

I gasped too. It felt like we had stepped into a cathedral—or maybe a massive old-timey ship, sailed by super-rich pirates. From the street, the store had looked like it was regular-sized, but inside it was huge. There was a magnificent wooden staircase in front of us with red carpeted steps and intricate patterns of animals and flowers carved into the railings. The ceiling was at least twenty feet high, and books hung from it like birds in flight. There was a stained-glass window as big as a swimming pool in the center of the ceiling, and its red-and-gold panes made the light that was streaming through it rosy, giving everything in the bookshop—including Belle, who was smiling at us proudly—a warm glow. I would have been proud too if this was my bookstore. The walls were lined with shelves, and every inch was filled with books. There must have been thousands of them.

"Hiya, Belle," said Hildee, kissing Belle on the cheek. "This is Cia, Romy, and John."

"'Allo, 'allo," said Belle warmly, looking at the three of us. "Come in, come in. . . . Follow me."

She led us into the bookshop and around the other side of the staircase. There was a sitting area tucked in beneath the staircase, a cozy spot in the middle of the vastness of the high ceilings and towering bookshelves.

"Sit down," she said, pointing at the comfy armchairs and sofa. "Make yourselves comfortable. This is my reading nook, my favorite place in the whole castle."

"So, this *is* a castle?" asked John, looking at Belle anxiously.

"Yes," said Belle. "From the street it just looks like a bookshop, but this"—she held out her arms—"takes up the entire block. All fifty thousand square feet. There's a courtyard in the middle . . . gardens . . . a ballroom . . . stables . . . dungeon . . ." She sighed in a bored way. "You know, all the stuff you'd find in any castle, really."

John nodded and pulled in his bottom lip. I wondered if he was trying to figure out where the Beast might be. I was wondering the same thing.

"I'll ask Claude to get us some refreshments." Belle pressed a button on a table, and almost immediately

Claude reappeared. He had changed out of his chauffeur uniform and was now wearing a very formal black suit with a black tie, gray vest, and high white collar. I'd never seen a butler in real life, but I guessed this was how they were supposed to dress.

"Mademoiselle Belle?" he said, clicking his heels together. "You called."

"Some refreshments for our guests, please," said Belle.

"Very good," said Claude, turning around.

"And Claude," said Belle hesitantly.

"Yes, mademoiselle?"

"You can wear something a bit more . . . comfortable if you'd like. . . . You know. . . . you don't have to go with the whole"—she waved a hand—"uniform. . . ."

"Mademoiselle," replied Claude, bristling and standing up even straighter. "Standards must be maintained."

He lifted his chin, turned, and stalked off.

"Oh, dear." Belle sighed. "He's going to bring out the full silver service now. . . . Linen napkins, the whole lot . . ."

"Mother would love it." Hildee giggled.

"She's not here, is she?" gulped Belle, craning her neck to see out the front of the store.

"No," said Hildee, shaking her head. She turned to me, Romy, and John and started to explain. "So, Mother took me to Paris to learn European manners." Hildee shrugged her shoulders. "Whatever that means. . . . Anyway, that's when I met Belle. Mother brought me into the bookstore because she wanted you—" She turned back to Belle.

"To get on with my wedding," continued Belle, rolling her eyes. "So that 'Ildee could get her pick of the guests. There's usually at least one count or baron or viscount who shows up. . . ."

"But Belle refused to do it." Hildee sighed. "Said it wasn't time yet." She pouted at Belle. "I'm still mad, you know. I wouldn't have minded marrying a count. . . . Not as good as a prince, but still royalty." She made big sad eyes at Belle, batted her eyelashes, and then stuck out her tongue to show—I guessed—that she wasn't really mad at all.

"Don't make that face at me," said Belle, laughing. "You're not even supposed to get married! I have to do it all the time. . . ."

Her eyes wandered to a large hourglass as big as a person on the floor beside us. The top part had about a third of sand left, and the bottom part was almost completely full.

"It?" asked John, looking confused. "You mean you have to get married all the time?"

"That's what my story says," said Belle, nodding. A look of pain crossed her face. "I get to do all this." She cast a loving look at the stack of books on the shelf next to her. "I read as much as I can . . . then I fall in love with old beastie boy upstairs." She rolled her eyes and pointed up at the staircase.

John jerked forward in his seat and stared for a moment at where Belle was pointing. This was good. The Beast was here. And if Belle was calling him "old beastie boy," then maybe he wasn't that fierce and he'd be okay meeting with John? I hoped so. I tuned back in to what Belle was saying. "And then . . . he becomes a man again and then we have a big wedding. . . ." She drummed out the words as if she had told the story a hundred times before—actually, it was worse than that; Belle had *lived* the story a hundred times before. "Then *poof*, it starts all over again."

"Your story starts all over again?" repeated John, looking like he was trying to make sense of what Belle was saying. "So, it restarts like a video game. You just go back to the start."

"Pretty much," said Belle.

John looked completely confused. His forehead was furrowed, and he was holding the side of his head, like he was worried his brain was going to fall out. I knew how he was feeling even though it had been a while since I'd thought about how weird it was that the fairy tales, like "Beauty and the Beast," were on repeat play. I remembered how I'd felt when I'd seen the wall of photos at Snow White's cottage, and I'd realized that she was stuck on a hamster wheel of marriage proposals and weddings. I wondered what happened to the Evil Queen when that fairy tale reset. Did she have to start her whole business over again?

"Isn't that horrible?" asked John. "Doing the same thing again and again? Like, do you not get bored?"

"No, not bored." Belle sighed. "But it's frustrating. I read as many books as I can, and then—*poof*—I restart and forget everything I've read. I have to start at the beginning all over again."

That would be awful. Like having to study for the same test again and again. But you could keep reading your favorite book, and every single time would be just as awesome as the very first time you picked it up. So, maybe Belle's situation wasn't totally awful?

"Last time when the hourglass was empty, I started learning Greek because I wanted to read *The Odyssey* in the original language, the way it was written. . . ."

"You're such a geek, Belle," said Hildee affectionately.

"There's some good stuff in *The Odyssey*, 'Ildee," said Belle. "You might like it. . . . Anyway, I got pretty far, but then after the wedding, I couldn't remember anything."

Okay. That would be awful. Poor Belle.

Claude reappeared, carrying a tray on one hand with a tower of tiny triangle-shaped sandwiches on it and a stack of silver plates on the other. He placed everything on the table in front of us and bowed deeply. Not only had he not changed out of his butler uniform, but he had also added another detail. Immaculate, dazzlingly white gloves.

"Will that be all, mademoiselle?"

"Would you get their rooms ready, please, Claude?" asked Belle.

"Of course," said Claude, still bowing. "I'll prepare the Blue Boudoir for the ladies and the Stag Suite for the gentleman."

"Oh, but Belle," said Hildee, "we're not staying. We're flying back home tonight." She pointed at John, who looked like he'd recovered from the shock of hearing about fairy tales on a constant loop and was busy making his own little tower of triangle sandwiches. "He has football practice in the morning. . . ." She paused and turned to Claude. "Actually, these three all need passports before we get on the plane tonight, if you could—"

"That can be arranged, mademoiselle," said Claude, bowing and tapping the side of his nose with two fingers.

I exchanged a glance with Romy. What was that all about? Was Claude a chauffeur/butler/expert forger? Romy shrugged and reached for another sandwich.

"And," continued Hildee, turning back to Belle, "the girls have to confront Elvira Queen—"

"Confront?" interrupted Belle, raising an eyebrow and looking at me, then Romy. "You can't just confront the Evil Queen!"

I filled in Belle on the skill extractions that we believed were going to happen at the tour of the Forever Young headquarters. I'd been hoping that Belle might have some ideas on how to take on the Evil Queen—something in one of her books, maybe?—but she seemed to be as freaked out as I was about the queen.

"So, she's expanding her repertoire," she said, taking a deep breath. Even though Belle had looked horrified as I told her what the queen was planning, I was happy to see that she wasn't surprised. So, I felt more certain than ever that we had done the right thing coming to Paris. "You know, she used to just be obsessed with being the most beautiful woman in the world."

"Oh, she's still obsessed with that," said Hildee. "A couple of months ago she was a judge at the Miss World contest." She paused to nibble on her sandwich. I exchanged a grimace with Romy. I didn't know those beauty contests still existed. Weren't they illegal now? "Anyway, a few days after the contest, the winner—Miss World—developed an addiction to peanuts. Couldn't stop eating them. But the thing is, she was *allergic* to peanuts. Her eyes swelled shut and she got enormous lips. Mother told me all about it. Said I should show the same level of dedication."

"To what?" I said, pushing away the awful image of what the poor contestant must have looked like. "Murder? That woman could have died!"

"Oh no," said Hildee, her eyes widening. "I hope that didn't happen. Mother didn't say . . ." She covered her mouth with her hand. "Mother just meant that I should be dedicated to finding a rich husband. You know what Mother's like . . . says I need to be prettier, smarter, thinner—just . . ." She sighed and slumped back into her chair. "Just not this." She pointed at herself.

"Your mother sounds—" began John. He looked shocked, holding his sandwich midway to his mouth as if his hand had suddenly frozen. "She sounds—" He glanced at me and Romy like he wanted us to fill in the blanks.

"Abusive," said Romy furiously.

"And demented," added Belle.

"You shouldn't listen to her, Hildee," I said, feeling so angry at Hildee's mother. Parents were supposed to be their kids' cheerleaders, not put them down. "You're amazing."

"You are," said Romy. "You're not afraid of anything, Hildee . . . you charged the Groac'h. And you're so positive about everything."

"Really?" asked Hildee, smiling at me and Romy and sitting up in her chair.

It was great that Hildee seemed to be listening to all

the compliments, but we needed to get back to talking about how we were going to stop the Evil Queen. I turned to face Belle.

"The awards ceremony is tomorrow, so we need to get to the Evil Queen before then and . . ."

"Well, she's got a book signing this morning," interrupted Belle.

John glanced nervously over his shoulder.

"Not here!" said Belle, catching John's eye. "I don't stock her books. They are absolute drivel. It's at the Musée d'Orsay."

"Could Claude take us?" I asked, looking up at Claude, who'd disappeared for a while (maybe to take care of the passports?) but was now standing at attention by Belle's side.

"Well, yes," said Belle hesitantly. She breathed on her glasses, rubbed them on the end of her sweater, and put them on. She gave me a firm look. "Claude can take you, but how are you going to stop the queen?"

Claude coughed and gave me a small bow. "Mademoiselle, I shall return to bring you to the Musée d'Orsay as soon as I am suitably attired."

"Oh Claude, you don't need to—" began Belle as Claude walked away. She shrugged her shoulders and shook her head. "At least someone around here enjoys dressing up. . . ." She turned her attention back to me. "How do you plan on stopping her? That woman is pure evil." Belle shuddered. "Last I heard, Snow White was afraid to eat because she's so scared of being poisoned."

I'd been wondering if the Evil Queen still bothered with Snow White, what with running a company and being an international celebrity. It seemed she still did. Poor Snow White. She'd been horrible to me, but that didn't make it okay for her to have to worry about the Evil Queen contaminating her food.

"How are you going to stop her?" Belle repeated.

Belle was staring at me, giving me a confused, critical look. Romy was smiling and nodding like she was expecting me to talk about some awesome plan I had. I hadn't had a chance to tell Romy that I had come up with something before I fell asleep on the plane. It wasn't awesome, but she'd probably tell me it was. And John, who'd been avoiding catching my eye since we'd got out of the car, was looking at me. He looked really interested, as if he couldn't wait to hear what I was going to say next. Hildee was the only one who wasn't staring at me. She had her head down, and she was filing her nails.

I sat up straighter and cleared my throat.

"So, I've been thinking about the queen's magic mirror." I thought about the words I had read in the Brothers Grimm book: "*Then she was satisfied, for she knew that the mirror spoke the truth.*" I looked at Belle. "Does the mirror answer all questions, or just ones about beauty? And does it answer anyone who asks it a question, or just the queen?"

"Oh, it answers whoever asks. And it answers all questions," said Belle. A worried look crossed her face. "But—" She raised a finger and pointed it at me.

"And where does the Evil Queen keep it?" I continued, speaking quickly, worried that I'd lose my nerve if I didn't keep talking. Belle looked annoyed, as if she didn't like what I was saying. It was making me very uncomfortable.

"She never lets it out of her sight. It's with her at all times," answered Belle sharply. "Why?"

"So, I just thought that we"—I looked at Romy, who nodded back at me—"could borrow the mirror and then—"

"I love it!" interrupted Romy loudly and excitedly. "Then we just ask the mirror how to stop the Evil Queen." She put her elbows on the table and looked at me. "Awesome plan, Cia!"

"Stealing the mirror is a terrible plan," said Belle.

"She said 'borrow,' not 'steal,'" said Romy, catching Belle's eye.

"That magic mirror," began Belle, shaking her head. She leaned back in her chair, then looked firmly at me, Romy, and John. "It's—"

There was a loud chime.

"Oh," said Belle, distractedly. "That's my ten o'clock appointment." She started to get up, but then sat back down again. She gave me an even firmer look. "The queen's mirror is dangerous. You have to be very careful with it."

There was another loud chime.

"I'd better take care of this," she said, getting to her feet again. "It's the Duke of Orlay. He's selling off books from the family library. . . . Lots of rare first editions . . ."

"A duke!" cried Hildee, reaching for her makeup bag.

"Take it easy, 'Ildee," said Belle, smoothing down her

turtleneck and taking off her glasses. "He's posh but poor. He's selling everything in the castle, and he has to live in the stables with the horses. . . ."

Hildee's hand, which was now holding her blush brush, stopped midway to her cheek. "Well, I'm not living with horses." She sighed, putting the brush away and zipping up her bag.

"I hope he has some first-edition Balzac," muttered Belle as she walked away.

There was a polite cough.

Claude had returned. He was wearing his chauffeur's uniform.

"I believe the book signing will commence in thirty minutes," he said.

"Okay," I said. "Let's go, Romy." What Belle had said about the mirror being dangerous didn't change anything. We had no other way of finding out how to stop the queen. Anyway, Belle seemed to know a lot about it, so we could just bring the mirror back here and she could tell us how to use it in a way that wasn't dangerous.

I stood up and felt a rush of adrenaline. In thirty minutes, I'd be standing in front of the Evil Queen.

"I'm coming too," said Hildee, buttoning up her blazer and tightening her scarf. She stood up.

"Five hundred is a more than fair price," said Belle, reappearing around the corner of the nook. She was talking to a man—it must have been the penniless duke—who was carrying a stack of worn-looking books. He was wearing a tweed jacket, a yellow checked shirt, and navy corduroy pants. He looked young, about the same age as Belle and Hildee, but his balding head and sad droopy eyes made him seem much older.

He turned his head toward us, nodded politely, and then stopped suddenly in his tracks, his eyes glued to Hildee. Hildee was staring back at him, her mouth hanging open ever so slightly, and her eyes wide as if she'd been stunned.

The duke stepped toward Hildee and stood in front of her. "Mademoiselle," he said as Hildee extended her hand to him. He took it and kissed it. "I am Hugo," he continued. He released Hildee's fingers and placed his right hand over his chest as if he were about to swear an oath.

"I am Hildee," said Hildee, sounding delighted and surprised as if she'd only just realized what her name was.

"This is weird," whispered Romy to me.

"If you'll just come this way," said Belle, looking worried and touching the duke on the shoulder. "I can pay you for the books."

The duke handed Belle the books and said, "Take them," without taking his eyes off Hildee.

Claude coughed again. A little more loudly than last time.

"Hildee," I said, leaning over to her. She was still staring at the duke. "We're going to go. . . ."

"Bye," she said, raising a hand in a wave but not breaking eye contact with the duke, who was gazing down at her. Had I missed something? Was he incredibly handsome? I stared at him for a moment. No, he wasn't. And now that I was looking at him more closely, I saw that the hem of his jacket was frayed, his shirt was missing some buttons, and there was a hole on the top of one of his shoes. Hopefully he'd use money from the book sales to buy some new clothes.

"I'm staying here, Cia," said Hildee calmly and decisively. "You go ahead." She shooed me away, her eyes never leaving the duke's face.

"C'mon, Cia," muttered Romy, getting to her feet.

I was worried that Belle might try to stop us from leaving, but her eyes were riveted to Hildee and the duke. She wasn't paying attention to me anymore. Could she be *that* worried that the duke wouldn't sell his books to her because he was distracted by Hildee? Maybe those first editions Belle was hoping for were a really big deal?

Giving up on Hildee, I asked John if he wanted to come with us. He hadn't signed up for confronting fairy-tale villains, but it seemed rude not to ask him, and I didn't want him to think that I was feeling awkward around him after what I'd said (and he'd *not* said) in the car. I *did* feel awkward, but I didn't want him to know that.

"Yes," he shouted, jumping up and throwing a fearful look at Hildee and the duke. He clearly wanted to get away. I couldn't blame him. Who'd want to be in a room with two people who were making sappy faces at each other and looked as if they were about to collide like a couple of magnets?

Chapter 17

WE GOT BACK INTO THE ROLLS-ROYCE, AND Claude sped off, navigating the Parisian traffic like a race-car driver. Romy and I agreed that while she distracted the Evil Queen—she'd played Juliet in the school play last year, and now she could faint and/or burst into tears on demand—I'd grab the magic mirror. Then I took deep breaths, trying to fight an icky, nauseating feeling of fear, but it just got bigger and bigger the farther we got from Belle's.

Every time I caught Romy's eye, she said, "We can do this, Cia." John didn't say a word. He just kept staring out

189

the window or looking at his hands. In what felt like a few minutes, Claude had parked and was turning around to tell us that we had arrived.

I looked out the window.

We were in front of another beautiful old castle-like building. There was a huge poster of Elvira Queen's face plastered to the front of the building, winking and holding a finger to her lips as if she were about to let everyone in on a big secret. She was holding a book up to her face that had the same photo of her on the cover.

"What does that say?" asked Romy.

"'One day only,'" read Claude. "'Meet with Elvira Queen and learn how you too can be Forever Young.'"

"There aren't any men here," noted John, sounding a little worried. I followed his gaze out the car window. There was a line of at least a hundred women snaking around the front and side of the building. They were all wearing fussy-looking party dresses, even though it was only ten o'clock in the morning. Some of them were jumping up and down and clutching each other as if they were going to burst from excitement.

"Maybe I'll just stay in the car with Claude?" said John.

"Very good, sir," said Claude, as if he thought that John was making a wise decision.

"Unless . . . you think you might need me," added John anxiously, tearing his eyes away from the window.

"It's okay," I said. It was true; we really didn't need John. Romy was going to create the distraction, and also, I figured that no one should meet the Evil Queen (or really, anyone who was evil) unless they absolutely had to. Romy couldn't avoid it, but John could.

"Let's go," said Romy.

Claude got out of the car and walked around to the passenger side. About a third of the people in the line looked over at him and started leaning forward and craning their necks to see who was in the back of the incredibly beautiful Rolls-Royce.

Well, they were going to be really disappointed when Romy and I stepped out and they saw it was just a couple of teenagers who hadn't even bothered to brush their hair.

Romy and I got out and walked toward the entrance, and the two security guards—who I'd thought would ask us for tickets—held open the doors and ushered us in.

"That's what happens when you show up in a fancy car," said Romy under her breath.

We stepped inside, and the doors shut behind us.

The place looked like a shrine to Elvira Queen. There were FOREVER YOUNG banners hanging from the ceiling, hundreds of copies of her book stacked in artful displays on tables, and huge pictures of her everywhere. I jumped back when I saw one of her holding out a shiny green apple. (It was just an advertisement for the Golden Delicious Deep Cleanser, but seeing the Evil Queen holding an apple made me feel sick.)

"Look at that," said Romy, tugging on the sleeve of my sweater. "It's Gavin."

I whipped around to see what she was talking about. Gavin wasn't supposed to be flying to Paris until tomorrow. But Romy was just pointing at a picture of him. It was an enormous photo of his face—so big and bright that I could see the blue brackets of his braces—and he looked really happy; maybe it was taken when he learned he'd won a spot to go to Paris. It was one of ten photos of equally happy, grinning winners. Underneath the line of photos were the words:

CONGRATULATIONS TO THE WINNERS OF THE ELVIRA QUEEN EXCELLENCE AWARDS.

My heart skipped a beat. So, these were the kids who were going to have whatever it was that had earned them a trip to Paris taken away from them. There were six girls and four boys. I stepped closer to the display so that I could read the word that was imprinted across the bottom of each picture. I knew that the word underneath Gavin's photo was "bravery." The girl next to him had huge brown eyes and was wearing a hijab, and her word was "generosity." Beside her was a boy with glasses that seemed too big for his face. "Idealism" was what would be taken from him. The next girl's was "kindness."

I couldn't read any more. It was too awful to think about how these kids would feel if their bravery, generosity, idealism, and kindness were taken from them. And what about their families? It would be awful for them too.

"Where's the queen?" I asked, scanning the huge hall. I didn't know if the rush of energy I was feeling was from fear or a determination to do something. It didn't matter. I had to see her.

"This way," said Romy, pointing at a line of women who were holding copies of Elvira Queen's book.

We walked over to the end of the line, and a security guard approached us, holding out books to me and Romy. "Approach Madame Queen when I give you the signal," he said. "Do not look Madame Queen in the eyes. . . . Do not engage Madame Queen in conversation. . . . Only speak when spoken to. . . ."

"Come on," muttered Romy as the security guard walked away from us. "That's stupid . . . I am *so* looking her in the eyes." She stuck out her chin.

The women in front of us stepped forward, and I caught a glimpse of the Evil Queen sitting at a table between two tall stacks of books.

"There she is," I whispered to Romy.

"Great outfit," observed Romy, standing on tippy-toes so she could see over the shoulders of the woman in front of us. "Very Snow Queen . . ."

Elvira Queen was wearing a long white dress with white fur-trimmed cuffs and collar, as well as a white headband studded with diamonds. She did look like the Snow Queen. It was a good look for her. She had an ice-cold heart, too.

I felt a hand on my shoulder. I jumped. The security guard was back.

"Madame Queen would like to see you now," he said.

"Great," said Romy, grabbing my hand and squeezing it. As we followed the security guard, she whispered to me, "I'll distract her. You get the mirror."

We approached Elvira Queen's table. She was waving goodbye to two women who were holding on to copies of her book as if they contained winning lottery tickets. She gave them a warm, dazzling smile, which changed into a disgusted grimace as soon as their backs were turned.

"Miss Queen," gushed Romy, leaning over the table. "I'm such a huge, HUGE fan."

"Are you really?" asked the queen, raising an eyebrow and giving Romy a look that showed she didn't believe a word Romy had said.

She turned to me. "What a treat," she said, leaning her head to one side and folding her arms, "seeing you and your mother both in the same morning."

"What?" I blurted out. What was the queen talking about? "But my mom is in—"

"Istanbul?" interrupted the queen, holding out her

hands and admiring her perfectly manicured nails. They were the same white as her dress.

Beside me Romy gasped. Was she thinking the same thing as me? How did the queen know Mom was supposed to be in Istanbul?

"Your mother didn't go to Istanbul." She looked up from her hands and stared at me. There was a hungry, nasty look in her eyes. She gave me a wolfish grin. "Your mother came to see me."

"But why?" I asked, swallowing hard. I wasn't sure why, but I felt terrified, as if I were receiving really, really bad news. My heart was contracting with fear.

"Well, she didn't agree with the Elvira Queen Excellence Awards. She said that extracting certain essences from children"—she curled her upper lip when she said "children," as if the word was really offensive—"was not entirely ethical. . . ."

Mom had come to Paris to stop the Evil Queen? But Mom had ignored me when I'd told her that the Evil Queen was up to something. So, Mom had believed me all along? My mind was bouncing from confusion to anger to relief, and then back to confusion and anger and relief.

"Well, I've never let anything as silly as," the queen continued, raising her arms and making air quotes, "'doing the right thing' stop me from doing what I want." She leaned forward and hooked her finger, beckoning me to come closer. "But she offered me a trade. So, I gave her my word that I wouldn't interfere with the winners' talents—and she gave me what I wanted." She leaned on the table and steepled her fingers. "Deal done."

"You mean, you're not going to siphon off Gavin's bravery?" asked Romy, sounding a little breathless.

"No," said the queen curtly. "Nor will I take Asma's generosity or Elisabeth's persistence or Ibram's sense of humor, though"—she sighed and glanced toward the display of all the smiling, happy winners—"it would have been so easy."

"And the reason you're not going to do this," I said, beginning to understand but not believing that the explanation I was coming up with was possible, "is because my mom gave you something?"

"Indeed," said the queen, looking at me. "Now," she added, pointing at the book I was holding, "shall I sign that for you?"

I felt like I was going to scream. Mom had believed me. She had gone to Paris. She had given the queen something to stop her from carrying out her plan. Why hadn't Mom told me about any of this? Why hadn't Mom said something when I was in her room, when she knew how upset and worried I was?

"What is wrong with her?" I said through gritted teeth. I was so mad. "She won't tell me anything." I turned to Romy. "She has all these secrets . . . like on her phone. In her contacts there's a 'sister number two.' Mom doesn't have a sister. Why does she have that contact? And—"

"Cia."

Romy said my name softly, but something in her tone made me stop. I looked at her. She glanced at me and then swiveled her eyes in the direction of the queen, who was sitting back in her chair, staring at me and looking like she had just eaten something really delicious. It was a look that filled me with fear.

"I think we'd better go," said Romy.

My heart started thumping. We couldn't leave now. Maybe everything the queen had said was true—and part of me knew that it probably was true and that Mom *had* given her something. (What could that possibly have been? Didn't the queen have everything?) Gavin and the others would be safe now. But what if there was a chance that the queen was lying to me and Romy? Wouldn't the magic mirror tell us if she was? And the magic mirror could give me answers to all the questions that I'd been asking Mom. This was my chance to find out everything.

But where was the mirror?

The queen raised her hand and beckoned to a security guard; then she reached into a beige purse on a stool beside her and pulled out a gold fountain pen, the tips of her fingers touching a wooden handle that was sticking out of the purse.

I felt adrenaline flooding me—that wooden handle had to be the handle of the mirror.

"Time's up, ladies," said the security guard.

I needed to do something. Now. I tried to catch Romy's eye, but she was scowling at the security guard. I needed to create a distraction just long enough so I could reach into that purse and grab the mirror.

I had to get Elvira Queen to look the other way.

What would make her look the other way?

Elvira Queen was obsessed with being the most beautiful woman in the world.

So, if she thought there was a more beautiful woman in the same room as her . . .

"That woman," I shouted, placing my hand on my chest. "That woman is the most beautiful woman I've ever seen!" I pointed at the book display behind the queen, where yet another burly security guard was standing, legs wide and hands on her hips as if she were protecting all the books from an imminent attack. "She's GORGEOUS!"

The queen dropped the fountain pen, jumped up, and turned around.

I reached into the purse, grabbed the wooden handle—it was a mirror!—and shoved it into the middle of the book I was still holding.

"We need to leave," I hissed at Romy. She was staring at Elvira Queen, who was now standing less than an inch from the security guard and inspecting her face closely. "NOW!" I grabbed Romy's hand.

There was a throng of people behind us—we'd taken so long with the queen that the line must have gotten backed up. Holding hands, Romy and I moved into the middle of the crowd and headed for the entrance. We walked fast, trying not to draw attention to ourselves, but as soon as we got outside, I ran to the car, pulling Romy along with me.

"What was that all about?" panted Romy as we scrambled into the back of the Rolls-Royce.

"Where to now?" asked Claude, turning to look at us over his shoulder.

"Please just drive!" I shouted. My hands and voice were shaking. "Sorry, I mean . . . just back to Belle's place, please."

I turned and looked out the rear window, expecting to see the Evil Queen and an army of security guards charging toward the car. She must have figured out by now that I had taken the mirror. But there was no one coming. No security guard. No Evil Queen. No one.

I sank back and put Elvira Queen's book on the seat between me and Romy. My arm and shoulder felt sore from clutching it so tightly.

I opened *Forever Young: The Elvira Queen Way* to the middle pages.

"I got the mirror," I said. "I got it."

Chapter 18

ARE YOU SURE YOU TOOK THE RIGHT ONE?" Romy asked, holding up the mirror and turning it at different angles. "It doesn't look very special."

The mirror did look ordinary. For one thing, it was small. About the same size as a hairbrush. The frame was made of wood, and it was a bit scratched up. There was no writing or decoration on the handle or the back. There was really nothing special about it.

"Yeah, this has to be it," I said, taking the mirror from her and putting it on the table. "Everything Elvira Queen has is fancy and designer and new-looking. She'd never have a beat-up mirror like this in her purse if it wasn't *the* magic mirror—"

"That's the magic mirror?" whispered John, a note of awe in his voice. He leaned forward and touched the mirror with the tip of a finger. "So, now you just need to ask it how to stop the Evil Queen?"

"Well, not exactly," I said, and then I explained to John how the Evil Queen had said that she wasn't going to siphon off anyone's talent.

"It turns out Cia's mom got to her before we did, and she had something the queen wanted, so they did a trade," said Romy matter-of-factly.

I glared at her. Why was she bringing up Mom? I was still getting my own head around it, and I was feeling really embarrassed. This whole trip to Paris had basically been for nothing. Mom had been going to take care of the whole thing all along. There had been no reason for me to come. Or Romy. Or John. I didn't feel that bad about Romy; it had been her idea to go to Paris, and she was just missing a day of school. But John? He'd practically been forced into it. And he'd almost been eaten. What if he had panic attacks for the rest of his life because of what had happened with the Groac'h?

"But this is good news," said John, looking confused and obviously trying to understand the worried, angry expression that must have been on my face. "Everyone's going to be okay. The queen's not going to do anything to anyone. We can all go home now—"

"Yeah," said Romy, leaning back in her seat. She sighed happily. "But let's see the Eiffel Tower first and let Hildee check out a couple of stores. We can still be back home in time for school tomorrow."

"Okay," said John, nodding at Romy. "But"—a concerned look crossed his face, and he glanced at me—"why did you take the mirror if you knew that the queen wasn't going to do anything?"

I looked down at the mirror. I could feel John and Romy staring at me, waiting for me to answer. They probably weren't going to like what I was about to say. I had to say it anyway.

I took a deep breath.

"Because there's stuff I want to know," I said, keeping my eyes on the mirror. "Things I can only find out about if I ask the mirror."

"Like what?" asked John softly.

I looked up at him, wondering whether I should tell

him about how frustrated I'd been with Mom. But Romy beat me to it.

"All the stuff her mom won't tell her. Like, what did she give the queen to make her change her mind? And the truth about magic and fairy tales." Romy shrugged and looked at me. "I get it, Cia. It's not fair. I'd want to know too. I do want to know! What is your mom not telling you?"

I nodded; the annoyance I'd felt at Romy had disappeared when she'd said the words *It's not fair*. She got it. It wasn't fair. If Mom had just told me everything, we wouldn't be sitting in this car in France, talking about the Evil Queen's magic mirror.

I stared down at my reflection in the mirror. I looked annoyed and worried. I *was* annoyed and worried.

"But," said John, reaching out and holding his hand over the mirror, "Belle told us the mirror is dangerous. Don't start asking it things."

"You could just ask Belle about it first," said Romy, chewing her lower lip. "I bet she knows way more about it than we do."

But I didn't want to wait. I grabbed the mirror and held it out in front of me. This could answer all my questions.

I was so tired of not understanding what was going on. Romy was giving me a concerned *let's be reasonable* look, but I knew that if the queen had said that *Romy's* mom had made a deal with her, Romy would have bombarded the mirror with questions before we'd even made it back to the car. There was no way she would have waited.

And there was no way I'd have let her do it.

If our positions had been reversed, I'd be the one telling Romy to wait until we'd spoken to Belle.

"Fine," I said, sighing and putting the mirror back on the table.

John exhaled loudly.

"Mademoiselles, monsieur, we have arrived," announced Claude as the car came to a stop.

I grabbed the mirror, leapt out of the car, and ran to the front of the store with Romy and John following me. I rang the bell, and as I waited to be let in, I started thinking through all the questions I'd ask the mirror as soon as Belle gave me the go-ahead.

But it was Hildee who appeared on the other side of the door, and when she opened it, I instantly forgot all about the magic mirror.

Chapter 19

"IS THAT A WEDDING DRESS?" ASKED JOHN, SIDE-stepping Hildee's outstretched arms as she barreled toward us.

Hildee grabbed Romy and me into a tight hug, and the bottom of her dress, which flared out like an enormous lampshade, almost knocked the two of us over.

"You're back!" Hildee shouted, eyes shining. "Did you stop the Evil Queen?"

"Not exactly," I said. "But she's not going to hurt those kids now." I put the mirror in the back pocket of my jeans. Dealing with Mom could wait. I needed to find out why

Hildee was wearing a wedding dress. We'd only been gone an hour; she couldn't have gotten engaged since we'd left, could she?

"You all need to talk to her."

It was Belle. She strode over toward us, scowling at Hildee.

"What's going on?" asked Romy, pulling away from the hug.

"I'm getting married," announced Hildee, her face breaking into a huge smile.

Belle groaned. Romy and I exchanged an uneasy look, and Hildee did a twirl, showing us the tiny yellow silk flowers embroidered all the way down the back of her dress.

John put his hands in his pockets, took a step back, and muttered something under his breath.

"You're getting married?" I said slowly, trying to buy some time. I knew you were supposed to say "Congratulations" when someone told you they were getting married—I think that was what John had just muttered—and Hildee looked so happy that I really did want to say it, but it felt like the right thing to say was, "What are you thinking?" She'd just met the duke—

assuming that was who she was marrying and that no one else had turned up while we were out confronting Elvira Queen.

"Yes," said Hildee, taking a step back and folding her arms across her chest. "I'm getting married this afternoon. In the courtyard. We don't want to wait a moment longer than we have to." She gestured toward the back of the store. "That way you can all be here. We'll get married, and then Hugo and I will fly back with you to New York."

Hugo? It was the duke.

"This afternoon?" gasped Romy, staring at Hildee. "Like, today? You're going to marry someone the same day you met them?"

"This is a really bad idea," said Belle, leaning so closely toward me and Romy that I could smell the coffee she'd been drinking. "You need to tell her that this is a really bad idea."

I agreed with Belle, but I had no idea how to change Hildee's mind.

"But Hildee, you just met him. . . . You don't even know him," I tried. "And what about the stables? You said you didn't want to live with horses?"

"Cia, I've been waiting for him my whole life . . . ," said Hildee dreamily. "And I'd live with Hugo in a box. I don't care if we have to live in the stables."

Belle rolled her eyes and let out a frustrated grunt.

"But what about Noah?' asked Romy. "This morning he was your snuggle bunny, and last night you were promising to call him every hour . . . and . . ." Romy paused and looked at the ground. I could see she was fighting with herself. She didn't want to push Hildee back into Noah's arms—not that his arms were open—but she also didn't want Hildee to marry a guy she'd just met. "How can you be in love with Hugo now, when you were in love with Noah just this morning?"

"Romy, Noah doesn't love me," Hildee replied matter-of-factly. There wasn't a hint of sadness or regret in her voice. "And I don't love him. Hugo loves me, and I love Hugo. I'm going to spend the rest of my life with him."

Was that even possible? Could you really fall in love with someone in a couple of hours? I didn't know anything about love, but I was pretty sure that it didn't work that way.

This time there was a loud groan from Belle.

Out of the corner of my eye, I saw John inching away from us and heading toward the reading nook. I'd have loved to run away too.

"Don't you want your mom and your sister to be here?" I said, trying a different tactic. "If you get married today, they won't be here. . . . Don't you want them at your wedding? Maybe just wait a couple of months, and that way you can plan a big wedding. . . ."

"No," said Hildee, shaking her head. Her eyes filled with worry. "Mother will be mad that he's not a prince." Her face fell for just a fraction of a second, and then she brightened. "When she meets Hugo, he'll already be my husband. Mother won't be able to stop me."

It was great that Hildee was realizing that she could make her own decisions and not worry about making her mom happy, but that didn't mean that this decision was a good one.

"You two will be there." Hildee grabbed my and Romy's hands. "And John. And Belle. You're the only people I need at my wedding."

Hildee sounded so different from the way I'd heard her talking about Noah. She was confident and calm. She sounded like a grown-up. I thought about the way she'd acted when she'd met Hugo. She'd been laser-focused on him, but she'd also been relaxed. She hadn't fussed with her hair or flapped her eyelashes or giggled the way she did when she was around Noah.

"And you two will be my bridesmaids, won't you?" said Hildee, her eyes starting to glisten with tears. "John will be the groomsman." She squeezed my hand. "You're like my sisters. My little sisters."

"Oh," I stuttered, surprised and moved by Hildee's words and how warm her voice sounded.

"That's really nice of you, Hildee—" said Romy.

"No bridesmaids!" yelled Belle, glaring at me and Romy as if Hildee's decision to get married was our fault. "There can't be a wedding!"

"Right," I said, Belle's tone bringing me back to my senses. I let go of the image of myself walking up the aisle carrying the train of Hildee's wedding dress. I'd never been to a wedding, and I sort of liked the idea of being a bridesmaid.

"No wedding," repeated Belle, as if she were sensing my weakness. "'Ildee cannot get married. She is not supposed to get married. She's a stepsister. Cinderella is the only one in that story who's allowed to get married."

"What?" I gasped, staring at Belle. I couldn't believe she'd said that. It wasn't like Belle even enjoyed her own story. She'd complained about having to marry the Beast every few months, and now, when Hildee had a chance to do something different with *her* story, Belle wanted to stop her?

"That's just mean!" said Romy, whipping around and glaring at Belle.

"A stepsister can't get married," said Belle through gritted teeth. "That's not in the story."

I couldn't believe Belle was so being so nasty. This was why she didn't want Hildee to get married? Because it wasn't part of the "Cinderella" story? I'd thought Belle had been against Hildee's wedding because she cared about Hildee, but it seemed like that wasn't it at all. She just cared that the story Hildee was in was told properly.

It was all right for Belle. She had a starring role in her fairy tale. She had a Beast waiting for her to turn him into a prince whenever she felt like it. Little girls all over the world dressed up as her. What did Hildee have? No prince had ever asked her to dance. No one ever wanted to dress up as her. Why shouldn't she get to live her dream too?

"Congratulations, Hildee," said Romy. She leaned in to hug Hildee and scowled at Belle over Hildee's shoulder. "I think it's fantastic news, and I'd love to be your bridesmaid!"

I couldn't tell if Romy had changed her mind just because, like me, she was so mad at Belle, or if she really was starting to think that Hildee marrying the duke was a good idea. Romy's grandparents had had an arranged marriage. The first time they'd seen each other was on their wedding day, and they'd always seemed really happy. Maybe Romy was thinking of them? And Hildee did look so happy. She was glowing. Who were we to tell her what to do? Romy and I were only thirteen. We didn't know anything about love. And Hildee was a fairy-tale character; they did things differently. In lots of the stories I'd read, the princes and princesses just met and got married straightaway.

"Congratulations, Hildee," I said, hugging her. "I'm really happy for you, and I'd love to be your bridesmaid too."

"Thanks, Cia. Thanks, Romy," said Hildee, wiping away a tear. "You'll both be beautiful bridesmaids."

"This is a really bad idea," said Belle, shaking her head. "A really, really bad idea."

She turned to Claude, who had been hovering close by the entire time, probably waiting for instructions/an opportunity to wear another outfit. "Showtime in an hour, Claude," she said wearily. "You know the drill."

"Indeed, mademoiselle." He made a small bow. "The gazebo in the courtyard? As per usual?"

Belle nodded.

"Congratulations, Hildee." She sighed, looking like she was resigning herself to the inevitable. She shrugged. "Maybe you'll get lucky. Maybe she won't show up. . . ."

She? Who was Belle talking about?

"Now, gotta find some gloves!" Hildee laughed, lifting up the skirt of her dress and running up the staircase. "See you in an hour!"

"She's going to be so mad . . . ," grumbled Belle to herself. She walked away from us and joined John at the table in the nook under the stairs. He was looking through a big hardcover book that had pictures of Roman ruins.

"Who are you talking about?" asked Romy as she and I followed Belle. "Who's going to be so mad?"

"Mmm?" said Belle, looking back at us distractedly. Then her face relaxed a little as if some good news—or the possibility of good news—was occurring to her. "Maybe they'll get away before she even finds out there's been a wedding. . . ."

"We could ask this," I offered, pulling the mirror from my back pocket. Although finding out whether an unwelcome guest was going to show up at Hildee's wedding was not the question I was dying to ask it.

"The Evil Queen's magic mirror," said Belle slowly. She stared at it and inhaled deeply as if she needed to steady herself. She looked firmly at me and then at Romy.

"Please tell me you haven't asked it anything."

Chapter 20

"N O," SAID ROMY, GIVING ME A LOOK THAT WAS just the tiniest bit smug. I couldn't blame her. Judging by the way Belle was staring at the mirror, as if it were a bomb that might explode, Romy and John had been right to stop me from using it.

"Good," said Belle firmly, putting on her glasses. She reached out her hand. "May I?"

I gave her the mirror.

Belle placed the mirror on the table and stared at it. She looked immensely curious and a little frightened,

as if she were looking at an insect that might fly off the table and sting her on the nose.

"What happens if you ask it a question?" asked John, leaning back so that Romy and I had space to sit down beside him. The three of us sat on one side of the table with Belle on the other, as if we were students in a class she was teaching.

"There's great danger in this mirror," said Belle, turning the mirror over so that it was facedown on the table. "It takes payment for every question it answers."

"What kind of payment?" I asked, swallowing hard. I almost didn't want to know what I'd just barely avoided. What if I hadn't listened to Romy and John?

"It takes a little piece of your soul," said Belle. "A little piece of the kindness and goodness and light."

There was a moment of silence as we all let that sink in.

"The Evil Queen wasn't always evil, you know," she continued. "But she was given this mirror, and bit by bit, answer by answer, it took her soul. And when all the kindness and goodness and light is gone, what's left?"

"Greed," I said. The Evil Queen wanted to be the richest woman in the world. "Jealousy." She couldn't stand it if she thought someone was more beautiful than her. "Cruelty." She'd told her huntsman to kill Snow White.

"Exactly," said Belle. "So, make sure your question is worth it before you ask. And ask only one."

Only one.

We needed to make sure that the queen had told us the truth and that Gavin and the other kids weren't in any danger. That was the reason we'd come to Paris. That was the question I had to ask, right? But this was my chance to find out about all the things that Mom wouldn't tell me. How could I not ask about that?

"I think Belle means we get one question each," said Romy softly as if reading my mind.

"Well, I'm not asking it anything," blurted out John, putting a hand over his chest. "I'm not messing around with that thing. . . ."

Belle gave a tiny nod, as if she thought that was a wise decision.

"I'll ask whether or not the queen told us the truth," said Romy, biting her lower lip. "Then you ask it about your . . ." She looked down at the floor and then back at me. "Well, then you ask it whatever you want."

"Okay," I said, exhaling loudly. I'd been holding my breath without realizing it.

Romy picked up the mirror and held it out in front of her so that both John and I could see her reflection.

"Do I need to say something special?" she asked Belle. "Like 'mirror, mirror.'"

Belle shook her head.

"The Brothers Grimm added that bit. They liked rhyming things. There's no special way to ask. You just ask a question."

"Okay," said Romy. She frowned and stuck out the tip of her tongue—always a sign that she was trying to fig-ure something out. "Here goes," she whispered. Then in a loud, clear voice she asked, "Was everything the Evil Queen told us this morning true?"

The surface of the mirror shimmered, and Romy's reflection disappeared. One word appeared on the surface.

YES.

I felt relieved. Gavin and the other kids weren't in any danger.

"Are you okay?" John asked Romy.

"Yeah." Romy sighed, putting the mirror back on the

table. Her hands were trembling, and her face was pale. Her shoulders sagged, and she leaned back on the sofa.

"I felt something when I asked the question," she said. She swallowed hard and looked over at Belle. "What you said about it taking a part of your soul . . . I felt it. Like I was being pricked by an ice-cold needle." She shivered.

"You were," said Belle, leaning across the table and giving Romy's hand a squeeze. She looked at me and John. "Hugs and supportive words and compliments will help to melt it." She pushed away from the table. "And a warm blanket. I'll go get you one."

I turned, gave Romy a tight hug, and said, "You're the best." Over her shoulder, I could see John looking uncomfortable, obviously not wanting to get in on the hug, but still wanting to follow Belle's instructions so that Romy would feel better.

"You're a really awesome friend," he said quietly, looking down at his hands. "And you're really brave and—"

"It's okay, John," said Romy, laughing and pulling away from my hug. "I'm feeling better."

"So, my turn now," I said, feeling nervous. But I was

excited too. I was finally going to find out what Mom was hiding from me.

I thought about the things she had said to me just before she left.

There is great danger in those tales.

There are forces that you don't understand.

What should I ask?

I picked up the mirror and held it out just as Romy had, so that she and John could see it.

"Do you remember the story of Pandora's box?" asked John hesitantly.

"Yeah," I said. "She opens a box even though she was told not to—"

"She's so curious, she can't help herself," interrupted John. "And she opens it, and she releases all this awful stuff that was in the box . . . diseases and worries and plagues—"

"I'm not like Pandora," I said, feeling my face getting hot. "She was just being nosy. This is about my mom." My voice started cracking, and I felt tears welling up. "She won't tell me things. This might be the only way I can find out what she's hiding from me."

"You kind of sound like Pandora," muttered John.

"Just let her do what she wants," said Romy. "How would you like it if your mother was keeping some massive secret from you?"

"I don't know," grumbled John. He was quiet for a moment. "Sorry, Cia."

But maybe John was right. What if there were really good reasons why Mom wouldn't answer my questions? What if she really was protecting me? Suddenly I felt bad that when she'd left last night, I hadn't told her I loved her. I'd been so angry at her, but she *had* taken everything I'd said seriously. She'd gone to Paris and confronted the Evil Queen. I wished I could see her right now. Maybe she was still in Paris?

"Where is my mom?"

It was only when I felt an ice-cold sensation in my chest that I realized I had spoken out loud.

The surface of the mirror rippled, and an image appeared.

I saw Mom standing in front of an enormous, incredibly intricate tapestry. She was leaning forward, peering at a spot on the tapestry, which showed a bored-looking young man with blond hair to his shoulders, sitting in a field surrounded by sheep.

"Is that your mother?" asked Belle, sounding shocked, as she carried in a pale purple blanket. She wrapped it around my and Romy's shoulders, and the frozen feeling in my chest started to disappear.

"I can't believe it," said Belle, leaning over my shoulder and pointing at the mirror just as the image started to fade. "She's at the Tapestry of Tales."

"The what?" I asked, placing the mirror back on the table.

"The Tapestry of Tales," repeated Belle excitedly. She walked away from us, cupping her hands over her mouth. Then she clapped her hands together.

"What's the Tapestry of Tales?" asked John.

"The Tapestry of Tales!" gushed Belle, her eyes shining. "No one has seen it for hundreds of years. Hang on. I read about it in one of these books." She ran over to one of the towering shelves. She climbed up the library ladder and grabbed a book from the top shelf, one leg dangling over the side of the ladder.

"Got it!" she yelled, scrambling back down. She

rejoined us at the table, holding the book to her chest. "This is really old, so don't touch it," she warned. "Don't even breathe on it."

She placed the book, which looked like a fancy leather-bound journal, carefully on the table. The brown material was worn and faded, and the edges of the paper that stuck out of the sides were frayed and yellowed. It looked like it hadn't been opened in a very long time.

"This," whispered Belle, as if talking normally would damage the book, "is the travel journal of Marco Polo. . . ."

"I know that name," said John, putting an elbow on the table and resting his chin on his hand. "He was an explorer, right?"

"Yes. An Italian explorer," said Belle, reaching for a pair of white gloves on top of a side table. She put them on and untied the leather strap that was wrapped around the journal. "About seven hundred years ago, when he was not much older than the three of you, he left his home in Venice."

"And he didn't return home for more than twenty years," continued Belle, putting on her glasses. "He traveled along what was called the Silk Road and visited

China, Persia, and India. He was received in the royal court of Kublai Khan, and there he saw . . . this."

She opened the journal to the middle pages.

The two pages Belle opened were covered with beautiful script in a language that I didn't recognize. I guessed that it was Italian. On the upper corner of one of the pages, there was an intricate sketch of a young man on bended knee gazing up at a beautiful lady with straight black hair that fell to her ankles. She was slipping a dainty foot into a shoe.

"What? Is that Cinderella?" said Romy, pointing at the page.

"Not exactly. That's Yeh-Shen," said Belle, shooing away Romy's finger. "She's the Chinese Cinderella. Almost the same story as the one you know . . . though the fairy godmother is a fairy godfather and there's only one stepsister."

"But what do Marco Polo and Kublai Khan have to do with where Mom is?" I asked. "This stuff happened forever ago."

"Because," said Belle, peering at me from over her glasses, "Marco Polo sketched a tiny part of what he saw in the great hall of Kublai Khan's palace. He described an exquisite tapestry that ran along the walls of the entire perimeter of the court."

She looked down at the book, her finger hovering over a line of the text.

"'The Tapestry of Tales is the greatest treasure of the royal court,'" she read. Understanding Italian was obviously another one of Belle's talents. "'It blazes with color and textures. The stories—amazing tales of adventure, the likes of which I have never encountered—leap from the fabric. It would take a man months to see each story that is woven here.'"

I turned to Belle. "And you're saying that Mom is at this tapestry now?"

Belle nodded.

"So, she's somewhere in Paris?"

"Oh no," said Belle, looking taken aback. "The tapestry's not in Paris. It hasn't been here since the French Revolution. It had been in the court of Louis the Fourteenth in Versailles . . . but then it was moved. Somewhere out of France."

"Well, where is it now?" asked Romy.

"No one knows," said Belle dramatically. She took off

her glasses. "Oh, I'd love to see it." She gazed into the distance, a dreamy look on her face. "Can you imagine all those stories . . . ?"

"But what's Mom doing there?"

"It's amazing that she found it," said Belle, a note of awe in her voice. "People have been searching for it for hundreds of years." She put her glasses back on. "Is your mother a treasure hunter?"

"No," I began, almost laughing at the image of Mom wearing an Indiana Jones–style hat that popped into my head. But then I started to feel hot and uncomfortable. I pushed the blanket off my shoulders. *Was* Mom some kind of treasure hunter? Was this yet another thing she was keeping from me?

Someone coughed behind me.

Claude was back, his eyes and forehead just visible above the layers and layers of blue tulle and taffeta that he was carrying in his arms. Dainty beige sandals and a pair of shiny black dress shoes dangled from his hands.

"The bride has requested the presence of her bridesmaids and groomsman," he said, laying the clothes on the back of a chair and placing the shoes underneath them.

"I've been instructed to give you these. The ceremony will commence in fifteen minutes. The bride will meet you at the entrance to the courtyard."

"These look awesome—thanks, Claude," said Romy, eyeing the dresses excitedly.

"The Blue Boudoir is ready for the ladies; it is the first door on the right at the top," said Claude, pointing up at the staircase. "The Stag Suite for the young gentleman is right beside it."

"Got it," said Romy, lifting up the dresses. "C'mon, Cia. Let's get changed."

I put the mirror in the back pocket of my jeans and took a deep breath. I'd get dressed up and go to Hildee's wedding. Then, as soon as the ceremony was over, we'd get our flight to New York—we could drop off the mirror at the Forever Young headquarters on our way, since it was too dangerous for anyone other than the Evil Queen to have it; her soul was already frozen solid—and as soon as Mom got home, I'd tell her she had to answer all my questions. She'd have to be impressed that I'd rescued John from a witch and stolen the Evil Queen's mirror from right under her nose. Okay, maybe she wouldn't be impressed with the stealing part. But Mom would have to realize that I was able to handle whatever secrets she was trying to protect me from.

"Okay," I said, grabbing the two pairs of shoes from under the chair.

"You guys know what a groomsman is supposed to do?" asked John, standing up and looking nervously at the tuxedo that Claude had left on a chair. "I won't have to make a speech . . . will I?"

"Nah," said Romy confidently. Had she ever even been to a wedding? "That's the best man's job. You just need to look good."

"Okay," gulped John, still looking nervous. "Look good. I think I can do that." He reached for the tux and shiny black shoes. "See you guys in ten minutes."

Romy and I separated from John and got changed in a beautiful room. Everything in it was in shades of blue, from the wallpaper with a pattern of tiny birds and the velvet pillows on the bed to the comfy chairs and huge vase filled with blue daisies and roses and poppies. It almost made me wish we were going to be staying the night.

"I bet John's gonna look cute in a tux," said Romy,

standing in front of a long mirror and adjusting the waistband of her dress. She looked over her shoulder and grinned at me. "Not that you'd care about that. Seeing as you don't like him anymore."

"You know that's not what I meant," I said, groaning. "Do you think *he* knows what I meant? That I had a crush on him before, but I don't, like, *like* him now?"

"Duh," said Romy, moving the skirt of her dress from side to side. It made a nice swooshing sound. "He's not an idiot, Cia. He knows what you meant."

"But do you think . . . ," I said, coming alongside Romy to check out my dress in the mirror. It had a pale blue top and a long satin skirt that made me feel like twirling. It was the nicest thing I'd ever worn. "Do you think I hurt his feelings? He looked kind of sad."

"He's fine," said Romy. "You had a crush on him, and now you don't. It's not a big deal." She gave me a sideways grin and wiggled her eyebrows. "You don't still *like* him, do you?"

"Definitely not," I said. But I wasn't really sure that was the right answer. I couldn't tell whether I still had a crush on John. If I did have one, it was buried too far underneath my embarrassment to matter. "I mean, of course I like him as a friend. John's really nice."

"He is nice," agreed Romy. "When he's not holding grudges or freaking out about stuff."

"Aww, that's not really fair, Romy," I said, thinking about all the things John had been through. I wondered if he'd completely recovered from his fear that I'd turn him into a beast again. And did he still want to meet the actual Beast? He hadn't said anything to Belle about it, but maybe he didn't know how to bring it up. Now that I was thinking about it, John hardly ever started a conversation, so maybe he was shy. As soon as I got a chance to speak to Belle, I'd ask her if she'd introduce John to the Beast. It was the least I could do for him, after everything I'd put him through.

"Do you think there'll be dancing?" asked Romy, doing a twirl.

"I hope so," I said. "But I don't think it'll be ballet," I added, laughing at Romy's pirouette and feeling a sudden burst of happiness. Everything was okay. It was better than okay. Maybe I didn't do what I'd come to Paris to do, but I'd figured out how to escape from the Groac'h and gotten the Evil Queen's magic mirror. How could Mom not be impressed with that? I'd finally get the answers to my questions.

I took one last look at myself in the mirror. I pushed my hair behind my ears and smiled, surprised at how much I liked my reflection. I hoped Hildee would let me and Romy keep the dresses. Then I put on the sandals. They had a tiny heel and felt tight. I'd be happy to hand them back after the wedding.

"Ready?" I asked Romy as I grabbed the magic mirror. I couldn't leave it lying around. My dress didn't have any pockets, so I just held it in my hand like it was a purse.

Romy and I locked arms and headed back downstairs.

It was time for a wedding.

Chapter 21

HILDEE WAS A BEAUTIFUL BRIDE.

She'd added some fancy touches to her outfit—white elbow-length gloves, a sparkly tiara, and a fifteen-foot-long veil that trailed on the ground around her. But it was her face that I couldn't stop looking at. I'd never seen Hildee without makeup.

It felt like I was seeing the real Hildee. The girl underneath it all. I saw that she had a smattering of freckles across the bridge of her nose and was much prettier than I had ever realized.

"Hildee, you look amazing," I said.

"Thank you, Cia. My cheeks hurt from smiling so much," she said, beaming. She grabbed the sides of her face.

John came down the stairs and joined us.

"Hey," he said softly.

I was preparing myself to see John all dressed up, but the first thing I noticed was a bruise under his left eye that I was pretty sure wasn't there when we'd all gone upstairs. I almost asked him about it before realizing it was probably just now developing after the run-in with the Groac'h, and I didn't want to remind everyone of that disaster. This was Hildee's moment.

"You look so cool," said Romy, nodding at John in his fancy tux and shiny black shoes. He'd parted his hair to the side and swept it all up to the left. He did look cool.

"You all look really nice," he said shyly, putting his hands in his pockets.

The grandfather clock chimed.

"Time to get going," said Hildee. I hadn't thought it was possible for her smile to get any bigger, but it did.

"John, will you walk behind us?" she said, bending down and gathering up the train of her veil.

"Sure," said John, swallowing hard and pulling his

shoulders back. "Whatever you need me to do. . . . You want me to carry your veil?"

"That'd be great," said Hildee, letting her veil fall to the ground. "You just grab the ends of it and lift it up and walk a few steps behind me and Cia and Romy."

"Okay," said John, eyeing the veil nervously. If I were him, I'd be terrified I'd step on it, or walk too fast or too slow and mess up the whole procession.

"And you two are going to walk me up the aisle," said Hildee, sticking out her elbows and grinning at me and Romy. "I'd never have met Hugo if it hadn't been for the two of you. You two made it happen."

"Thanks, Hildee," I said. I felt proud, but also guilty and nervous. What if marrying Hugo did end up being a really bad idea?

Romy showed no hesitation and linked arms with Hildee.

"John, can you put this in one of your pockets?" I said, holding out the mirror to him. I couldn't walk Hildee up the aisle carrying it.

"Sure," said John. He took it from me and placed it in the inside pocket of his jacket.

I linked arms with Hildee.

The doors to the courtyard opened, and the three of us stepped outside.

I felt like I was walking into a fairy tale. Every tree and rosebush in the courtyard was covered with light bulbs as tiny as fireflies, casting a twinkly glow over everything. There were garlands of purple and white flowers draped around the pillars and hanging from the roof of the gazebo, framing a beaming Hugo, who kept his eyes glued on Hildee as she came down the aisle. The guests on either side of us turned and let out "oohs" and "aahs" of delight as they gazed at Hildee. Somewhere violins were being played and beautiful music accompanied our procession. I don't know if it was the violins, the way Hugo was grinning at Hildee, or all the smiling faces (except for Belle, who scowled as we passed her) but I felt almost teary with happiness when we reached the gazebo.

"*Ma chérie,*" said Hugo, bending down to kiss Hildee's gloved hand. She stepped into the gazebo. With the flowers and the size of the wedding dress, there was barely enough room in there for Hildee, Hugo, and Claude, who was suited up in the robes of a minister, ready to perform the wedding ceremony. (Was there nothing this guy couldn't do?) Romy and I followed John back up the aisle and sat in the empty seats next to Belle.

"We are gathered here tonight," began Claude, "to join Hildee Winnifred Graff and Hugo Alexandre Didier Emile Victor . . ."

"How many names does this guy have?" Romy sighed to herself.

". . . Dubois, Duke of Oraly, in matrimony," finished Claude.

I looked at the people on the other side of the aisle, wondering where they had all come from. There were at least twenty guests here. Maybe they were all members of Hugo's family? There was a woman in the front row who had the same round, wide nose as him.

"Cia," whispered Romy. "Cia . . ."

I shushed her and fixed my eyes on the gazebo. Hugo and Hildee were holding hands. I didn't want to miss the "Do you, Hildee, take Hugo to be your husband?" bit that I'd seen in the movies.

"Cia," hissed Romy, poking me in the ribs.

"Ouch," I said, still not looking at her. I'd need to talk

to Romy after the ceremony about taking her bridesmaid responsibilities more seriously.

"You need to see this," she hissed in my ear. "Beside Belle."

She wasn't going to give up. I turned my head and looked at Romy. She seemed like she was about to burst. She cocked her head to the left. I leaned forward ever so slightly and looked at Belle. She was staring up at the sky, a worried expression on her face. Was she afraid it was going to rain? Then I noticed the guest sitting on the other side of her.

She'd changed her hairstyle and gained some weight. But there was no mistaking who it was. The woman who had cursed me with a spell when I was a baby was sitting at the other end of the row, smiling at the happy couple.

It was Madame Fredepia.

Chapter 22

WHAT WAS MADAME FREDEPIA DOING AT Hildee's wedding? What was she doing in Paris? The last time I'd seen her, she'd been running a fortune-telling business behind the frozen yogurt shop near my middle school.

Applause broke out around me, interrupting my thoughts. I glanced back up at the gazebo, annoyed that I seemed to have just missed the "I now pronounce you man and wife" part. Hugo was leaning in to kiss Hildee's upturned face, and they both looked so happy.

Then I heard a crack of thunder and felt the ground

beneath my feet and the seat of my chair begin to vibrate. The light bulbs on the trees and rosebushes exploded, sending shards of glass flying. It was as if a tornado had touched down on the courtyard. Suddenly a wind was blowing through the gazebo and down the aisle, ripping apart the carefully arranged flowers and pelting the screaming guests with petals. I glanced at the gazebo. Hugo had his arms around Hildee and was shielding her from the flying debris. Claude was tearing off the garlands of flowers that had landed on his head and yelling at the guests to stay calm, as some of them ran back inside and others threw themselves on the ground. There was a ripping sound, and I was thrown forward onto the chair in front of me.

"Is this an earthquake?" shouted Romy. She was sprawled on the ground, grabbing onto the legs of her chair. I pulled myself back up and crouched down beside her.

"I said this was a bad idea!" yelled Belle. "I knew this would happen!!"

What was Belle talking about? Did she mean that she'd known that Hildee getting married would trigger a natural disaster? How could she possibly have known that?

"You need to do something!" screamed Belle.

For a second, I thought Belle was talking to me; then I realized she was shouting at Madame Fredepia, who was standing on her chair. She had her hand outstretched and was holding a stick. Wait, no, it was a wand! It was gold and had a star at the end of it. (Where was that thing when I needed her to break my spell?!) She narrowed her eyes and pointed it at the gazebo.

I wanted to stay with Romy and John, who were both crouched underneath their chairs—was that what you were supposed to do in an earthquake, hide under chairs?—but I wanted to see what Madame Fredepia was going to do with her wand. Real magic might be about to happen. I stood up and stared at the gazebo, holding on to my hair with one hand so it didn't get blown in my eyes and grabbing my dress with the other to stop it from flapping over my head. I felt like I was on a boat being bounced around in the middle of a storm.

"Do a reset!" yelled Belle, running up to the gazebo.

"It won't work if this is true love," shouted Madame Fredepia, who sounded pretty calm for a woman whose hair was being whipped up into a cotton-candy cone by the wind that was barreling through the courtyard.

"That's not true love!" screamed Belle.

"Looks like it is," shouted Madame Fredepia, as a confetti of fire sparks exploded from her wand. She went flying off her chair and landed on the ground.

I leaned over and reached out my hand to help her get up.

"You can't do a reset when it's true love," she said, shooing away my hand. If she recognized me, she didn't show it. She sat up and leaned her hands on her knees. "The reset won't work." Looking over at the gazebo, Madame Fredepia smiled. "And it looks like this one is a double whammy. Love at first sight *and* true love. Haven't seen anything like it for twenty years. . . . Lovely when it happens."

I looked over at the gazebo. Belle was standing in front of Hildee and Hugo, hands on her hips, looking furious. Hugo was removing petals from Hildee's veil, and she was brushing off leaves from his jacket. They were both smiling at each other.

Madame Fredepia pushed herself up to a standing position. "I need to get them out of here. Before Bossy Face shows up." She took off running.

The wind was dying down, but it felt like it might pick up again at any moment. The temperature had dropped, and it seemed darker, but maybe that was because all the twinkly lights had been shattered. I pushed my hair out of my face and pulled out some twigs that had gotten tangled up in it.

Romy and John scrambled out from underneath the chairs.

"Apparently someone called Bossy Face is on the way," I said, shaking out the soil that had landed on my dress.

"And this is good news . . . or bad news?" said Romy, leaning down as she put on her shoe. It must have fallen off when she dived under her chair.

"Bad, I think. Madame Fredepia doesn't like her."

Or Belle. This had to be the same "she" that Belle had been worried about earlier.

"What is going on?" said John, dusting off bits of glass from his shoulders. "What just happened?"

"I don't know," I said, looking at the chaos around us. All the chairs were overturned, and one of them was on top of the gazebo. The trees and rosebushes had tipped over, and the red-carpeted aisle was a mess of soil and rose petals and glass fragments. All the guests had taken off. The only person left in the courtyard other than the wedding couple, Belle, and Madame Fredepia was Claude, who had grabbed a broom and was sweeping up the mess, whistling while he worked like it was just another chore on his list.

"Madame Fredepia and Belle know what's going on, though," I said, surprised by how angry I felt. Why hadn't Belle tried harder to stop the wedding if she knew that there was a possibility of flying chairs and an earthquake and gale-force winds? Or did bad things just happen whenever Madame Fredepia was around?

I walked over to the gazebo, Romy and John following behind me.

Madame Fredepia was waving her hands and talking excitedly. "I need something big . . . bigger than a pumpkin. . . ." She scanned the courtyard and then pointed at a large flowerpot. "That'll do!"

She ran to the flowerpot—one of the few that was still intact—pulled out the roses inside it, and threw them on the ground. Then, seeing something on the ground, she bent down and picked it up.

"Bit small," she said, walking back toward us, holding up a beetle between her thumb and forefinger and staring at it appreciatively. "But I think he'll get the job done."

"Now, go get the flowerpot," she said, looking at me, Romy, and John as she walked toward the gazebo. "Not a minute to lose. Old Fish Face is on the way. I can feel it."

I ran to the flowerpot. I didn't know who Madame Fredepia was talking about or what she was planning, but it was obvious that she wanted to help Hildee and Hugo. So, I'd help her. It looked like Romy and John, who were running beside me, were thinking the same thing. We got to the flowerpot and hauled it back to Madame Fredepia, gasping from the weight of it. It was only after we placed it in front of her that I wondered, with a flash of annoyance, why she hadn't just used the wand that she was holding to magic the flowerpot over.

"Get behind me," she said, tapping her wand on her shoulder. Romy, John, and I stepped behind her and squeezed into the gazebo beside Belle, Hildee, and Hugo. Hildee and Hugo were still holding hands and watching Madame Fredepia.

"Do you know what she's going to do?" I asked Belle,

though I already had a good idea of what was about to happen. That beetle was going to become some sort of getaway driver for Hildee and Hugo, and the flowerpot would become . . . what? A car? No, how could anyone drive a car out of here? The courtyard had walls on all sides. Maybe a horse that would fit all three of them? You could ride a horse through a house.

Madame Fredepia raised her wand. There was a blinding flash of light, and when I opened my eyes, I saw the getaway vehicle.

It was a helicopter.

"Awesome," gasped John.

"I don't think it's for us," I said.

"Get in it," yelled Madame Fredepia to Hildee and Hugo. "It'll take you north to the mountains. There's a house, a cottage in the woods. It's not much, just four walls and a roof, but you'll be safe there."

Hildee hugged me. "Almost as good as the stables!" She laughed. Hildee had really meant it when she said she'd live with Hugo in a box. She looked even happier than she had in the moments before her wedding. She moved on to hug Romy and John.

"You don't need a chaperone," she said. "You don't need me to get you where you need to go. You just need each other." She smiled at each of us. "You all just stick together, okay?"

"No time for the emotional goodbyes," interrupted Madame Fredepia. "You need to get out of here!"

Hildee linked hands with Hugo, and they walked toward the helicopter. The beetle had become a small, mustachioed, barrel-shaped man dressed in a navy pilot's uniform. He looked up for the job as he ushered Hildee and Hugo into the tiny helicopter. Hildee had to cast off her veil so that there was enough room for her and Hugo to sit on the two passenger seats.

The beetle pilot hopped in, and the helicopter blades started to spin, pushing air through the courtyard and spraying Claude's carefully swept piles of petals and debris all over the place. The roar was so loud that we all held our hands over our ears as we watched the helicopter rise up into the sky. I could see Hildee's face pressed against the window, her hand raised in a wave like she was a princess in a carriage.

I felt a surge of happiness as I looked up. Hildee was

writing her own story now. She was flying in an enchanted helicopter with a man whom—according to Madame Fredepia, who should know about these things—she really had fallen in love with at first sight. It was the real deal.

We all looked up and watched the helicopter until it disappeared from sight.

"I just love a good happily ever after." Madame Fredepia sighed.

"That," said Belle, pointing up at the sky, "remains to be seen."

Chapter 23

SWIRLING GRAY CLOUDS APPEARED OVER-head just as the lights inside the castle turned off.

There was a whooshing sound above us, and I looked up to see a figure diving through the air, as if she had emerged from one of the clouds. A black cape spread out behind her like wings.

"Is that Bossy Face?" I asked Madame Fredepia.

"The one and only," said Madame Fredepia. "Though she prefers to be addressed as Carabosse." Madame Fredepia rolled the *r* and lengthened the *e* so that the name sounded like a fancy Italian pasta.

Carabosse landed soundlessly on her feet in front of the gazebo, her cape falling to the ground. She pulled a wand out and pointed it at the top of the gazebo, creating brilliant sparks, and then light shone down from the roof, bathing us all in floodlight. It was so bright, I had to squint my eyes.

"Just loves to make a dramatic entrance," sniffed Madame Fredepia disapprovingly.

"There has been a wedding here," said Carabosse, picking up Hildee's veil and shaking it at us like it was a crucial piece of evidence, "involving a fairy-tale character...."

I shook my head. Maybe if we denied everything, we could delay Carabosse's investigation, and Hildee and Hugo would have more time to make their getaway. But why did she care?

Carabosse stared at me, but then her eyes flicked over to Belle, who was ever so carefully and slowly backing out of the courtyard and moving toward the castle.

"And you," she snapped. "No more dillydallying. You've dragged out your tale long enough. Get upstairs and turn that Beast into a prince." She pointed her wand at Belle's head. "And your hair is a disgrace!"

Masses of brown hair sprouted from Belle's head and tumbled down past her shoulders.

"Why can't you just leave us alone?" she blurted out, furiously pushing her hair behind her ears. Her voice was shaking. "Hildee's not hurting anyone by getting married. Just leave her alone. Why can't you leave us all alone?"

"So you can study in your library?" sneered Carabosse. "You're not here to *read*. You trade imprisonment with your father, fall in love with the Beast, turn the Beast into a prince, and then you get married. End of story."

"Please," pleaded Belle. "Just give me a week. . . . Just a few more days . . ."

"You will finish your story," roared Carabosse. "Or I will end it."

"No!" Belle gasped. She looked terrified, bending down and backing away from Carabosse as if she'd just been hit. "I'll do it. I'll go now."

She ran back inside, her new hair flowing out behind her.

"Such insubordination," commented Carabosse to no one in particular. "That girl's lucky to get a happily ever after."

Madame Fredepia snorted loudly.

"Ah, Fredepia," sneered Carabosse, her cape swishing as she whipped around to face her. "You. Are you the mastermind behind this unauthorized wedding?"

"Just a guest, Carabosse," answered Madame Fredepia, lifting up a hand and checking her manicure. "And it was a beautiful ceremony. Pity you missed it."

"I wasn't invited," snapped Carabosse.

"As if . . . ," muttered Madame Fredepia under her breath.

"You know that Cinderella's stepsister cannot get married!" bellowed Carabosse. "They won't get far. Wherever you've sent them, I'll find them."

"Just—just . . . leave them alone," said John, folding his arms and sticking out his chin. I could tell he was trying to act like he wasn't scared, but the shake in his voice gave him away. "So what if Hildee's Cinderella's stepsister? She's allowed to be happy."

Carabosse glared at John. There was something vampire-like about her, and it wasn't just the cape. She had pale skin and dark grayish lips, and her pupils were unusually large. She was . . . scary.

"And who are you?" scoffed Carabosse, still staring at

John. "Ah, a groomsman," she continued, answering her own question.

She took a step back, and her eyes flitted from John to me and Romy, and then back to John.

"How lovely. It's the whole wedding party." Carabosse smiled, but it wasn't a nice one.

I glanced down at my flouncy, lacy dress. It might as well have had the word BRIDESMAID emblazoned on the front. Would Carabosse punish us too? I glanced at John, who had broken out in a sweat. He took off his bow tie and shoved it in the lapel pocket of his jacket. As if that would make him look less guilty.

"So," said Carabosse, striding back and forth in front of the gazebo like a detective about to crack a case. "You three have participated in . . . no, *facilitated* an unsanctioned wedding. This is a very serious offense."

"It was a wedding," said Romy dryly. "Not a bank robbery."

Carabosse stopped midstride and stared at Romy.

"Now, Carabosse," said Madame Fredepia. "They are just children." The note of concern in her voice was scarier than Carabosse's accusations. What was Madame

Fredepia afraid that Carabosse would do to us?

"Fredepia," roared Carabosse, taking out her wand. "That is enough! They have upset the balance of the tales."

I exchanged a glance with Romy. She mouthed the word "run," but it was too late. Carabosse was already pointing her wand at Romy.

"You like to talk," she said. "The moment you turn sixteen, you won't be able to stop talking. You will talk even while you sleep. You will talk while others are talking; you will talk while you are eating. You will simply talk. All the time."

Romy gasped, and I clutched her arm. Could Carabosse really do this? Thinking of what had happened to me as a baby, I knew she could. But no one could live that way! And no one could live with someone who talked all the time. Romy would end up a shut-in or an outcast.

"Always with the sixteenth birthday," tutted Madame Fredepia. "No originality."

"Don't you try to run away from me," continued Carabosse, pointing her wand at John, who was attempting to do just that. He had bolted around the side of the gazebo. "On your sixteenth birthday, whenever you try to run, you will dance."

"Just for the day, right?" said Romy, the words coming out in a panicky squeak. "I'll just have to talk all day for one day . . . on my birthday? Right?"

Carabosse ignored her. She turned her gaze on me.

"You. You thought you could deceive me. On your sixteenth birthday, your nose will grow a foot."

"What?" I yelled, touching my nose. I'd just shaken my head when Carabosse asked a question. I didn't deserve to be turned into Pinocchio over that! None of us deserved these curses!

"She won't get away," hissed Carabosse, addressing Madame Fredepia now. "There will be no happily ever after for Cinderella's stepsister."

Carabosse pulled her cape around her, and then, with a crackle of thunder and a flash of light, she disappeared.

"Loves the dramatic exits as well." Madame Fredepia sighed, managing to sound both annoyed and impressed at the same time.

"She put a spell on me," gasped John, stumbling

toward us as if he had just woken up. "She said I'm not going to be able to run and that I have to dance?"

"Can she do that?" Romy asked Madame Fredepia in a shaky voice. "Are those things actually going to happen? John has to dance? I won't stop talking? Cia gets an enormous nose?"

"Well, Carabosse does know her magic," said Madame Fredepia. "But . . ." She tapped her nose and narrowed her eyes. "She's not the only one with a wand."

Chapter 24

WE ALL FOLLOWED MADAME FREDEPIA OUT of the courtyard and then through the castle, walking along silent hallways that were empty of people except for Claude, who was polishing the floors. Looking sad, he told us he was getting the place ready for another wedding. I guessed he meant Belle and the Beast's. Romy, John, and I wondered if we should try and find her to say goodbye, but we figured that it was more important to stick with Madame Fredepia and her wand. So, we followed her through the castle and then out onto the street.

"She can stop this from happening, right?" said John, pointing at Madame Fredepia, who was a few steps ahead of us. "I can't play football if I can't run. I can't dance across a football field."

"Well, I can't do anything if I'm just talking nonstop all the time," added Romy testily. "Everyone will hate me."

"You could still play football," grumbled John.

"C'mon, guys. She turned a flowerpot into a helicopter and a beetle into a pilot," I noted, wanting to stop John and Romy's weird who's-been-spelled-worse competition. Plus, I didn't want to get pulled into it. A super long nose didn't seem too bad compared to what they might have to deal with. "She can totally undo a few spells. . . ." I forced myself to sound upbeat, but I wasn't feeling it. My own personal experience with Madame Fredepia's spell-breaking had been that she was terrible at it.

"Hang on," said Romy suddenly, stopping in her tracks. "Wasn't her license to practice magic revoked? Remember the signs we found outside her business?"

"I don't think she cares about those signs," I said. Turning to John, who was looking confused, I started to explain. "So, that's the woman who spelled me." I pointed at Madame Fredepia, who was a few steps ahead of us. "But," I added hastily, seeing John's face, "she *is* nice."

"But she's still got her wand?" said John frowning. "She's still practicing magic. . . . She's going to help us, right?"

"Yeah," I said. "Looks like it."

"Lucky for us, she doesn't care about breaking a few rules," said Romy, looking pointedly at Madame Fredepia.

"And what about the other one . . . Carabosse?" asked John. "What was her problem? Why was she so mad about Hildee getting married?"

I'd already been thinking about that. My guess was that Carabosse was the evil fairy from the "Sleeping Beauty" story. That fitted with the way she'd acted at the wedding. She had been annoyed about not getting an invite, and she had cast spells on me, Romy, and John that wouldn't happen until our sixteenth birthdays—that was just like the "Sleeping Beauty" story. But why would she care so much about Cinderella's stepsister getting married and Belle transforming the Beast into a prince? They had nothing to do with the "Sleeping Beauty" fairy tale.

"I think I know who she is, but let's ask Madame Fredepia."

I'd been so busy thinking and talking to John that I hadn't noticed that Madame Fredepia had stopped outside a shuttered storefront. The word BOULANGERIE was painted on the sign above it.

"Just looking for the key," she said, jangling a huge key chain.

"Why doesn't she just use her wand?" whispered John.

"Needs to give it a rest," I suggested, and then immediately regretted saying anything. Why was I commenting on wands? This was exactly why John thought I knew about magic stuff.

Madame Fredepia opened the door and led us up a narrow staircase. We had climbed up about three flights of stairs—Romy and I had to lift up our long swishy bridesmaid dresses so we wouldn't step on them, and John complained about how much his shoes pinched—when Madame Fredepia stopped in front of a door.

"This is it," she said, stepping aside and ushering us into her tiny apartment. From the doorway I could see the kitchen, the living room, and the bedroom, which was just a little alcove off the living room with the sign HAVE SWEET DREAMS dangling from the ceiling. I felt like

I was stepping into a jewelry box. The walls in the entry-way were painted a deep sapphire blue, the living room had emerald-green wallpaper with a delicate gold-leaf pattern, and the chairs were all pink velvet. The fireplace was painted black and topped with a display of yellow and purple orchids.

"It's small, and storage is a bit of a challenge. But I've made it my own," said Madame Fredepia proudly. She took off her tartan jacket and threw it on top of a coat stand. "Would have tidied up a bit if I'd known I was going to have company!"

"Oh, it's just beautiful," said Romy warmly.

"Go in, go in," said Madame Fredepia, pointing into the living room. "I'll get us a plate of almond croissants. Just trying out a new recipe before I sell them down-stairs . . ."

"You're a baker now?" I asked. I'd wondered what Madame Fredepia had been doing since she'd left her fortune-telling business in Brooklyn, but I'd never have guessed that she'd be running a bakery.

"Oh yes," she said winking at me as if she'd just read my mind. "Baking's a lot like magic. You mix different ingredients together, and then"—she clapped her hands—"*poof!* You end up with something quite magical." She pulled her wand from the pocket of her skirt and tapped it on her chin. "And quite delicious too."

"I don't care how delicious it is; I don't think we should eat anything made with a wand," whispered John as Madame Fredepia stepped away into the kitchen.

"Well, I'm hungry," said Romy. "I'd eat a candy apple if the Evil Queen gave it to me."

We walked into the living room. Romy and I sat on the pink velvet sofa, and John sat on a pink wingback chair.

"So, how have you been?" asked Madame Fredepia, looking at me as she placed a tray on the small table in the middle of the living room. She settled herself into the other wingback chair and reached for the teapot. "Who'll have a cup?" she asked, acting like we had all just popped in for a chat and hadn't, less than an hour ago, been cursed by an angry wedding crasher. "I see you've taken care of that other business since I last saw you."

"Well, yeah," I said, assuming she was referring to the spell—*her* spell—that I had broken. "I did." For a moment I wondered if I should tell Madame Fredepia that in the course of taking care of that "business," I'd been kidnapped by Snow White, just narrowly escaped from the Sea Witch and her revolting eels, negotiated with the Evil Queen, and even transformed into a mermaid to save my brother's life. But I had an idea that she already knew all that.

"You did a very fine job," she said. She sipped her tea, and peering at me over the rim of her teacup, gave me an approving look. "Well done."

"No thanks to you," muttered Romy grumpily, reaching for a croissant. But the way Madame Fredepia was looking at me made me feel happy. It was strange, but also good, to realize that the woman who had set in motion all the fairy-tale craziness I had experienced seemed to be proud of me. Romy had told me that everything I'd done was awesome and cool, but she was my best friend, and her compliments didn't really count, and Mom—the only other person who could comment on what I'd done— wouldn't let me talk about it. So, it felt really good to hear Madame Fredepia say, *Well done.*

I glanced at a clock on the wall. It was almost ten o'clock. There was no way we were going to be able to fly home tonight. Plus, we couldn't head home until we'd broken Carabosse's curses.

"What time is it in the States?" I wondered aloud. "I don't think we're going to be able to get that flight home tonight." We needed to ask Noah to get us another flight and check back in with Claude about the passports. We'd have to do that as soon as Madame Fredepia broke Carabosse's spells.

"Yeah," said John, looking at the clock. "My parents are going to be worried if I don't check in." He leaned forward and looked at Madame Fredepia. "Do you have a phone I can use? I need to tell them I'm okay."

Madame Fredepia raised both hands and shushed him. "I've a better idea than that. And I don't have a phone anyway—you never know who's listening in on your calls; much better not to use them. I'll just cast a teeny spell, and they won't even notice you're missing."

She reached over and pulled a hair from John's head.

"OW!" he yelled, glaring at Madame Fredepia and grabbing the spot on his head where she had pulled his hair.

"What are your parents' names?"

"Seo-yeon and Michael," said John, still wincing.

"What about you two?"

"I think we'll be okay. As long as we get back by tomorrow night, Noah won't be worried," said Romy, reaching up and touching her head as if she were protecting it from Madame Fredepia.

"I'm okay too. Dad thinks I'm staying with Romy."

Madame Fredepia got up and took a ruby-colored bowl down from the mantelpiece. It looked like a fishbowl. Without the fish. Madame Fredepia put her hand over it and muttered something that I couldn't make out. The bowl filled with white smoke, and she placed it on the table.

The faces of a middle-aged man and woman appeared in the smoke. Judging by the stunned expression on John's face, I guessed that they were his parents.

"So, where do they think you are now?" asked Madame Fredepia.

"They think I'm staying with a friend," mumbled John.

Madame Fredepia tapped the bowl with her wand and recited:

"Where is John, you say? Is it possible he has gone
  away?

No, no, no. He is safe and sound.
He has homework to do, good food to eat,
and a friend in whose safe hands he'll stay until
      next you meet."

She tapped the bowl again, and through the smoke, I could see John's parents smiling at each other.

"There," she said. She blew away the last bits of smoke. "That'll do it."

"But where do they think I am?" asked John, staring at the ruby-colored bowl as the image of his parents disappeared.

"Oh, wherever makes most sense to them," said Madame Fredepia, wiggling her fingers in the air. "They might think you're taking extra training sessions, or that'd you've left town with your team for a couple of days to play a game. That's the beauty of this spell . . . whoever you use it on just adds in the details themselves."

She put the bowl back on the mantelpiece and sat back down.

"That was fun." She sighed in a satisfied way. "Haven't done an amnesiac enchantment for ages."

"Amnesia?" shouted John, Romy, and I at the same time.

"They're not going to forget that I—" John gulped. "Exist?"

"Oh no. No, no, no," said Madame Fredepia. I'd never seen her look so serious. "Don't worry about that. I would never do that. Never. A person can be forgotten completely. As if they never lived at all. That's an appalling use of the spell.

"There *are* those who use the amnesiac enchantment that way, though. In my opinion they shouldn't have wands at all." She folded her arms and shook her head slowly. "Now, if you ask me—"

"So, what about Carabosse's curses?" I asked, cutting off Madame Fredepia, who seemed like she was getting ready to give us a lecture on ethical spell-casting, which might have been interesting, but there were way more important things to talk about.

"Yeah," said John, leaning forward in his seat. He grabbed his leg with two hands, like he was worried that it was about to fall off. He turned to Madame Fredepia. "So, you can stop me from having to dance, right?" There was a slight shake in his voice as he spoke. "And"—he gestured at me and Romy—"you can break those other spells that that

Carabosse lady did. You can stop all of them, right?"

"Well, now, that Carabosse," said Madame Fredepia, reaching under her chair and bringing out a small wicker basket. She opened it and pulled out a piece of beige fabric about the size of a handkerchief, a pincushion, and a spool of brown thread. "Have to keep my hands busy since I gave up the ciggies," she said as she threaded a needle.

We sat in silence for a moment as Madame Fredepia started stitching the fabric. Romy elbowed me in the ribs and jerked her head in the direction of Madame Fredepia's lap. I swallowed a snort of laughter. She was embroidering a picture of a cigarette.

"You three got off lightly, you know," she continued. "Forced dancing, nonstop talking, and an exceptionally long nose. Carabosse's been known to do a lot worse than that. . . ."

"Like Sleeping Beauty?" I asked. "She's the Evil Fairy, right? She didn't get invited to the christening, and she turned up and cursed the baby princess and said that on her sixteenth birthday, she'd prick her finger on a spinning wheel and die."

Madame Fredepia nodded.

"You'd think she'd get invited to everything now," commented Romy. "Like, who'd leave her off a guest list?"

"And then another fairy—a good fairy," said Madame Fredepia, lingering on the words "good fairy," "downgraded the 'prick the finger on a spinning wheel and die' spell to a 'prick the finger on a spinning wheel and fall asleep' spell."

Madame Fredepia smiled proudly and looked at us. Why was she looking so delighted with herself? Did she expect us to be impressed that she'd remembered all the details of the "Sleeping Beauty" story?

No, that wasn't it. . . .

"That was you!" gasped Romy, figuring out Madame Fredepia's identity just as I was getting there. "You were the fairy who made sure that Sleeping Beauty didn't die and would just fall asleep for a hundred years."

"Okay," said John, sounding slightly stunned. "Does that mean you can break the spell this time? The stuff that Carabosse said, you can stop that from happening, right?"

"Not quite," said Madame Fredepia. She put her sewing on the arm of her chair and then looked directly into John's eyes. "I can downgrade a Carabosse spell. Dilute it. You'll hardly even notice it's there."

She pulled out her wand and pointed it at John.

"Carabosse said that on your sixteenth birthday, you'll lose the ability to run and will be compelled to dance. I can reduce the dancing to hopping."

A spray of silvery filaments shot out of her wand and landed on John's leg.

"Hopping!" whimpered John. "I can't hop around a football field."

Madame Fredepia ignored him and turned her attention to Romy.

"And yourself," she said to Romy, not missing a beat. "You're scheduled to start talking all the time. I'm sure I can improve on that a bit." She paused, looking deep in thought. "Got it! You'll be able to stop talking, but you'll have to repeat everything you say three times."

Romy stared at her, opening and closing her mouth, but no sound came out.

"Right, we'll go with that, then," continued Madame Fredepia.

There was another wave of the wand, and more silvery airborne threads made their way over to the sofa. Romy leapt up as if she were trying to run away from them, but they still landed on her mouth.

"Remind me," said Madame Fredepia, looking at me. "What did she have planned for your nose?"

"One extra foot," I said. "But Madame Fredepia, the hopping and the repeating . . ." I looked at Romy and John. Romy was glaring at Madame Fredepia, and John had gone pale. He was clutching his legs and muttering to himself.

"Your nose," said Madame Fredepia, tapping her own nose with her wand. "I can get that down to two inches. Much better than a foot."

She flicked her wand again.

"Or," she added, smiling, as if inspiration had suddenly hit her, "I can move the location. . . . What about two-inch earlobes? Or eyebrows with a depth of two inches?"

"No!" I shouted, my mind scrambling to imagine what either of those things would look like. "No."

"All right, nose it is," she said, waving her wand in my direction.

"Now, who'll have another cup of tea?" she said, sounding like a gracious hostess.

"I don't want tea!" wailed John. "I want to be able to run and play football!"

"Look, Madame Fredepia, I know this isn't your fault," I began. "And we are grateful for you, you know, trying, but—"

"Do you have a more powerful wand?" interrupted Romy.

"Hops can be fixed, though, can't they? Like, with physical therapy?" I suggested. Even if Madame Fredepia had another wand, was she powerful enough to undo Carabosse's curses? Maybe there were non-magical ways to make things better. "And maybe the repeating things could get fixed with speech therapy?"

"No, no," said Madame Fredepia, looking at me like she had never heard such stupid suggestions. "Modern methods have no effect on magic. You get a spot of surgery on your nose, it'll grow right back. And there's no modern mending of bewitched speech and a hop."

"Okay," said Romy, taking a deep breath. I could tell she was trying not to lose it. "You can't do it. Is there someone else who can?"

"Well, I suppose we could ask Anansi," said Madame Fredepia.

Chapter 25

ANANCY?" ASKED ROMY. "WHO'S SHE?"

"Anansi is not a *she*," said Madame Fredepia, getting up from her chair. "Now, we need to summon him. . . ."

Who was Anansi? The name sounded sort of familiar, but I couldn't place it. It was good that Madame Fredepia was getting help, but judging by her magic, this Anansi guy might not be much help at all.

"Is it difficult to summon him?" I asked.

"Getting him here is easy," said Madame Fredepia as she walked into the kitchen. "It's getting him to stick

around that's difficult. He gets bored easily, and if Anansi gets bored, he'll"—she clapped her hands—"leave."

She came back into the tiny sitting area carrying a tray, on which she'd placed a large glass tumbler filled to the brim with an amber liquid and a plate of chocolate croissants. Madame Fredepia put the tray on the table. She opened the window, lit a big, fat cigar—I couldn't tell if she'd taken it from her pocket or magicked it out of thin air—and placed that on the tray. Then she lifted the tray, and with hands outstretched, she held it out the window.

"He'll be here in a moment," she said, putting the tray back on the table. "Whiskey, chocolate, and cigars . . . Anansi can't resist them."

The air blowing in through the open window was cold, so I joined Romy on the sofa to wait. I assumed that Anansi was going to make his entrance through the window. Would he have to use a ladder, or would he fly through it Carabosse-style? I hoped he wouldn't come with a ladder; it wouldn't say much for his magical powers if he needed one of those.

But I didn't really have to worry. It turned out that Anansi didn't need a ladder. He could climb up any wall.

That's the sort of thing you can do when you have eight legs.

"Is that a tarantula?" gasped Romy, pointing at the dinner-plate-sized spider that was outside the window.

I stared at it as it crawled over the window and into the room, transforming as it moved from a spider into a long-legged Black man. It was done in one seamless movement, like turning a page. One moment it was a spider, and the next it was a man. A man with a beautiful purple, gold, and green blanket draped around him, wearing a necklace of colorful beads.

He sat in the big armchair by the window.

"Now, how about a fire?" he said, rubbing his hands together. His blanket only covered one shoulder; it looked like a toga. Flashing a smile at me, he commented, "I am used to the warmer temps, you know."

Madame Fredepia pointed her wand at the unlit hearth, and a roaring fire sprang to life.

"Thank you, Fredepia," said Anansi, stretching out his legs and placing one ankle over the other. "And may I say that you are looking lovely." He reached down, picked up the lit cigar from the tray, and passed it through his fingers, like it was a coin that he was about to make disappear; then, putting the cigar in his mouth, he blew a big smoke ring that hung in the air. After another puff, he pursed his lips together and moved his head ever so slowly as he blew out a stream of smoke that made the letter *F*. Through a haze of smoke, I saw him winking at me and Romy. The *F* floated through the smoke ring.

"Been a while since I've seen her. . . ." He grinned, nodding in Madame Fredepia's direction. "You girls know what she wants?"

"It's these children who want to see you. Not me," corrected Madame Fredepia, but she smiled in a way that made it clear that she wasn't upset he'd climbed through her living room window. "They have a question for you."

"So, that will need an answer," said Anansi, picking up the glass from the tray. He raised it to his lips, nodded at me and Romy, and then drank the whole thing. "But what will you give me for an answer?"

What could I give him? I felt a knot of panic in my stomach. I didn't have anything.

"He means a story," said Madame Fredepia, sitting in

the chair on the other side of the fireplace. "Anansi always wants a story."

"An original story," he said, pointing a finger at me. "And I don't want a love story." He puckered his face as if he'd just bitten into a lemon.

"It's okay. I don't know any love stories," I said, realizing that I didn't know any stories at all. Instantly my mind went blank. It was as if I'd never read a book. Not that it mattered—Anansi wanted an original story. I couldn't just use something he'd have heard before.

"Spin me a tale," said Anansi, biting into a croissant. "You got a tragic comedy? Or a good rags-to-riches? A little fable with a moral?"

He finished the croissant and polished off another in two bites. He had smoked the cigar, drunk the whiskey, and almost finished the pastries. If I didn't start talking soon, he'd take off.

"I have a story," I gulped. It wasn't a rags-to-riches story, and I didn't think it had a moral, but at least it was original. "About how to get away from a man-eating witch . . ."

And then I kept talking and told him the whole story

of our encounter with the Groac'h and how I had sabotaged her potion by spitting in it.

When I finished, Anansi clapped his hands.

"I like this story," he said, nodding and smiling at me with twinkling eyes. "I'm going to take this story."

He threw his head back and laughed a big, deep belly laugh, which was odd, because I hadn't thought my story was that funny. Then he stopped laughing and looked at me, suddenly serious.

"You live by your wits, girl."

I couldn't tell if Anansi was giving me a compliment or a piece of advice.

"So, you gave me a story. Now, what will I give you?" Anansi asked, holding out his hands—he had beautiful, long fingers—as if he were expecting me to place something in them.

"Carabosse," I said. "She put spells on me and my friends and . . . Madame Fredepia, she's helped a lot, but"—I glanced at Madame Fredepia, who nodded at me in an agreeable way and shrugged as if to say *what can you do*—"Well, she's helped a lot . . . but Romy"—I pointed at Romy—"she's going to have to repeat herself all the time, and John"—I looked around the room; where had John gone?—"he's going to have to hop around everywhere, which is not okay because he wants to be a football player. . . ."

"And I might be an actor," added Romy. "So, you know, having to repeat everything is really not going to help with that. . . ."

"And I'm going to get a really big nose," I finished. "So, what we need to know is, how do we break Carabosse's spells?"

"That Carabosse. Always making trouble with her wand," mused Anansi, getting up from his chair and standing in front of the fire. He adjusted his blanket, scratched his nose, and cleared his throat.

"You know, one time I had a terrible, creeping, crawling itch between my blades. And I couldn't reach it." He turned a little to the side, showing us his back. He angled his hand around and pointed in between his shoulder blades, pinpointing—I guessed—the impossible-to-get-at itch. "So, I went down to the watering hole, and I saw a warthog scratching his back on a big old tree, and he was snuffling and sighing, so happy to be scratching an itch.

And I said to him, 'Warthog, I've got a present for you. You're so happy scratching your itch, I'm gonna give you mine.' And the warthog, he took it off me, and that's how I got rid of my itch."

Romy and Madame Fredepia burst into applause as Anansi made a theatrical bow. He beamed at us, looking like he'd just told us the secrets of the universe and not a tiny tale about an itchy pig. I glanced at Romy, who was still clapping. Was she applauding sarcastically? No. She was smiling up at Anansi, looking genuinely impressed by what he'd just said. What was I missing? How was Anansi's story going to help us to break Carabosse's spells/Madame Fredepia's half-baked remedies?

I looked back over at the fireplace. Anansi was gone. I jumped up, ran to the window, and looked out. I saw a spider scuttling down the wall into the darkness.

"Anansi," I shouted after him.

"He won't come back," said Madame Fredepia. "You told him a story, and he told you a story. There's no more to be done."

"Well, he was awesome," said Romy, joining me at the window.

"He was so not awesome," I muttered. "Well, the spider thing, that was cool . . . and his toga blanket . . ."

"And the stuff with the smoke ring," added Romy.

"Sure, the smoke ring." I sighed. "But he didn't tell us how to break Carabosse's spells."

"Yes, he did," said Romy.

I just stared at her.

"Oh c'mon, Cia." She laughed. "He totally told us how to break them. He gave his itch to a warthog!"

She looked at me expectantly. I still didn't know what she was getting at.

"This Anansi, he's from Africa, right?" She looked at Madame Fredepia for confirmation.

Madame Fredepia nodded.

"And in the African fairy tales, there are a lot of animals," continued Romy. "C'mon, Cia, didn't you read any of them?"

I shook my head. I hadn't made it even halfway through the Brothers Grimm book. I hadn't read anything close to the number of stories that Romy had.

"Well, the animals, they can take on whatever your curse is, because it isn't a curse to them. So, I'll give my repeating spell to an animal who likes repeating things. That's gotta be a parrot. And John will give his hop to a frog or a kangaroo, and you just give your big nose to—well, you've loads of choices! An elephant or an anteater or a . . ."

"Proboscis monkey?" offered Madame Fredepia. "They have very long noses."

I was beginning to see how Anansi's story made sense. But I wasn't completely convinced yet. "We don't have to go to an actual watering hole, though, do we?"

"Oh no," said Madame Fredepia. "Anansi's from Africa, so sometimes his stories have watering holes in them, but no—whatever lesson Anansi teaches, you can use it anywhere."

"We can just go to a pet store . . . ," said Romy.

"Well, you can. I'll have to go to a zoo . . . ," I said, thinking. I was starting to feel better. Anansi did know what he was talking about.

"Let's give John the good news. He was really freaking out," said Romy. "We can tell him he can just give his hop to a frog. Where is he, anyway?"

It took us less than a minute to figure out that John was not in the apartment. We checked the bedroom, bathroom, and kitchen—no John.

"Where is he?"

We'd figured out how to break Carabosse's curses; we should have been able to head back home, but now we couldn't. Why did John take off in the middle of the night? How long had he been gone? I couldn't remember if he'd been in the living room when Anansi turned up, so that would mean John had been gone for almost an hour.

"Why would he just leave?" asked Romy. "He doesn't even have any money. . . ."

"Yeah, what was he thinking?" I added. Walking around a strange city without a phone or a dollar (or euro) in your pocket was a really not-smart thing to do. Then I remembered. John did have something in his pocket.

"The mirror," I gasped. "John has the mirror."

In all the chaos of the wedding, I'd forgotten that I'd given it to John to hold on to for me.

"What mirror?" asked Madame Fredepia.

"Well, it's Elvira Queen's. The Evil Queen's . . . ," I said, wincing a bit as I spoke; I knew that I'd have to admit that I'd taken it. "It's the magic mirror, the one you ask questions—"

"I know how the magic mirror works," interrupted

Madame Fredepia, narrowing her eyes at me. "What I don't know is why your friend has it."

I explained that I had taken the Evil Queen's mirror.

"She just borrowed it," clarified Romy. "She didn't steal it. We're going to give it back."

Madame Fredepia laughed. "Oh, I know you didn't steal it. There is no way you could steal anything from the Evil Queen. If you took that mirror, you took it because she wanted you to take it."

"What?" I asked, starting to feel sick. I remembered how lucky I'd felt that we'd made it back to Belle's without the Evil Queen stopping us. But this made much more sense. The Evil Queen hadn't chased us because she had wanted us to take the mirror. But why?

"Why would she want us to take the mirror?" I asked.

"Because she wants someone to do something for her," tutted Madame Fredepia. "That woman is just plain lazy sometimes."

"But what does this have to do with John?" I asked. "He's got the mirror now. . . . Why would he just take off?"

"The queen probably has him running some errand for her," continued Madame Fredepia. "I told you, she's just plain lazy. She casts an enchantment through the mirror so that the person holding it has to do what she wants."

"An errand?" I asked, feeling queasy—I'd had that mirror for a couple of hours; what if the queen had enchanted me?—but also hopeful. "An errand" didn't sound too terrible. Maybe John was okay? "What kind of errand?"

"My bet would be that he's gone to steal the *Mona Lisa*," said Madame Fredepia matter-of-factly.

I looked over at Romy. Had Madame Fredepia just said that John was, at this moment, stealing the most famous painting in the world?

"Like, THE *Mona Lisa*?" asked Romy. "The one Leonardo da Vinci painted?"

"Is there another one?" said Madame Fredepia dryly.

"Oh c'mon," I said, almost laughing. There was no way John was going to be able to break into a maximum-security museum and walk out with the *Mona Lisa*.

"The Evil Queen has been behind every major museum theft in the last thirty years," said Madame Fredepia, getting down on her hands and knees and peering underneath the sofa, muttering about a lack of storage space. "She won't leave Paris without the *Mona Lisa*."

She angled her arm underneath the sofa. "Do either of you have any experience breaking and entering?"

"No," Romy and I said at the same time. My heart dropped a little. Why was Madame Fredepia asking us if we had any criminal experience?

"These'll help," she said, standing up and holding out the objects she had found.

"Wands!" gasped Romy, grabbing one of the sticks and swishing it above her head.

"What do they do?" I asked, taking the wand that Madame Fredepia offered me. I half expected to feel a jolt of magic or electricity or something when I held it, but all I felt was a prickle of anxiety. I'd seen what wands could do. Madame Fredepia's wand had transformed an insect into a man, and Carabosse's had almost changed me, Romy, and John forever.

Romy, though, looked thrilled as she waved her wand around. She pointed it at her feet.

"Can I turn these into sneakers?" she asked Madame Fredepia.

"No," said Madame Fredepia. "These are level-one wands. You'd need at least a level twelve for a transformation."

"Oh," said Romy disappointedly, eyeing her wand skeptically. "So, what can a level one do?"

"It can momentarily stun whatever you point it at . . . and it's the only level that doesn't require any special training or skill."

"That's it?" said Romy disgustedly.

"Do you have to say something when you point it?" I asked. Being able to stupefy people—if only for seconds—just by waving a stick at them sounded incredibly useful and potentially dangerous, no matter what Romy thought.

"Point it and shout 'zap that,'" explained Madame Fredepia.

I felt a sudden pang of homesickness. *Riley would love this*, I thought. He'd think this was the best game ever, running around with a wand, shouting "Zap that."

"So, what are we zapping?" asked Romy.

"Hopefully nothing," said Madame Fredepia. "But it's always good to be prepared."

I was about to ask what exactly we needed to be pre-pared for, but Madame Fredepia walked away and went into the kitchen. She came right back holding a heart-shaped I LOVE THE LOUVRE fridge magnet. She placed it in the middle of the floor.

"I need to go pick up something anyway," she said, as if we'd all been talking about running out to the grocery store. "Now, stand beside me." She patted the sides of her legs, and Romy and I positioned ourselves on either side of her.

"Eyes on that," she continued, pointing at the magnet with her wand.

"What level is your wand?" asked Romy.

"It's a twelve," shouted Madame Fredepia as a loud buzzing noise filled my ears. "Ideal for making soufflés and transferences!"

Then she shouted, "Transfer!"

The fridge magnet started spinning, going faster and faster until the heart and words melded into a mesmerizing red-and-black spiral. I couldn't take my eyes off it. It got bigger and bigger until it was all I could see. It was as if the rug disappeared. Then I felt myself fall as if the ground had just opened up, and I had the horrible feeling that I was being sucked down a plughole. But as quickly as it had begun, it stopped. My knees buckled, and I fell onto the floor.

The floor of the gift shop at the Louvre.

Chapter 26

"THAT WAS AWFUL," WHIMPERED ROMY BESIDE me. I looked over at her. She was pale and clutching her stomach. "Like the worst roller-coaster ride ever."

"You get used to it," said Madame Fredepia, reaching down and helping us both to our feet. Standing and brushing myself off, I took in the glass cases, bookshelves, and postcard displays at the store.

"Can you do something about these?" asked Romy, pulling at the skirt of her dress. "It's so flouncy. Can you just change us into jeans or, like, something comfortable?" She pointed at Madame Fredepia's wand.

"No time for that."

I didn't think it was fair of Madame Fredepia to refuse to flick her wrist and make us more comfortable when she had changed out of her own wedding outfit into a cozy-looking velvet sweat suit, but she was the one with the wand.

"The museum maps and guide books are over there," she said, pointing at a display stand.

"Are you not coming with us?" I said, my heart skipping a beat. Stopping an art heist was hardly a job for a couple of teenagers with level-one wands.

"No. I have to head to Greek Antiquities. It's upstairs." She put her hands on her hips and looked at me and Romy. "You girls can do this. You don't even need to worry about the cameras." She pointed her wand at one on the ceiling just above the cash register. "She'll have turned them all off. Just watch out for the security guards."

And then, before I'd even thought to ask her what she was picking up in Greek Antiquities, she had opened the door of the gift shop and taken off.

"We have to go up the escalator, then take an elevator to the first floor and we'll get to the gallery with the *Mona*

Lisa," said Romy. She was holding a map in one hand and a guidebook in the other. She opened the book. "Says here the Louvre has one thousand two hundred guards."

"One thousand two hundred security guards?!"

"Yeah, but they can't all be here at the same time," mused Romy, looking up from her book. "What'll we do if we meet one?"

"Run?" I suggested.

"That's why I wanted to get changed," moaned Romy. "I can't run in five layers of lace."

I looked around me. The museum floor that we were on—or at least, as much of it as I could see—was empty. And it was so quiet. We weren't too late. If John had already made it to the *Mona Lisa*, there'd be sirens blaring and guards running all over the place. I saw the escalator that Romy said we needed to take.

We headed toward the escalator and stepped on. I didn't know what to do with the wand, so I just held it out in front of me like it was a flashlight.

"Says here that this is the biggest museum in the world," said Romy. "And that the *Mona Lisa* is worth eight hundred and fifty million dollars. It's France's greatest national treasure, even though Leonardo da Vinci was Italian—"

"Shh," I whispered as we stepped off the escalator. This wasn't the time for Romy to start acting like a tour guide. I looked around me trying to figure out which direction we should run in if we spotted a security guard.

Romy looked up from her book and gasped. "I think I see him."

I stared straight ahead of me. It was John, and he was carrying a painting.

Romy and I ran toward him.

"John," I hissed, coming alongside him. "You need to put that back."

He kept walking without even turning his head. It was as if he couldn't hear or see me.

"Please, John, put it down," I pleaded. He was holding the painting out in front of him with straight arms, like he was impersonating Frankenstein. It *was* the *Mona Lisa*. It was much smaller than I'd expected, about the size of a picture book. How had John taken it off the wall without activating all the alarms?

"John, put it back," said Romy firmly. She waved her

hand in front of his face, but John didn't blink. Romy turned to me. "It's like he's a robot."

I saw the handle of the mirror in his jacket pocket and thought about grabbing it—if I took it from him, maybe whatever spell it had on him would break—but what if he moved suddenly and I accidentally stuck my finger through the *Mona Lisa* or fell on top of it? What if I damaged or destroyed the most famous painting in the world?

"What about our wands?" asked Romy, raising hers and pointing it at John. "We could just zap him. I stun him and you grab the *Mona Lisa*?"

"NO!" I yelled on impulse, before clearing my throat and whispering, *"No."* I looked around, but no guards came running—hopefully my shout hadn't alerted any. "Romy, we can't. This is the most famous, the most loved thing in France. . . . It's been preserved for five hundred years. . . . We can't mess around with this."

"Okay, well, what are we going to do?"

We were still following John, who seemed to know exactly where he was going—even though his brain was offline—and we followed him around corners and through gallery rooms.

"Let's just see where he's heading," I said.

I almost wished we'd bump into a security guard—
where were they?—because that would mean that the
Mona Lisa would be returned, no harm done, to her
spot on the wall, but I couldn't see how us getting caught
would end well for me, Romy, and John. There'd be police
officers asking questions we couldn't answer and probably news cameras with reporters shouting at us for trying
to steal France's number one national treasure. And we'd
be locked up.

"Put it down, John," I whispered again, even though I
realized it was pointless.

"He's heading for one of the restaurants," said Romy.

She was right. The double doors of the restaurant
swung open on their own and we followed John into the
empty dining hall. We walked in between the tables and
then into the kitchen, past countertops and sinks and
white uniforms hanging on pegs. John never changed his
pace or his posture, striding purposefully on and holding
the *Mona Lisa* straight out in front of him.

"There's an exit right over there," said Romy, pointing
at a green exit sign.

John and the *Mona Lisa* were headed toward it.

This door also swung open as if by magic, and we followed John outside. The door slammed behind us.

We were standing in an alley. There were piles of empty boxes and full-to-the-brim trash cans ready for the garbage pickup. I waved my hand in front of my face to bat away the smell of rotting food.

"The Louvre's security system is totally useless," said Romy, throwing her map into a trash can and leaving the guidebook in front of the closed door. "Lucky for us."

"Or maybe the Evil Queen's magic is ridiculously powerful," I said as a red limousine with a FOREVER YOUNG license plate pulled into the alley. John walked toward it, and a door of the car slid open. He got in.

"Let's go," I shouted at Romy, running to the car and holding up my wand, wishing that Madame Fredepia had given us something stronger than a level one. We'd need about a level one hundred if the Evil Queen was in that car.

I jumped in, Romy following behind me, and just as the door slid shut, an alarm loud enough to wake up all of Paris started blaring.

Chapter 27

I'D SEEN LIMOUSINES IN MOVIES, BUT I WAS STILL surprised by how big it was inside. My entire basketball team could have all fit on the U-shaped leather seats. John was sitting opposite me, still holding the *Mona Lisa* and looking like he was sleepwalking, and Romy was banging on the partition window that separated our side of the limousine from the driver. The partition glass was completely black, so I couldn't see who was on the other side. Was the Evil Queen driving?

"Tell us where we're going!" said Romy, putting her face right up to the partition window and pounding it

with both fists. "I know you can hear me!" She looked over her shoulder at me. "See if you can find a button that'll open this thing."

I started pressing buttons. There were a bunch of them on a panel beside my seat. None of them did anything to the window that Romy was pounding on, but I did turn on a peanut dispenser, the music system, and three TV screens.

I stared at the screens. They were all showing footage of police cars swarming around the Louvre. A picture of the *Mona Lisa* flashed on the screen. Then there was a picture of an ancient pair of scissors. (Was that what Madame Fredepia had gone to pick up?) The word VOLÉS ran across the bottom of the screens. I didn't know any French, but I guessed that *"volés"* meant stolen.

"Oh no," I whimpered. I felt a bit dizzy. Even though the security cameras had been turned off, what if a guard had spotted us and given a description of what we looked like to the police? "This is awful."

"Oh, stop being so dramatic," came a voice from the other end of the limousine, making Romy and me jump. I knew that voice. It was the Evil Queen.

My heart felt like it was about to leap out of my chest. She leaned forward, her face still partially hidden in shadow, and flicked a wand, causing the three TVs to burst into flames.

There was a moment of stunned silence as the fires sizzled out, and then Romy blurted, "What have you done to John?"

"Oh, no harm done," said the Evil Queen, reaching into John's pocket and removing her mirror. She took the *Mona Lisa* from his hands and placed it on her lap.

"I'm so glad I had you pick this up for me," she said. "It's such a chore getting in and out of the Louvre at night."

"Pick it up for you," sputtered Romy. "PICK IT UP FOR YOU? You made him"—she patted John's shoulder; he appeared to be waking up and was rubbing his eyes— "steal the *Mona Lisa*!"

I was just as angry as Romy, but I wished she'd stop shouting at one of the most evil people on the planet. We were speeding along in a car going who-knows-where with a woman who, if she felt like it, could turn the three of us to a pile of ashes. Now was not the time for my best friend to be throwing out zingers.

"Stop fussing," snapped the Evil Queen. "I disabled all the security. There was no fear of him getting caught. Now, let me take a look at it."

She stared at the painting. What was she going to do with it? Sell it for a fortune to some evil art collector? Magic up some copies and sell those for an even bigger fortune to more evil art collectors? How much money did this woman need?

"What's going on?" gasped John, shaking his head as if he were trying to get water out of his ears. "Are we in a limo?" His eyes darted around, taking in the vast leather seats, incinerated TV screens, and the Evil Queen, who still had her eyes on the painting.

"Who is she?" said John, staring at the queen.

"Snow White's stepmother," muttered Romy out of the side of her mouth.

"I am Elvira Queen, CEO of Forever Young, recipient of the French Legion of Honor and the Nobel Peace Prize. According to *Fortune* magazine, I am one of the richest women in the world," said the queen, glaring at Romy. "Being stepmother to that stupid wedding-obsessed girl is the least interesting thing about me."

"You can say that again," said Romy. She leaned over to John and pointed at the queen's lap. "She just made you steal the *Mona Lisa*."

"WHAT?!" roared John, jumping up and banging his head on the roof of the car. He stared at the painting. "I didn't steal the *Mona Lisa*. There's no way I stole the *Mona Lisa*." He threw me a desperate look. "Cia, what is she talking about? There's no way I stole the *Mona Lisa*."

"Well, you kind of did," said Romy gently.

"But it wasn't your fault," I added. I wished Romy hadn't said anything. John was just waking up from his sleepwalking coma (or whatever it was the queen had put him into). But then again, was there a right time to tell someone that they had stolen the most famous painting in the world? "You didn't know what you were doing. You were under the influence of a magic mirror."

"And if it makes you feel any better," said Romy, "we know how to fix your leg now . . . so you don't have to worry about having to hop everywhere."

"NO!" roared John. "That does not make me feel better." He sat back down and put his head in his hands. "I'm going to go to prison," he mumbled. "The *Mona Lisa*?

They'll lock me up forever. I haven't even started high school. . . ."

"Oh, do shut up," snapped the queen. "I'll put it back when I'm finished with it."

John looked up and rubbed his eyes. The three of us stared at the queen.

"I'm hosting a little dinner party next week. The theme is Italian." She raised an eyebrow as if that was supposed to explain everything. "I needed some Italian art to go with the Italian food . . . and, well, you can't get more Italian than Leonardo da Vinci. It'll be a nice complement to the pasta and bruschetta."

I could feel Romy tensing up beside me, trying to control her temper. I felt the same way. Somehow stealing the *Mona Lisa* just so you could impress your dinner guests seemed much worse than stealing it so you could sell it.

"I thought about getting that statue of David by Michelangelo or the pope's hat as a centerpiece for the table, but when you all turned up, I just thought, 'well, it might as well be the *Mona Lisa*.'"

The pope's hat? What kind of dinner party was the Evil Queen planning?

"Hope that all goes well," I said, struggling to sound polite and keep the panic out of my voice. "Sounds like you have a lot of planning to do, you know, for the party, so you can just drop us off . . ." Where? Where could the queen drop us off? Anywhere. Anywhere would be better than this car. We just needed to get away from her before she made us kidnap Ed Sheeran or some other celebrity to perform for her guests.

The queen gave me a nasty look, like she thought what I had just said was stupid.

She took the mirror that she had placed on the seat beside her and gazed into it. "Now, let's see what questions you asked," she said, swiping a finger across the surface of the mirror. "Always interesting to find out a person's deepest desires."

"Did I tell the truth?" she sneered, looking at what must have been an image of Romy asking her question. Mine was up next. I flinched. I felt like the queen was about to read something private, like my journal.

"You asked for this?" she said, turning the mirror around so that I could see Mom standing in front of what Belle had told me was the Tapestry of Tales. "So, your mother is here."

The queen turned the mirror around and stared at it. Her face didn't show any emotion, but I noticed that she was gripping the handle of the mirror so tightly that she had clenched her hand into a fist.

"And you know what this is?" she asked.

"Yes, it's the Tapestry of Tales."

"And do you know what they're going to do to her?"

"Who's 'they'?" I said. My mouth was suddenly dry.

"The fairy godmothers," said the queen. She stared at me. What did fairy godmothers have to do with the tapestry? Belle hadn't said anything about any fairy godmothers. My heart started thudding in my chest. I felt like the Evil Queen was about to tell me something terrible. Something terrible about Mom.

The queen looked back at the mirror. "They've been looking for her for a long time. And now—" She paused and tapped on the mirror. "And now, it seems they are planning on stitching her into the Tapestry of Tales."

"What?" I said. Too much information was coming too fast. Why had fairy godmothers been looking for my mom? And why would they want to stitch her into the tapestry? Was something like that even possible? "How? Why?"

"If I'd known that this was what they were planning," continued the queen, "perhaps I wouldn't have told them where she was—"

"You told them where she was?" I was shouting now.

"Don't look so judgmental, darling," said the queen, placing the mirror into a crocodile-skin purse on the seat beside her. "It was you who really clarified things for me."

I couldn't speak. I didn't understand what the queen was talking about.

"What do you mean?" asked Romy.

"When you came to the book signing this morning," said the queen, looking at me. "You mentioned that your mother had certain contacts in her phone."

Had I? What had I said? I glanced at Romy to see if she understood what the queen was talking about. No, she looked confused too.

"And it confirmed that your mother was the one the fairy godmothers have been looking for—"

"But they're nice, right?" said John, leaning forward in his seat and looking back and forth between me and the queen. "Fairy godmothers are nice—"

"Not if they're stitching people into tapestries," whispered Romy.

"We'll just go and get Mom," I said, my heart skipping and thumping. "We have to go to the tapestry."

The doors slid open and pale early morning light filled the back of the limo.

"Out," said the queen.

Before I knew what was happening, the queen had hit an eject button or used magic to throw me, Romy, and John out of our seats and onto the street.

By the time the three of us stood up, the limo was gone.

Chapter 28

MAYBE THE EVIL QUEEN DIDN'T KNOW WHAT she was talking about?"

Romy was standing in front of the fireplace in Madame Fredepia's living room. The limo had stopped right in front of her apartment—I didn't know if that was where the limo had been headed all along, or if it was just weird timing that that was where it had stopped when the queen decided to throw us out. We'd climbed the stairs. I'd been planning to ask Madame Fredepia to help us find the tapestry and answer all the questions that were bouncing around in my head about fairy godmothers and why they'd been looking for my mom and why they were planning on stitching her into a tapestry.

But the apartment had been empty. So, it was just the three of us trying to figure out what to do next.

"Like, how does she even know that your mom is going to get stitched into the tapestry?" continued Romy. "Why would anyone do that?"

"Well, the Romans, they used to stick people into walls . . . like, they'd build the wall around them," said John as he reached for a chocolate croissant that he'd found on a plate of pastries in the kitchen. I guessed he was too hungry to worry about the fact that Madame Fredepia had probably used her wand to make them. I was too nervous and jumpy to eat anything. "It was called immurement."

"And how is that information useful?" said Romy, scowling at John.

"I just mean that the Romans, they used to, you know, punish people that way. I think the Greeks might have done it too. . . ." John blushed and looked down at his hands.

Romy was glaring at him, but I could tell John was just trying to help.

"So, maybe Mom's being punished for something?" I wondered aloud. Why would anyone want to punish my mom? What could she possibly have done? "And," I continued, looking at John, "the people who got stuck in the walls. Would they be, you know, okay afterwards?"

"Well, no," gulped John. "I mean . . . they'd be, you know . . ."

I wouldn't make him say it. "Dead," I muttered, feeling a knot in my stomach.

Wanting to be alone, I walked into the kitchen. I took a deep breath to try to slow down and sort through the thoughts that were racing through my head. Was it my fault that Mom had been taken? What had I said? And why couldn't the queen have just kept it to herself? I felt so angry, but I wasn't sure who I was angrier with: me or the queen.

We had to find Mom. But what if we were already too late? The knot in my stomach got tighter and tighter. I looked around the tiny kitchen, looking for—I didn't know what—something that would tell me what to do next. I saw an empty bottle of whiskey on the counter. I picked it up and ran back into the living room.

"We could call Anansi again!" I said to John and Romy.

"Yesss!" shouted Romy, giving me a hug. "Brilliant idea!"

"Anansi?" asked John.

"He's cool," explained Romy. "He's a spider man."

"Spiderman?" said John, his eyes widening with excitement. "Like Superman?"

"No. Not *Spiderman*. He's a spider man," said Romy. "He's a man who can change into a spider. Or maybe he's a spider who can change into a man." Romy shrugged. "Anyway, you'll like him. He knows things. He told us how to break Carabosse's curses."

"I'll see if I can find the summoning stuff," I said, walking back into the kitchen as Romy explained the chocolate, whiskey, and cigar requirements to John.

I opened the cabinets and found a bottle of cooking sherry and a candle—not exactly what I was looking for, but it was the best I could do. Now, all I needed was some chocolate. There wasn't any. Not even a jar of cocoa powder. Why had John eaten all those chocolate croissants? I went to the fridge to check if there was any chocolate ice cream—that might work. Then I stopped, my hand in midair, and stared at the door.

There were hundreds of magnets on it, so many that

the white surface of the fridge was only visible in just a few tiny spots. There were magnets of every shape and color, and some were as big as coasters, while others were as small as stamps. They all had the names or images of places printed on them, and I'd never heard of most of the places. Where was the Ulriksdal Palace and Eritrea? Some had really fancy designs, like the one from Germany that was a miniature cuckoo clock with two tiny girls with braids standing by it like soldiers.

"Romy! John! You need to come see this!"

They ran into the kitchen.

"Look," I said, pointing at the fridge.

"Yeah," said Romy. "I saw that earlier. I guess Madame Fredepia travels a lot?"

"Cool collection," added John.

"No," I said, my voice was shaking with excitement. "Look at it! That's not what I mean. Just—just look."

Romy and John stepped so close to the fridge that their faces were inches from the magnets.

"We're looking," muttered Romy.

There was a moment of silence, then Romy let out a shout.

"That's how we got into the Louvre!" She grabbed my shoulders. "Cia! That's how we got into the Louvre."

Romy turned to John. "This," she said breathlessly, gesturing at the fridge. "Is how we're going to get to the Tapestry of Tales."

"The fridge?" said John looking confused. "We're going to go through the fridge? This fridge is a portal?"

"No," I said. I took a deep breath. I felt giddy with excitement. And hope. This could work. We didn't need Madame Fredepia. We didn't need Anansi. We could get to my mom and save her all on our own. "So, this is going to sound impossible . . . but these magnets are like keys."

"Um, okay," said John, peering at the fridge.

"When we needed to get into the Louvre to go after you, Madame Fredepia put a magnet on the floor," I continued. "It said, 'I LOVE THE LOUVRE'—and we stood around it, and she shouted, 'Transfer,' and then it felt like we were falling—"

"That bit was pretty awful," added Romy. "I thought I was going to vomit."

"But she didn't," I added hastily, seeing John go pale. "And then we just sort of landed in the gift shop inside the Louvre. I bet that's where Madame Fredepia got the magnet in the first place."

"Whoa," said John. "This is amazing. You think we can just go to any of these places?" He gazed at the display of magnets, his mouth hanging slightly open the way Riley's did when he was standing in front of the counter in an ice cream shop.

John reached over Romy's head and picked a magnet off the fridge.

"So, how does this work?" he asked, staring at a magnet that said BUCKINGHAM PALACE. "We can just use this to get us to London?" He turned the magnet over in his hand.

"I think so," I said.

"'The Temple of Artemis'... 'the Library of Alexandria,'" John continued, sounding more and more excited as he read the print on the magnets. "'The Hanging Gardens of Babylon' . . . 'the Statue of Zeus at Olympia' . . ."

He grabbed his forehead and took a step back as if he'd been hit.

"These places—some don't even exist anymore. These are like the wonders of the ancient world. You're saying we can go, like, back in time? We could meet the Romans?" His eyes were popping out of his head. I hadn't known John was such a history nerd.

"I don't know. Maybe," I said, feeling a bit overwhelmed. "I just want to find the one that'll take us to the Tapestry of Tales."

"Of course," said John, putting back a magnet that had a picture of a friendly-looking dinosaur with the words LOCH NESS MONSTER underneath it. "Sorry, Cia. Yeah, the tapestry. That's the one we have to find."

"I mean, I don't know for sure if there's a magnet that'll take us to the tapestry," I said. "But it seems like it's possible, because Madame Fredepia is a fairy godmother."

"I think it's the best plan we've got," said John. "Let's do it."

"You guys figure out the magnets," said Romy. "I'll find us a wand."

"A wand?" asked John, not looking away from the fridge.

"Yeah, a level twelve," I reminded Romy. "Madame Fredepia said you need a level-twelve wand to do a transference."

"I'm on it," said Romy. "I bet there are wands all over this apartment. Madame Fredepia pulled ours out of the sofa, remember? You guys figure out which magnet will take us to the tapestry, and I'll get us a wand. Level twelve, coming right up!" She raced over to the drawers beside the kitchen sink and emptied them, flinging utensils onto the kitchen counter.

"There's about three hundred and fifty magnets," said John, a note of apprehension in his voice.

"Three hundred and fifty." I sighed, my heart dropping as I stared at them all. How would we figure out which one to use? "I guess if we tried all of them . . ."

"It would take at least thirty hours to visit all of them," said John. "And that's if we just spent five minutes in each place."

"We don't have thirty hours," I said, gulping. "I don't know how much time we have before Mom is, you know . . ."

"Nothing in the kitchen!" yelled Romy. "I'm going to check the bedroom."

"None of the magnets say 'Tapestry of Tales,'" said John.

"As if," I blurted out. "That would be way too easy." But I was glad that John had thought to look for it.

"The only thing we know for sure is that it was in China like hundreds of years ago . . . ," I said, remembering what Belle had told us.

"At Kublai Khan's court," said John. "Wasn't he an emperor? We could try a palace. Maybe it's a royal thing?"

I picked up the magnet that said BUCKINGHAM PALACE and then found the ROYAL PALACE OF MADRID, and I grouped them in one spot on the fridge. Then a magnet in the top corner caught my eye. It looked more worn than the others, and it had a green background and a black outline of a tree on it. My heart jumped. It was exactly like the tree Mom had on the scarf she always wore when she traveled.

I placed the magnet on the counter.

"I can't find any wands," shouted Romy, running back into the kitchen. "And that's not all. . . ."

John and I turned around to face her.

"A police car's just pulled up outside."

Chapter 29

I WAS JUST CHECKING BEHIND THE DRAPES IN THE living room window, and I looked down and saw it," said Romy.

"No!" wailed John, running to the window in the living room. Romy and I followed him, all of us crowding around the window to look down. Romy was right. There was a white car with the word GENDARMERIE on it. You didn't need to speak French to know what that word meant. So much for the queen scrambling the Louvre's security system. The two front doors opened, and a woman who looked like she was about my mom's age got

out on one side. She was wearing a dark navy suit and a white shirt. On the other side of the car, another woman got out. This one was dressed in a police uniform. She was holding a piece of paper that fluttered in the breeze. I gulped. Maybe it was a warrant for our arrest?

"I'm going to jail," gasped John, pointing at the piece of paper.

"Maybe they just want to get breakfast at the bakery," said Romy. "The croissants are really . . ."

The shrill ring of the doorbell cut her off midsentence.

"Don't answer it!" whispered John. "Shouldn't we, like, call an attorney or the US embassy? Why isn't there a phone in here?" He started running around the living room, throwing cushions off the sofa. When he ran back into the kitchen, Romy and I followed him.

"Just summon that Anansi guy," he panted, rifling through the cupboard and pulling out a bottle of olive oil. "This'll work, right?"

John was sweating and shaking.

I glanced at Romy. She mouthed the words "panic attack."

I was panicking too. The French police were probably

seconds away from getting the front door open, climbing the three flights of stairs, and then breaking down the door to the apartment if we didn't let them in. (Had a security guard seen us after all? And how did the police know we were here? Did the Evil Queen tell them?) They'd arrest us, and we'd never get to the Tapestry of Tales in time. We'd never get to Mom in time. We had to get out of here.

I looked around the kitchen and saw the pile of utensils that Romy had thrown on the counter. I felt a little sliver of hope. I saw a possibility. The Groac'h's wooden spoon had been her wand. Maybe she wasn't the only one who used kitchen utensils to cast her spells? What if Madame Fredepia did the same thing?

"We're getting out of here," I said. I swiped at the magnets on the fridge, and they fell into my hand like candy spilling out of a dispenser. I stuffed them into the pockets of John's jacket. "Fill up John's pockets," I yelled at Romy. Romy moved fast, pushing magnets into John's pants pockets. He was standing still, looking stunned and mumbling, "I'm going to prison."

I grabbed the magnet I'd set aside on the counter

and placed it on the floor. It didn't matter where we were going. We just needed to get out of here fast.

"Cia, we don't have a wand," said Romy.

There was a loud knock on the front door followed by two more knocks.

"*Gendarmes!* Open up!"

"Just a moment," I shouted back, forcing my voice to sound steady and calm. "Just getting dressed."

John let out a garbled whine, and Romy repeated what she had just said, whispering, "Cia, we don't have a wand!"

I ran to the utensils. "What do you use to make a soufflé?" I said, remembering what Madame Fredepia had said about her wand just before we transferred to the Louvre.

"What?" gasped Romy.

"A soufflé!" I said again, flinging aside a spatula, wooden spoon, peeler, rolling pin, and bread knife. "Is it this?" I held up a whisk. I'd never made a soufflé, but I'd eaten a chocolate one and it was light and fluffy; I'd also used a whisk to make scrambled eggs before, and they were light and fluffy.

"Maybe?" said Romy, sounding alarmed and confused.

I ran back to Romy and John, grabbed the tree magnet I'd taken off the fridge, and placed it on the floor.

"Now, stare at the magnet," I said, pointing the whisk at it.

There was another knock on the door.

"Eyes on that!" I said, remembering the words Madame Fredepia had used. I gripped the whisk with both hands.

"I'm going to be sick," said John.

"Transfer!" I shouted.

The magnet on the floor spun, increasing in size with every rotation, and in what seemed like a nanosecond, it became so big that it covered the entire kitchen floor. Just like last time, I felt myself falling. I heard Romy shout, "It's working!" and John screaming. And then it was over.

Chapter 30

"WHOA! IT WASN'T NEARLY AS BAD THIS time," said Romy, standing up and stretching. "Maybe you're better than Madame Fredepia at this transferring thing, Cia!"

I stared at the whisk I was still holding, amazed that it had worked. I wondered how powerful of a wand it was. Madame Fredepia had said we'd needed a level twelve to do a transference, so this one had to be at least that strong; would it be powerful enough, though, to fight fairy god-mothers? I held it tightly, getting ready to use it. I looked around me. Where were we? I had only chosen the magnet because it reminded me of Mom, and I had no idea where it had taken us.

John was sitting on the ground with his head between his knees. He groaned.

"You okay?" said Romy, touching his back.

"No," he moaned without looking up. "Just tell me there's no police here."

"There's no police," I said. "Or anyone else."

We'd landed on a bed of moss and leaves at the base of a huge, towering tree. I gazed up at the vast, green canopy. The tree must have been at least thirty feet high, and above it—where there should have been sky—was a ceiling. We were sitting in a woodland setting inside a—what? I got to my feet and looked around me.

We were in the middle of a very long, very wide, brightly lit tunnel. It reminded me of the subway back at home, though this place was clean and new-looking and there weren't any tracks. And other than the spot where we had landed, there was no grass or bushes or anything outdoorsy.

Could the tapestry be somewhere along the tunnel? Had I just randomly picked the right magnet? I felt a little pulse of pride and then nervousness. If the tapestry was here, so were the fairy godmothers. The magnet we'd used was on the ground. I picked it up. The words ENTRY MADE had appeared on it.

"'Entry made,'" I read.

"Entrance to what?" John asked.

"We could ask that guy," said Romy.

A man was walking toward us from the other end of the tunnel. My heart had jumped when Romy pointed him out, but I calmed down when I saw that he didn't look like a police officer or anyone threatening. His arms were full of files and papers—nothing that looked like, or could be used as, a wand. Not a fairy godperson, then. He had the intense, busy look of someone on their way to an important meeting. But the long-tailed coat and top hat he was wearing were so strange that I wondered if we had actually time-traveled. Coming alongside us, he walked right by without a glance in our direction, which made me think that he was used to seeing people hanging out (arriving?) at the tree.

"Hey," said Romy, running after him. "Can I ask you something?"

The man didn't slow down or turn around, but he pointed an arm over his shoulder and shouted, "Information is that way!"

"Thank you!" Romy shouted back. She turned to me. "Awesome! How cool is that? There's an information desk!"

"Information on *what*?" asked John, getting to his feet.

"Well, maybe everything," said Romy excitedly. "C'mon, let's go."

"Hang on," I said, holding up the ENTRY MADE magnet and the whisk. I didn't want to walk around clutching a kitchen utensil, and I couldn't stuff anything else into John's already bulging pockets. "Hold this," I said to Romy as I handed her the magnet. "I want to try something."

A level twelve wand should be able to magic up a backpack, right? I pointed the whisk at the ground and in a firm voice said, "Backpack."

Nothing happened.

"You need to have something to turn into a backpack," said Romy. "I don't think you can just make it appear out of thin air. Remember, Madame Fredepia turned a beetle into a pilot. . . ."

"And a flowerpot into a helicopter," added John.

I looked around me. No beetles or insects. And no flowerpots. I reached down, grabbed a handful of leaves, and placed them at my feet. I pointed the whisk at them.

"Backpack."

In place of the leaves, a green-and-black backpack appeared.

Romy clapped her hands. "Fantastic!"

"Let's do something about these," she said kicking off the shoes we'd both been wearing since the wedding.

"Sneakers?" I asked.

"I'd love a pair of Doc Martens, actually," she grinned. "In burgundy. Please. And I'll need socks too."

"I'll try," I said, focusing on the shoes. I pointed the whisk and made my request, and a shiny, brand-new pair of Doc Martens with socks hanging out of them appeared.

"You're really good at this," commented Romy, sitting down and putting on her new boots.

"It's just the wand," I said. I didn't like the idea that I was good at spell-casting, or transforming leaves into bags, or just magic of any sort. I hadn't done anything. It *was* just the wand. I held it out to Romy. "Here, you do it."

"You okay in those?" she asked John, waving the wand at him. "Want me to change it?"

"No." John paled, stepping away from Romy and putting up his hands. "Don't . . . don't point that thing at me."

"Just get me some sneakers, Romy," I said, taking off my shoes and placing them in front of her.

"Any preference on brand?" she asked. "What about color?"

"I don't care," I said impatiently. We needed to get to that information desk and find out about the tapestry, not spend time thinking about shoes. "Just sneakers."

She pointed the whisk at my bridesmaid shoes. "Sneakers."

Nothing happened.

Romy stuck out her tongue, shook the whisk, and bent down so that the tip of the whisk was just an inch or two from the shoes. "Sneakers!" she shouted.

Nothing happened. Again. The pale beige sandals were unchanged.

Romy stared at them for a moment. "Is this thing broken?" she muttered, giving the whisk another shake before handing it back to me.

I took it from her and pointed it at the shoes. I

whispered, "Sneakers," and in an instant there were sneakers in the spot where the shoes had been.

I kept my eyes glued to the sneakers as I put them on. I didn't want to see the look on Romy's or John's face.

"Let's check out the information desk. Or office or whatever," I said, straightening back up. I stuffed the whisk into the bottom of the backpack and threw the magnet in on top of it. I could feel Romy and John staring at me, but I didn't want to talk about what had just happened. I knew what they were thinking. I was thinking the same thing.

Why had the wand worked for me, but not for Romy?

I handed the backpack to John. "You wanna put the magnets in here?"

"Sure," he said, transferring the magnets into the backpack. "Want me to carry it?"

"It's okay. I got it," I said. John was looking at the backpack as if it contained some really smelly socks.

"Next stop, information desk," said Romy.

There was no way to miss the desk. A huge, boulder-like piece of wood as big as a car and almost as high as a van, it stood out like an island in the middle of the vast tunnel.

My shoulders just about reached the top of the desk, and Romy had to stand on tiptoes to get to chin level. Only John was tall enough to reach over and ring the bell that was dangling from the INFORMATION HERE sign.

A voice came from behind the desk. "Be right with you."

There was a sound of something scraping the floor and steps being taken; then a head popped up on the other side of the desk.

"It's a troll," whispered Romy excitedly.

I'd never seen a troll in real life—*obviously,* I thought to myself—and I was pretty sure that Romy hadn't either, but "troll" did seem like the right description for the green-skinned man standing in front of us. He seemed to be slightly hunchbacked and had a huge warty nose and an underbite that thrust his chin out so far that it was parallel with the tip of his nose. He had masses of black hair brushed back and up so that it looked like he was wearing a wig, and his eyebrows were extraordinary: big tufts of black wiry hair that stood out over each eye like sturdy perches for tiny birds. He was huge, but really he looked very friendly and welcoming. I could just imagine baby birds nesting comfortably in his eyebrows.

"Hello, hello," he said, peering down at the three of us. "It's been quiet around here for a few days. Nice to see you. You're a bit late, though. Nearly closing time here."

A bit late? Had we traveled across time zones? It had been morning in Paris, and we'd only just come from there. Where were we? And, most importantly, was this where Mom was?

"We're looking for the Tapestry of Tales," I blurted out. "Is it here?"

The troll reached down behind the desk and pulled out a book so huge, he had to use both his hands to place it on the top of the desk. It must have been ten thousand pages long. It had a shiny red leather cover and was either new or really well taken care of.

"Is there something about the Tapestry of Tales in there?" I asked, feeling hopeful—the book was enormous; it had to have something in it that would help us find my mom—but I also felt nervous. The troll was moving very slowly and didn't seem to be paying attention to what I was saying.

"Are you all from the same story?" said the troll.

He wasn't listening to me! *From the same story?* Why

was he asking us that? I glanced at Romy and John. They were staring blankly at the troll, looking confused.

"Different stories then?" said the troll. "What stories have you come from? Look, we need to get it all down in here. . . ." He tapped a well-trimmed fingernail on the cover of the book.

"I'm from a Nordic folktale myself," he offered encouragingly. "And very happy to get away from it, I was. I'd only a tiny part, and I'd had enough of the bloodthirsty, fearsome carrying-on." He bared his teeth and growled, giving us a glimpse of what he must have spent his time doing before he'd taken on his current meet-and-greet role behind the information desk.

"We're not from . . . ," I began. I took a deep breath. "We just need to find something called—"

"So, it *is* different stories," he interrupted me, holding up a finger. "Should have guessed."

"What is he talking about?" whispered John through gritted teeth.

"You're from an Asian tale, I presume?" said the troll, looking at John.

"I'm Korean American, actually," said John. "But . . ."

"Korean," said the troll flipping through the massive book. "Yes, we've got plenty of Korean stories in here."

I wondered if I should just grab the book away from him—that way he'd have to listen to me.

"And you ladies." He gave me and Romy an appraising look. "Those dresses nearly had me fooled. I was thinking you were straight out of a Brothers Grimm, but no, now I'm guessing a Slavic fairy tale?"

"Slavic?" repeated Romy, turning to me and flashing a grin. "That sounds glamorous."

"No," I said to both Romy and the troll, wondering how to stop him talking and get her back on track. "We are looking for the Tapestry of Tales, and we are not—"

John beat me to it.

"We are not fairy-tale characters!" he shouted.

"Very good, very good," said the troll, tapping his huge nose and winking at John. "You are absolutely right. You are not"—he paused and winked at me and Romy—"fairy-tale characters. Anymore." He leaned forward onto the desk. "It takes a while to get used to life on the other side, but you're already getting the hang of it. And look at you!" He gave each of us an encouraging nod. "You'll all fit

right in, no problem at all. Bit harder for the likes of me."
He gave us all a significant look and raised his eyebrows.

"Now, don't get me wrong, I'm proud to be a troll." He
puffed up his chest. "But I'd stand out a bit walking up
and down the aisles in a grocery store, now, wouldn't I?"
He chuckled. "Sorry. You don't know what that is yet.
'GROW-ser-eee stoar.'" He pronounced the words slowly
and carefully as if he thought we had only the most basic
grasp of the English language and/or shopping habits.
"You've a lot to learn, but they'll sort you out here. Lots of
workshops—I can sign you up for them. There's more to
food than baking and boiling, if you'd like?" He beamed
at us all enthusiastically.

"Please," I said, starting to feel desperate. At this point
I was happy to tell him I was Cinderella if it would stop
him talking and get him to answer my question. "Do you
know where the Tapestry of Tales is?"

"Tapestry of Tales?" repeated the troll, shaking his
head and finally looking at me. "Never heard of it."

"Would there be anything about it in there?" I asked,
reaching over the desk and pointing at the enormous
book—only then noticing my hand was shaking.

"No, no," said the troll firmly. "There's no mention of a Tapestry of Tales in there."

"Are you sure? It's a very big book," said John, turning to me and giving me a small, encouraging smile.

"And I know every page of it," answered the troll firmly, tapping on the book again. "Nothing about a tapestry in here."

I felt a bit dizzy. I had chosen the wrong magnet. I crossed my arms, trying to steady myself. I had a horrible feeling that we were wasting time. This troll didn't know anything. We needed to try another magnet and keep looking for Mom.

"Look, is there anyone around who might know something about a tapestry?" asked Romy. "It's supposed to be massive and really, really old. This tapestry is a big deal."

The troll scratched his nose and looked thoughtful. I looked around the atrium. Was there anyone else around? Maybe we'd try one more person before we picked the next magnet? I caught a glimpse of a woman just as she disappeared from view around a corner. I didn't get a chance to see her face, but the moment I saw the swirly, psychedelic skirt and the oversized red basketball shoes, I knew who she was.

"That's Miss Pesky," I gasped, pointing after her.

"What?" said Romy and John together.

"She went that way," I yelled, sprinting away from the desk, the backpack slapping against my shoulders as I ran. Romy and John weren't far behind me.

"There's a seminar on how to use something called a shower just finishing up now—you can catch the last five minutes!" the troll shouted after us.

Chapter 31

MISS PESKY WAS DELIGHTED TO SEE US.

"You three are in my eighth-grade science class," she gushed.

We had followed our teacher around a couple of sharp turns and finally caught up with her when she slowed down in the middle of a busy intersection. There were lots of people and a few fairy-tale-like creatures milling around, and Romy kept gasping and grabbing my arm every time she thought she spotted a goblin. John had gone quiet again, muttering under his breath and looking worried.

"You three are in my science class," repeated Miss Pesky.

"Yeah," I said, wondering why she wasn't asking us why we weren't at school. Actually, why wasn't *she* at school?

"What are you all doing here?"

"We're looking for something called the Tapestry of Tales," I said, getting straight to the point. I also wanted to ask her about her FFTC tattoo and confirm that she, like Captain Argus, was a former fairy-tale character. And then find out what all that meant. But I'd get to that later.

"Never heard of it," she said, shaking her head. She had on big dangly earrings that swayed from side to side. "Did you ask at the information desk?"

"Yeah," said Romy. "He didn't know anything."

"Well, Enutrof knows everything about everything," mused Miss Pesky, rubbing her chin. "If he hasn't heard of a tapestry . . . well." She shrugged. "No one here would know anything about it."

My heart dropped, and I felt a wave of panic. How was it possible that Belle and the Evil Queen were the only ones who knew about the Tapestry of Tales? Enutrof—a troll in charge of INFORMATION and a huge fairy-tale book—had never heard of it. A former fairy-tale character had never heard of it. If they hadn't heard of it, how were we going to find someone who had? Maybe we should go back to Paris and wait for Madame Fredepia to show up? But there were police there. . . .

"Want to join me for dinner?" asked Miss Pesky, cutting into my thoughts. "We can go to the Happy Hearth."

Miss Pesky looked at me, Romy, and John, and then Romy and John looked at me, obviously waiting for me to make the decision.

The Happy Hearth sounded like a restaurant. There'd be people there. People I could ask about the tapestry. We could try another magnet or we could ask more people, and Miss Pesky might have helpful information, even if she didn't realize it. She was a former fairy-tale character. She might have met fairy godmothers.

"Okay," I said.

"It's just over here," said Miss Pesky, pointing at a cottage that looked like it had been airlifted out of a fairy-tale forest and dropped into the tunnel. It was storybook perfect, with a slanting thatched roof, windows with tiny glass panes, and wild white roses growing up the walls and spilling over the top of the front door. There was even smoke coming out of the chimney. A sign saying THE HAPPY HEARTH was hanging on the front door.

"This looks a bit too perfect," said John. He stared at the cottage and grimaced. "You know, like, too perfect . . . like 'Hansel and Gretel' perfect . . ."

"You think there's a witch in there who'll want to eat you," observed Romy knowingly.

"Wouldn't be the first time," muttered John.

"Miss Pesky, are there any witches in there?" I said, pointing at the cottage. "Or really, anyone"—I added; witches weren't the only ones in fairy tales who ate people—"like an ogre or a giant or really anything or anyone who would be interested in eating us?" I couldn't blame John for feeling anxious after the close encounter he'd had. And he was right; the cottage did have a gingerbread-house "Hansel and Gretel" vibe.

Miss Pesky looked thoughtful for a moment. A little too thoughtful. Thoughtfulness is not what you want to see when you've asked someone if there is a chance that you might be eaten.

"Well, I've never heard of anything like that happening

at the Happy Hearth," she finally replied. "You go there to eat, not get eaten."

"Well, that's good enough for me," said Romy, starting to move toward the entrance.

"And the food is so much nicer here than at the school cafeteria," said Miss Pesky. "The bibimbap is delicious."

"There's Korean food?" asked John, brightening.

"Kimchi . . . galbi . . . ," continued Miss Pesky.

That seemed to settle it. John moved so quickly, he got to the front door before Romy. He held it open as Romy, Miss Pesky, and I walked in.

A hum of conversation hit me as we entered. The place was tiny—not much bigger than Madame Fredepia's apartment—and it seemed like every table was packed with happy diners. "It smells amazing," said Romy as she inhaled deeply.

Whatever was cooking had onions, garlic, and spices in it, and it smelled delicious.

"You grab a table," said Miss Pesky, gesturing at four women who were leaving a table in the farthest corner of the restaurant. "I'll get the food."

We walked toward the table. The four women smiled

at us as we approached. They were all wearing white coats as if they worked in a hospital or a laboratory. I realized that a lot of the diners were wearing uniforms. On the way to our table, we passed a fireman, a policewoman, a postal worker, a construction worker with a hard hat and a bright yellow vest, and even a man in a race-car driver's uniform. Everyone seemed to know each other; there was a lot of conversation and smiles and passing of plates going on between tables. I wondered how they'd all react if I stood on a chair and said, *Does anyone know anything about the Tapestry of Tales?* That was probably what I'd have to do if Miss Pesky didn't have any helpful information.

The three of us sat down. Miss Pesky joined us a few moments later and put a tray in the middle of the table. "Help yourselves," she said. We reached for the bowls of steaming noodles and started tucking in.

"So, Miss Pesky, you're a fairy-tale character, right?" I asked, taking a forkful of noodles.

"*Former* fairy-tale character," answered Miss Pesky, emphasizing the "former" as if she were really proud of it, like "former" meant "general" or "professor" or "doctor."

"Like Captain Argus," mumbled Romy, speaking with her mouth full.

"Yes," said Miss Pesky. "We're all former fairy-tale characters." She stretched out her arm and pulled up her sleeve, revealing the tiny tattoo on her wrist that I'd seen during class. Just like the one Captain Argus had.

"Everyone here?" whispered John, holding up his spoon and gesturing at the table next to us. "Everyone here is a former fairy-tale character?"

I was surprised that John sounded totally shocked and amazed; then I realized he might not have known, like Romy and I did, that Miss Pesky had the same FFTC tattoo as Captain Argus. But really, so what if Miss Pesky had been a fairy-tale character and all the people in the restaurant had been too? Compared to the other news we'd had today, that my mom was going to be stitched into a tapestry, it wasn't that shocking.

"And you're a science teacher now," said Romy matter-of-factly.

"Well, I thought I'd be better at home economics, but there was an opening for a science teacher, and I'm taking some classes here—"

So, there was more than learning how to get around a grocery store and take a shower on offer for the former fairy-tale characters; that was good. What was this place? I glanced around at the other diners. Had they been trained for those jobs here? Was this where Captain Argus had learned to fly too?

"Oh, I forgot the salt," said Miss Pesky, pushing back her chair. "I'll be right back."

"I'm glad people are getting out," said John, looking around at the diners. "You know, out of their fairy tales." He took a bite of his food. "When you guys were getting ready for the wedding, I went and I met the Beast."

Romy and I looked at each other. I didn't know what to say.

"I don't know," said John, even though Romy and I hadn't asked him anything. He shrugged his shoulders. "I just wanted to talk to him—to see him—I guess after, you know, what happened to me—"

Romy and I nodded. Yeah, we knew.

"Anyway, it was awful. Really sad. He's in a room, and it's a nice room . . . it's big . . . but he can't leave it because of the way he looks. So, it's a prison. And he's really angry.

He did this." John touched the bruise under his eye. "Not deliberately; he just started throwing things, and the side of a candlestick hit me. And I remembered feeling that way. How I felt so mad, like I wanted to burst out of my skin. Sure, he gets a break when the wedding happens and he gets to be normal for a bit, but then it's back to being a monster. It's not fair."

"Salt," announced Miss Pesky, putting the saltshaker on the table.

John reached for a plate of pickled cabbage.

"Which fairy tale are you from, Miss Pesky?" he asked.

"You wouldn't have heard of it," said Miss Pesky, shaking the salt over her food. "It's not a very exciting story. Though I've been told the Brothers Grimm might have written it down."

"Can you tell us?" asked Romy. "Cia and I have read a lot of them."

"Well, there was a young herdsman," began Miss Pesky. "And he wanted to get married, and he knew three sisters. Each one was just as beautiful as the other, so it was impossible for him to choose which one to marry. So, he asked his mother for help and she said, 'Invite all three and set some cheese before them, and watch how they cut each slice.' So, he did just that. The first one ate the cheese with the rind on. The second hastily cut the rind off the cheese, but she cut it off so quickly that she left a lot of good cheese on it and threw that away also. The third peeled off the rind carefully and cut off neither too much nor too little. The herdsman told all this to his mother, who said, 'Take the third as your wife.' And so he did, and they lived happily ever after."

There was a stunned silence as the three of us let the details of Miss Pesky's story sink in.

Romy spoke first. "So, is the cheese a metaphor for something else?"

Miss Pesky shook her head, her earrings brushing against her cheeks. "I don't think so."

"That's it? That's the whole story?" wondered John. "Nothing else happened after all the cheese was eaten? No one had to find something or rescue someone? You know, like a quest?"

Miss Pesky shook her head again.

"Is that actually a fairy tale?" asked John, turning to me. He lowered his voice. "Shouldn't there be some magic or something?"

"Doesn't have to be," I whispered back. "A lot of them don't have any magic in them. At all." A lot of them were also really boring. But there was no way I was going to say that in front of Miss Pesky.

"So, who were you in the story?" I put as much enthusiasm into the question as possible. Miss Pesky looked sad, staring into her bowl as if she might find a better plot for her fairy tale at the bottom of it. I thought about what Mom had said about how important it is that people get to tell their own stories. And I remembered the rush of pride I'd felt when Anansi had whooped and applauded after I'd finished telling him about how I'd destroyed the Groac'h's potion. None of us had applauded Miss Pesky's story. We'd just sat silently and asked her (possibly rude) questions. No wonder she was trying to disappear into her bowl.

"I was the second sister," she answered.

"Ah, you cut off too much cheese with the rind," said Romy, as if she too had often cut off too much cheese with the rind.

"Sister number two," said John.

Sister number two?

"You know my mom, Helena Anderson. Don't you?" I asked excitedly. "Sister number two" was the contact name I'd seen on Mom's phone. How had I not connected it to fairy tales? Most of the characters in the Brothers Grimm tales had no names; they were just known by their jobs. "Herdsman," "swineherd," "miller's daughter," "baker," or "the second sister" . . . I'd read so many of them; how had I not made the fairy-tale connection when I saw Mom's phone?

Something else hit me. This was the information the queen had given to the fairy godmothers—that Mom had a "sister number two" in her contacts. Because that was the information that I'd blurted out in front of the queen. I got a sickening feeling in my stomach.

"Yes!" gushed Miss Pesky, her face breaking into a huge smile. "I know your mom!"

"How do you know her?" asked Romy, glancing quickly at me and then back at Miss Pesky.

"She led me out of my fairy tale," said Miss Pesky matter-of-factly. "She led all of us out."

"Led you out," repeated John, putting down his bowl so suddenly that broth splashed onto the table. "What do you mean, she led you out?"

What was Miss Pesky talking about? I caught Romy's eye. She smiled at me, but she looked worried too. What had Mom been doing?

"I was on my way to the herdsman's cottage to—" She took a sip of her water.

"Eat cheese," added Romy encouragingly.

"That's right," continued Miss Pesky. "And Helena—" She paused and smiled at me. "Your mother. She turned up and explained everything to me. She said that I was living in an abandoned adventure and that there was a whole world outside of the forest, and that I could . . ."

"Write your own story," I said, finishing Miss Pesky's sentence.

"That's right," said Miss Pesky, grinning. "How did you know?"

"That's something my mom always says," I explained to Miss Pesky and John. *To me.* That was something my mom had always said to me. Why was she telling fairy-tale characters to do it? The more Miss Pesky spoke, the more confused I got. Why was Mom swiping characters out of fairy tales?

"If it wasn't for your mom, I'd still be eating cheese

and never getting picked," said Miss Pesky with a sigh. "Only having the one dress to wear over and over again." I guess that explained why she wanted to wear as many things as possible now. "She's helped so many of us—" She gestured around the Happy Hearth, but it had emptied out. There was only one diner left besides us and the rosy-cheeked man serving food behind the counter.

"Mom helped all of you," I repeated, thinking about all the people we'd seen since we'd landed in this strange place. There had to have been at least fifty. My mom had helped all of them?

I was starting to feel light-headed. My heart was thumping too fast in my chest, but it felt like it was sinking into my stomach at the same time. Was Mom running some kind of resettlement program for fairy-tale characters? She must have led Captain Argus out of his tale too. And what about that double-crossing goblin, Tragus? How long had this been going on? Was that why she'd taken all those research trips? Was "research" just a cover for what she was actually doing—breaking people out of fairy tales?

"Your mom," said John, leaning back in his chair. He sounded a bit awestruck. "Your mom's a—"

I could tell he was about to say a bad word to describe something good, but he caught Miss Pesky's eye. "Awesome. Your mom is awesome," he repeated.

"Thanks, John," I muttered. I guessed it was awesome that Mom had saved Miss Pesky from a lifetime of eating cheese and wearing one boring dress and never being picked—and who knew how many others from their not-so-exciting fairy-tale lives.

"I have to head back to school," said Miss Pesky, getting up from her chair.

"Back to school?"

At some point since entering the Happy Hearth, I'd forgotten that Miss Pesky was our science teacher. It took me a moment to understand what she had just said.

"Yes," she said, lifting up her arm and showing me the tattoo on her wrist. "I flash this at the gate at the end of the tunnel and back I go." So, that was why she had the FFTC tattoo—it was like a bar code or a key. Maybe it acted like one of Madame Fredepia's travel magnets?

"Oh," I said, suddenly feeling deflated, though I guessed this was good news for Romy and John. I looked at them. "I guess you guys can just go back, too." There was no reason they should stay with me, especially since it could get dangerous. It was my mom that was in trouble, not theirs.

Romy made a sound that was half laugh, half grunt. "What is wrong with you?" she said, frowning, reminding me of the way she'd looked when I told her I thought I'd failed a math test last semester. "There's no way we're just going to leave you!"

"This is a rescue mission," said John. He sat up straight in his chair and looked me firmly in the eyes. "You don't walk away from a mission."

I couldn't help it—I started laughing. It was mainly nervous, borderline hysterical laughter, but there was some real laugher in there too. John sounded like he was a marine and the three of us were an elite trained fighting unit, not three kids with a backpack of magic magnets and no clue what to do next.

"Okay," I said, looking down at the table, afraid that if I looked at either Romy or John I might start crying.

"Well, I have to go," continued Miss Pesky. "Thanks to your mom"—she beamed at me—"I have a class to teach!"

Romy, John, and I sat in silence for a moment,

watching Miss Pesky bounce happily out the door. I guessed teaching eighth grade would be a total dream if you'd spent years (how long had it been?) trapped in a cheese-themed fairy tale.

I thought about what Miss Pesky had told us. So much of it didn't make sense. If Mom was leading characters out of fairy tales, why was Belle still trapped in hers? Why hadn't Mom led her out of her story? Why didn't Belle just walk out the way Miss Pesky had?

Belle had looked terrified when Carabosse showed up. What was it Carabosse had yelled at me, Romy, and John before she had spelled us? She had shouted, *They have upset the balance of the tales.*

They have upset the balance of the tales.

I felt a wave of nausea hit me. Mom had upset the balance of the tales. No, it was more than that. She had turned them upside down. A sister number two had become a middle-school teacher; a woodcutter was now a pilot. I'd seen a woman in a police uniform at the table next to us. . . . What had she been before joining law enforcement, a shepherdess? How many fairy tales had Mom interfered with?

Carabosse had been furious at us for helping Hildee

get married and at Belle for delaying her wedding. How would she feel about someone who had upset hundreds of tales?

She'd be furious. She'd be furious enough to . . .

"It's Carabosse," I croaked. My throat felt tight. Romy and John were staring at me. "It's Carabosse who wants to stitch Mom into the tapestry." I grabbed the backpack off the ground.

"Carabosse used a spindle and a spinning wheel to activate her curse in the 'Sleeping Beauty' story," I explained to John and Romy. "Sewing is her thing."

Why had it taken me so long to connect her to the tapestry?

Chapter 32

I OPENED THE BACKPACK AND TIPPED IT OVER AS Romy and John raced to move away the plates and bowls and put them on the tables beside us. The magnets came pouring out, clattering as they hit the table. I spread them out so we could see each one clearly. It seemed like there were even more of them than before. It was as if they'd multiplied while they were in the backpack. "We have to find Carabosse. We find her, we find the tapestry. And we'll find Mom."

"Okay. We'll find her," said Romy firmly.

I scanned the mass of magnets for one that would

make me think of Carabosse, but I didn't know what I was looking for. I grabbed one that said THE EMPIRE STATE BUILDING and put it inside my sneaker.

"I bet she's in Italy," said Romy, holding up a magnet that had POMPEII written on it. "That's where the 'Sleeping Beauty' story started." She put the magnet to one side and stared intently at the table. "I'll find all the Italy ones," she muttered, reaching over and seizing one that said FLORENCE. "I'm sure I saw Rome somewhere."

"I see Milan," said John, pointing at the table. He sounded a bit breathless, even though he was sitting down.

My stomach was cramping; I wished I hadn't eaten so many noodles. I stared so hard at the table that all the magnets blurred together. What if Romy was wrong about Italy? There were French versions of "Sleeping Beauty" too. We couldn't waste time focusing on the wrong country. Carabosse might be threading her needle right now.

Carabosse might be threading her needle right now.

"Look for one with a needle on it," I yelled. "Or a thing of thread, or a spindle." I didn't actually know what a spindle was, but I felt like I'd know it if I saw it.

We all put our hands on the table and leaned over it. It

was so quiet in the Happy Hearth that I could hear Romy and John breathing. An image popped into my head. The massive hourglass in Belle's castle with the sand spilling out. What if we were out of time? What if the sand had already run out for Mom? What if she was already in the tapestry?

I let out a groan.

"Got it!" shouted Romy, punching the air with her fist. She flung herself across the table, sending dozens of magnets flying. "I got it, Cia!"

I held out my hand, and Romy dropped a red magnet into it. It was one of the smaller ones, no bigger than the tip of my thumb.

"Yeah, this is it." I took a deep breath and stared down at it. The image on it was definitely a needle, but it made me think of something else too. Something that made me shudder. It made me think of a wand. One end for gripping, the other for pointing. "Yeah." I exhaled. "This has got to be it."

I held the backpack open, and John pushed the magnets off the table into it. Romy picked up the ones that had fallen onto the floor and dropped them in.

I zipped it up, tightened the straps, and put it on my back.

"Let's go," said Romy, handing me the whisk that I'd left on the table. "You need this."

We stepped away from the table. I placed the magnet on the floor, and the three of us stood in a tight circle around it.

"You all ready?" I asked. Feeling a swell of gratitude for Romy and John, I wiggled the back of my foot and felt the smooth edges of the Empire State Building magnet in my sneaker. We'd get Mom, and then we'd all go home together.

Romy reached out her arms and grabbed one of my hands as well as John's. John placed his other hand on the lower part of my arm just as I pointed it at the magnet. We all stood so close to each other that I could hear John and Romy breathing. I squeezed Romy's hand and glanced at John, who gave me a small, determined smile.

"Transfer!" I shouted just as a buzzing noise started to rise from the magnet.

It was the third time we had used a magic magnet—as John had called them—and this time it felt different. It was as if I were riding in a very fast elevator, traveling up at a tremendous speed. The air that I pushed through felt cool and then warm and then cool again. Then, just like the previous two times, just seconds after it had started, it was all over.

Chapter 33

THE TAPESTRY WAS ALL I COULD SEE, AND FOR A microsecond—in the moment we arrived—I forgot about everything. I forgot about finding Mom and worrying about a mean, control-freak fairy. I was so mesmerized by what I was seeing, by the vastness and beauty of the tapestry, that there wasn't space in my brain for anything else.

Beside me Romy and John gasped. That was all I could do too. Just gasp.

Staring at the tapestry gave me the same feeling I'd had when I'd seen the Grand Canyon on a sixth-grade class trip. It had been so big, it had made me feel absolutely tiny. I felt the same way now.

"It's like I want to yell and shout," said Romy softly. "But I want to whisper too."

Romy's words reverberated around us.

I turned in a circle, taking in our surroundings. The tapestry was in front of me and behind me and on both sides of me. I stepped back, trying to get a better view. But I felt like even if I was looking at it from the distance of a mile, I still wouldn't be able to find where it began and where it ended.

The air felt cool and smelled of pinecones as if we were outside, but I looked up and saw an enormous vaulted ceiling above us.

"Looks like we're in the right place," said Romy, gazing around her.

"I thought a tapestry was just a big rug on a wall," said John, sounding stunned. "This is . . . this is . . ." He stopped and stood openmouthed, staring all around him. He couldn't seem to find the right words to describe what he was seeing. "Marco Polo was wrong. It would take years and years to look at all of this."

It felt like we were standing in the middle of a maze. All around us the tapestry rose up on huge pillars as high and wide as skyscrapers. There were narrow paths in between the pillars, wide enough to walk through, and the tapestry continued—inasmuch as I could make out from where I stood—down along the sides of these pillars, each path extending to some point that I couldn't see.

"It's so beautiful!" Romy sighed.

"There's a unicorn," said John, pointing at a spot on the tapestry.

The tapestry was ablaze with colors. Greens, blues, reds, oranges, purples, and pinks. The colors and images were so bright, it seemed like they were moving. My eyes swept across the swath of fabric in front of me. I saw animals . . . bears, wolves, horses, pigs, and sheep. There were magnificent castles with turrets and charming cottages, paths weaving through forests and waterfalls cascading down hills. There were sweeping vistas of green valleys and mountain ranges and clusters of picturesque villages. There were people too. I saw what had to be kings and queens, princes and princesses, all wearing magnificent robes and crowns. They were so lifelike that a horrible thought struck me. Could they once have been actual people? The Evil Queen's theory bounced around in my head. *Your mother will be stitched into the Tapestry of Tales. . . . Your mother will be stitched into the Tapestry of Tales.* We had to find Mom.

"What's that?" asked John, a note of alarm in his voice.

I looked in the direction John was pointing and followed his line of sight. There was movement on a patch of the tapestry, like ripples on the surface of a still lake just after a stone is thrown into it. It was there and gone in a second.

"There it is again," said John, pointing to another spot on the tapestry. There was the same rippling motion and then stillness.

"No," said John. "It couldn't be. Could it?" He ran his hand through his hair and stared at the tapestry. He looked amazed and confused, just like when Belle had told him about her having to get married over and over again.

What was John talking about? What was he seeing?

"It's code," he said. He took a deep breath and looked at me and Romy. "Guys, it's code."

"What?" asked Romy, glancing at me. "What does that mean?"

"Coding's like an instruction manual," said John excitedly. "So, when you code something you give instructions to a computer, and then the computer does what you want it to do."

"Okay," I said slowly, sort of understanding what John was saying, but also not really understanding. "But what's that got to do with the tapestry?"

"This is all the code," said John breathlessly, gesturing at the tapestry. "For the stories! You said there were, what? Thousands of them?"

Romy and I nodded.

"Well, there are thousands of stories here," continued John.

"Looks like it," I said, even though I didn't see any of the stories I knew on it. But that didn't mean anything; I'd only looked closely at a tiny bit of the tapestry.

"So, I think that the way the stories are shown here is how they"—John paused, obviously trying to find the right words—"play out, like, happen in our world. . . .

"Look, there it is again!" He pointed at another

rippling of the fabric. "Remember how Belle said that her story just ends when she marries the Beast, and then it restarts? Well, this—this tapestry—is what's controlling that. 'Beauty and the Beast,' that story, it's somewhere on this tapestry. All the stories are on the tapestry. . . ."

"Okay," said Romy slowly, like she wanted John to know she understood what he was saying, but she wasn't as excited as him about it. "That's all great. But remember, we're here to find Cia's mom."

"Yeah," said John, exhaling loudly and nodding. "Which way do you want to go, Cia?"

"I . . ." I thought about what I'd seen in the Evil Queen's mirror, what Mom had been standing in front of. "It's a scene with a field that's full of sheep, and there's a man with blond hair too."

"Okay," said John. "So, we're looking for sheep." He gazed at the yards and yards of tapestry and gulped. "That narrows things down a bit."

My heart dropped. This was a needle-in-a-haystack operation. There were thousands of stories on the tapestry, and hundreds of those probably had sheep in them. It would take years—with all three of us working separately—to find the spot that Mom had been standing in front of when I'd seen her in the mirror. And how did I know she was still even there?

I stood rooted to the spot, intensely aware of Romy and John waiting for me to say something. Should we split up and cover as much ground as possible? But the tapestry had a mazelike layout—we might all get lost and never be able to find each other. Should we just yell out Mom's name? But there was an echo; the fairy godmothers— where were they anyway?—would hear us. I stared at the whisk. What else could the wand do? I felt a little pulse of hope. Maybe it could tell me what to do? Maybe, if I asked, it would point us in the right direction?

"Oh no," whispered John. "It's her."

I whipped around and saw Carabosse flying toward us, her black cape flapping behind her like wings. And she wasn't alone. There was a man approaching us too, though he was walking. He wore an orange-and-yellow robe.

"That's Anansi," I whispered, the dread I was feeling at seeing Carabosse easing a little. I turned to John. "He's nice. He's the one who helped us at Madame Fredepia's." But what was he doing here?

I wasn't sure if John had heard me. His eyes were glued to Carabosse, who was now within a couple of feet from where we were standing.

"Where is Fredepia?" she roared. "Her wand was just used!"

I instinctively put the wand behind my back. But it didn't make any difference.

"How dare you enter the hallowed ground of the tapestry!" she boomed.

My hand jerked forward, and the whisk flew out of it and into Carabosse's outstretched hand. She stuck it into a fold of her cape. "I'll take that too!" she yelled, and my backpack fell to the ground and went sliding toward Carabosse.

Beside me Romy muttered a curse under her breath.

"You need to hold your tongue," she snapped, pointing her finger at Romy. Romy's hands flew to her face, and she slapped both palms in a crisscross pattern across her mouth. Her eyes filled with fear and shock. She whimpered and grunted and pumped her elbows up and down as she tried to break free of the spell that had superglued her hands to her mouth.

Every bad word I knew exploded in my head. I wanted to scream them all at Carabosse. She was a monster. Out of the corner of my eye I saw John clenching and unclenching his fists, struggling like me to control his anger. But we wouldn't be able to help Romy if Carabosse spelled us too. I glanced at Anansi, willing him to do something. He was standing a little apart from us with his arms folded, a slightly amused expression on his handsome face.

"Temper, temper, Carabosse," he said, examining the sleeve of his robe. He looked up and took a step closer to Romy. "Let's hear what the girl has to say." He placed two fingers on her hands, and they fell away from her mouth. Romy gasped for air and clutched her chest as if she'd just been pulled, almost drowning, from water. She leaned over and grabbed her knees, shaking and whimpering.

I ran over and put my arms around her.

"What are you all doing here?" asked Anansi, looking at us with an interested smile.

"We want . . . ," I began, loosening my grip on Romy and standing up straight so I could look Anansi directly in the eyes. I wanted to talk to him, not Carabosse, who was glaring at me, Romy, and John and tapping her foot impatiently as if she couldn't wait to be rid of us. "We want my mother. I've come to take her home."

"Your mother?" said Carabosse disbelievingly.

"Yes," I answered, still looking at Anansi. "I know she's here. And I know she upset some of you . . . because she . . . " I paused, feeling my heart thumping in my chest. Mom had upset the balance of the tales, but I didn't want to use the same words as Carabosse. I remembered what Miss Pesky had said. "Because she led some people out of their fairy tales."

Anansi exploded with a big booming laugh that reverberated all around us. I exchanged an uneasy glance with John—Romy was still doubled over—that I'd been hoping Anansi would help us. Why was he laughing? What had happened to Mom wasn't funny.

"Your mother is a thief!" roared Carabosse. "Stealing characters from their tales. Causing havoc! Meddling and interfering! She thought we wouldn't notice if she didn't touch the big stories, thought she'd get away with it if it was just a woodcutter who went missing, or a sister number three who didn't play her part—"

"Well, you didn't notice for ages," said Anansi matter-of-factly. "Took you years and years."

"She messed with your work too, Anansi," snapped Carabosse. "She interfered with our masterpiece." Carabosse raised her arms and gestured at the tapestry all around us. "Hundreds of years of work. We created and she—"

"Modified?" interrupted Anansi, winking at me.

"DESTROYED!" roared Carabosse. "She destroyed our work."

Carabosse marched up to the tapestry. She pulled out her wand, and using it like a laser pointer, lit up a section of the tapestry about twenty feet from where she stood.

"There," she spat out the word. "Look at that. . . ."

There was a hole in the fabric, with blackened threads around the edges as if it had been burned.

"There! And there! And there!" shouted Carabosse, moving her wand around and lighting up other spots on the tapestry that were marked with black holes.

I began to understand what John had been talking about when he said that the tapestry was like code. When Mom led a character out of their tale, the portion of the tapestry that contained their tale was changed, and in the spot where the character should have been, a hole was created.

But I didn't care about all that. I only cared about

seeing my mom. "Where is my mother?" I shouted, wishing Carabosse would stop yelling. Anger flooded me. How dare she call my mom a thief? So what if Mom had made some holes in her precious tapestry? Mom had been helping people. Miss Pesky was happy now because of Mom. Captain Argus too. "Where is she?"

"Back where she belongs!" said Carabosse furiously.

"What?" I gasped. What did that mean?

"Your mother is back in her fairy tale."

Chapter 34

WHAT?

Had Carabosse just said that my mom was a fairy-tale character?

I turned to John and Romy, who was standing upright, her breathing back to normal. They both looked completely confused.

I looked at Anansi. He shrugged like what was going on had nothing to do with him.

My mind and heart were racing. It felt like the room was moving, and all the colors in the tapestry seemed to be blending together and swirling. Romy grabbed my hand.

"It's okay," I muttered, trying to clear my head. It was okay. So what if Mom was a fairy-tale character? She was still my mom. She was still the same person she'd always been. I'd met loads of fairy-tale characters, and they were just people—well, a few weren't actually people—but they were just like everyone else. I took a deep breath. All that mattered was finding Mom. It didn't matter that she was a fairy-tale character.

"Where is she?" I asked again, looking Carabosse firmly in the eyes. I squeezed Romy's hand tightly.

"Where she belongs," repeated Carabosse. "She's been stitched back into the tapestry."

I felt a rush of blood roaring in my ears. My knees buckled, and Romy and John caught me before I fell to the ground. We were too late.

"Unstitch her!" I shouted, leaning on Romy and John. I fought against the awful tightness in my chest, resisting the urge to burst into tears.

"You want to take her place?" said Carabosse, giving me a wolfish grin.

"NO!" shouted Romy, letting go of my hand and stepping in front of me.

Carabosse pulled her wand from her robe and tapped it against her palm.

"We do have a lot of vacancies." She sighed, gazing up at the tapestry. "You—" She pointed at Romy. "You were so supportive of Cinderella's stepsister getting married. It was quite touching. How about you take her place?"

Romy stumbled backward and grabbed my hand.

"And you," said Carabosse, turning her attention to John. "We're always short on woodcutters." She gave him an appraising look. "You'd make a fine woodsman."

"The tale of the black raven, that's missing one, isn't it?" Carabosse looked at Anansi for confirmation.

Anansi nodded.

"Your mother interfered with that one too," she sneered at me.

Carabosse rolled up her sleeves and rotated her wrists as if she were getting ready to spell someone. Spell three someones. I glanced at Anansi, who was puffing on a cigar, acting like he couldn't care less about what was going on.

"You don't get all three, Carabosse," he said, talking with the cigar in his mouth. "I need one for the tale of

Iyawo and her baby." He took out his cigar. "Your mother swiped wife number two out of that one," he said, winking at me.

No. Anansi wasn't going to help us.

"RUN!" I shouted, pulling on Romy's hand and whipping around to face John. "RUN!" We couldn't just stand here waiting for Carabosse (and Anansi) to do something awful. John sprinted toward a path in between two folds of the tapestry. If we could all make it down the narrow passage, maybe we could find something . . . someone to help us . . .

"AARGH!"

I was running, but my legs weren't touching the ground. I was being lifted into the air. My body started spinning, and something wrapped around me, pinning my arms to my sides and my legs together until I was completely immobile. I heard Romy and John screaming and jerked my head to see that, other than their heads, their bodies had been covered completely in silvery silk bandages. I looked down at myself. The three of us were wrapped up like mummies.

A web had been spun around us, anchored on the

opposite folds of the tapestry. We were each stuck in our separate cocoons, and each cocoon was suspended in the web. I was in the middle. If I turned my head to the right, I could see Romy, and I could see John if I turned to the left.

"Comfortable?" asked Carabosse sweetly.

Behind her, Anansi, now a massive black spider, crawled away.

"Why are you doing this?" screamed Romy.

"I am guarding our stories," hissed Carabosse. She paused dramatically and gazed at the tapestry. "We are the creators of these tales. We have to protect them."

Some part of me recognized that this was really big news. It was possible that Romy, John, and I were actually the only people in the world who knew who had created the fairy tales. (Although maybe Mom had known all along too?) But I didn't care. I just wanted to not be stuck in a web. I just wanted to get my mom. I just wanted to go home.

"Now, don't go anywhere," joked Carabosse, wagging a finger at us. "I'll just get the bowl I use for the amnesiac enchantments."

"You're going to make our families forget about us?" said John in a heartbreakingly small voice.

"Of course!" said Carabosse brightly. "We're not monsters, you know. This way no one will ever notice you're gone. No one will miss you at all."

She turned and strode off, her dark cape flying out behind her.

No one will miss you at all.

I thought about Dad and Riley. Would I just be wiped out of their memories? So, it would be as if Dad had never had a daughter. Riley had never had a sister.

"NO!" Beside me John was straining against the bindings, trying to break out. His neck muscles bulged from the effort as he used all his strength to push against the cocoon, but it made no difference at all. He let out a desperate sigh.

"I'm glad Hildee made it out," he said, his voice breaking. "I'm glad she married Hugo. I hope they made it to the mountains."

"Maybe she'll come get us," said Romy. "She'll find our fairy tales and break us out. . . ."

I turned to look at my best friend. Tears were streaming down her face. We both knew no one would be able to find us.

"Romy and John, I'm so sorry," I said. "I'm so sorry for everything."

"It's okay," whispered Romy.

"Not your fault," muttered John.

But it wasn't okay, and it was my fault. My heart felt like it was breaking into a million pieces.

BANG!

A blinding flash of pink light illuminated the tapestry, and I closed my eyes, bracing myself for Carabosse's return, but when I opened them, Madame Fredepia was standing in front of us.

Chapter 35

"WE'RE SAVED!" SHOUTED ROMY.

"You are not saved," said Madame Fredepia, giving Romy a stern look. "I'm in enough trouble already without breaking the three of you out of that web." She waved a piece of paper at us.

"They're shutting down my bakery. Saying I've been practicing magic without a license," she said, reading from the piece of paper. "It is outrageous. So what if I sprinkled a little love potion into my apple fritters? You can hardly call that practicing magic! That's just helping people!"

"Madame Fredepia, please," I pleaded. How much

time did we have before Carabosse came back? "It's Carabosse. She's going to stitch us into fairy tales. You have to help us!"

"I can't take on Carabosse," said Madame Fredepia, but she looked like she was thinking about it. "Who else is here?"

"We just saw Anansi," I said.

"Not great." She sighed. "Sometimes he helps. Sometimes he doesn't. You never know with that guy.

"No," she said, shaking her head and sounding resolved. "You'll have to figure this out for yourselves. I'm hanging on by a thread as it is." She pinched two fingers together to show us. "Just a thread with these people."

Madame Fredepia turned on her heel and walked away from us. Something dropped on the ground beside her, making a clanging noise. It was a pair of scissors. "Whoops," she said without turning around. She kicked her leg out behind her, and the scissors came flying toward us. The blades landed on the web within inches of my and Romy's faces. We both screamed. Madame Fredepia, still not turning around, raised one hand in the air and strode away.

I wriggled and pushed my body against the gash in the web between my and Romy's cocoons, trying to make it bigger. Beside me Romy was doing the same thing.

"Why couldn't she have just cut us out?" she asked, panting.

"Maybe this way she won't get in trouble," said John, angling his head awkwardly so he could see the scissors. "Cia, you've almost got it," he said excitedly. "The rip is getting bigger."

I forced my shoulder against the edge of the opening the scissors had made, concentrating every ounce of strength on that spot. It worked. The split got bigger and bigger. I pushed again, and my arms broke free of the cocoon. I grabbed the scissors and slashed at the web, slicing at the sticky threads that were trapping me, Romy, and John.

The three of us fell to the ground.

We were free. Relief flooded through my body.

It lasted about two seconds.

There was an enormous black spider crawling toward us.

Anansi was back.

"He's going to be so mad we ruined his web," whispered Romy, sounding terrified.

I gripped the scissors with two hands and held it out in front of me like it was a sword, but the thought of stabbing Anansi was so revolting and terrifying and impossible that my hands shook.

The spider came within three feet of where we were standing and stopped. It was monstrous. Its pincers, each one about the size of a man's leg, stuck out like two black fangs, and its four black eyes—the two in the middle were as big as bicycle wheels, and the two on the side were the size of dinner plates—stared unblinkingly at the three of us. There were yellow-and-orange stripes on the spider's head, just like the stripes on the robe Anansi had been wearing.

"I thought you said he was nice," whimpered John.

My whole body was shaking with fear. Now that I saw the huge hairy monstrousness of Anansi the spider, I realized that the scissors would be useless. Unless I got him right in an eye—and he had three more of them, so how much damage could that even do?—he'd hardly even feel a scissors piercing him.

"T-t-tell him a story, Cia," stuttered Romy.

"Yeah," I said, my voice shaking. A story. Anansi liked stories. "I ha-have a story," I said to the spider.

The spider's eight legs moved, and it came even closer to us.

"Make it a good one," whispered Romy. She had wrapped her arms around herself and was shivering.

I took a deep breath. I wanted to wipe my hands—my palms were dripping with sweat—but I was frozen like a statue. I couldn't move.

The spider turned and crawled away from us.

"No story then?" asked Romy.

"What's he doing?" said John.

The spider had moved about ten feet way. It turned around, faced us, came a little closer, and then turned again and crawled in the opposite direction. It did this three times.

"I think it wants us to follow it," said Romy. "Look, it just waved one of its legs. It wants us to follow it. . . ."

"What?" said John. "Into a bigger web?"

Romy was right. It did seem like Anansi wanted us to follow him. But what if John was right too?

Anansi had helped us once before, and then he'd

trapped us in a web. Madame Fredepia had said, *Sometimes he helps. Sometimes he doesn't.* What if there was some pattern to Anansi's actions? And now he was being helpful again? Or maybe it was more like flipping a coin, and there was no way of knowing what Anansi was going to do?

"Let's follow him," I said, putting down my arms and wiping my hands on my dress. What else could we do? Stay put and wait for Carabosse to show up with her wand and her amnesiac enchantment bowl?

As soon as we stepped forward, the spider picked up its speed and crawled onto the tapestry. We ran after it, racing to keep up as it scuttled across the walls of tapestry, following it along passageway after passageway until we were deep into the maze of colors and fabric that surrounded us.

"He's stopping," said John, panting and pointing upward.

John, Romy, and I stood and stared at the spot of tapestry that Anansi was covering.

"He's shrinking," said Romy. "Look!"

Anansi the spider got smaller and smaller, and the

smaller he got, the more the area of the tapestry that he had been covering was revealed. I saw a clearing in a forest. There was a woman standing in the clearing, peering at an iron box that was as big as a man.

The woman was my mother.

"It's Mom," I said, my voice catching in my throat.

I pointed up at the tapestry. Anansi was now about the size of a dime. I had to squint to make out that he was still a spider.

"Your mom?" whispered John, a note of awe in his voice.

I stared at Mom. She looked so young. She looked the way she did in the photograph that Dad had by his side of their bed. Her hair was so long, it reached her waist. I reached out to touch the tapestry.

"The scissors, Cia," shouted Romy. "Use the scissors!"

"Cut her out!" shouted John.

My hands were shaking so much that I wasn't sure I could do it. I put my left hand on the tapestry to steady myself, holding the scissors in my right. As I pushed the tip of the blades into the fabric, I felt heat rising from the tapestry. There was no resistance at all; it was as if I was pushing the scissors into butter. I snipped. A burst of brightness shot up through the tapestry, and Mom was outlined in tiny twinkling lights.

"It's working!" shouted John.

I made another snip along the outline of lights and Mom disappeared, a hole in the tapestry appearing in the spot where she had stood.

"Cia!" yelled Romy.

I turned around.

Romy and John were standing over a figure lying on the ground.

It was Mom.

"Mom!" I said, running over and getting on my knees. I threw the scissors down. "Mom, are you okay?"

She looked up at me and then Romy and John.

"Who . . . who are you?" she said weakly. She tried to get to her feet but started coughing and leaned back into a sitting position.

"Mom, it's me, Cia," I said. It *was* Mom. It was my mom. But it was Mom from fourteen years ago. The wrinkles around her eyes were gone. She had no gray in her hair. And she was looking at me like she'd never seen me before.

"Mom, your name is Helena Anderson," I said firmly, though my heart was skipping and thudding in my chest. "You live in Brooklyn. I'm your daughter, Cia. You have a husband. You have a son named Riley. He's only six. And . . ." She was listening to me, but the more I spoke, the more confused she looked. She had a dazed expression on her face. "You love them, Mom. You love us."

"No," she said shaking her head. "I have to try to rescue the prince."

"Cia," said Romy, kneeling down beside me. "It's got to be the amnesiac enchantment. She can't remember anything."

No. My heart dropped. No. This couldn't be happening. I'd found the tapestry. I'd found Mom. I'd cut her from the tapestry. She was *my* mom. She belonged with me and Riley and Dad in Brooklyn. She didn't belong to them. She didn't belong to Carabosse and Anansi. She belonged to us.

I felt rage flooding me. I wanted my mom back.

"Guys," said John nervously. "We've got company."

Chapter 36

I LOOKED UP. CARABOSSE HAD APPEARED AT ONE end of the passageway, and she wasn't alone. There were four caped figures with her. They were still too far away for me to make out faces, but none of them seemed round enough to be Madame Fredepia or tall enough to be Anansi.

This was bad.

I stood up and grabbed the scissors.

One pair of scissors against Carabosse and four others.

We were doomed.

"There's a dragon!" shouted John.

I stared down the passageway. The figures were getting closer, but I didn't see a dragon. What was John talking about?

"On the tapestry!" he yelled, waving his arms furiously.

I saw it. It was sleeping, but it still looked terrifying. Its huge body of red and green scales and enormous wings were wrapped around a pile of gold. Its mouth was slightly open, showing teeth that were as long as my fingers.

I understood what John wanted me to do. He wanted me to release a dragon. My heart skipped a beat. I felt like I was going to pass out. He wanted me to release a dragon.

"Just do it!" screamed Romy.

I plunged the scissors into the tapestry, right at the edge of the dragon's sleeping head, and cut the fabric—and, just as had happened with Mom, a trail of lights outlined the dragon and it disappeared.

"Run!" screamed Romy.

I grabbed Mom's hand and pulled her off the ground. She was still muttering about the prince, but I just held on to her hand and started running. Romy ran beside me, and John was a little farther ahead, sprinting with long strides. I didn't know where we were going or even what we were doing, other than trying to get as far away from Carabosse and the dragon as quickly as possible. I could sense the creature stirring, but I couldn't bring myself to look over my shoulder to see what was happening.

The ground beneath us started to shake. The dragon was waking up.

There were voices echoing through the passageway.

"Stun the beast!"

It was Carabosse.

"Don't let it burn the tapestry!" she cried. There was a note of panic in her voice.

I felt a blast of cold air push me forward. Mom screamed, let go of my hand, and fell to the ground. John wheeled around and ran back.

"I got her," he said, bending down and staring at Mom. "She's okay, Cia." He picked up Mom. She was as limp as a rag doll. He threw her over his shoulders, putting one of his arms across the back of her knees and the other on her elbow.

"They iced the dragon," whimpered Romy.

I looked behind me and saw a thirty-foot-tall ice sculpture. It completely filled the passageway, but through the ice, I could see Carabosse and the rest of her crew on the other side of it.

"Won't take them long to get through that," said Romy.

"I need a wand," I said, rubbing my heel against the magnet I'd put in my sneaker. We had Mom. We had the magnet. I just needed a wand to get us out of here.

Our eyes all turned to the tapestry. No one needed to say anything. I knew we were all looking for the same thing. A wand.

A shard of ice came flying toward us, narrowly missing hitting Romy in the head.

They were coming.

"What if you don't need one?" asked Romy as we took off running down the hall.

"You need a level twelve wand for a transference, Romy!" I said. Romy knew that. We'd done three of them already.

"But what if *you* don't?"

Romy and John stopped running and turned to face me. I couldn't stand the look of hope in their eyes. This wasn't going to work.

I kicked off my shoe and grabbed the magnet anyway.

Romy and John, with Mom on his back, stood beside me. I stared at the tiny Empire State Building, stretched out my hand, and pointed at it.

Just as millions of pieces of ice rained down on top of us, I shouted, "TRANSFER!"

Chapter 37

I FELT MY FEET HITTING A FLOOR.

Romy, John, and Mom landed beside me with a thud, sending a display stand of postcards crashing to the ground. We were in a gift shop full of tourist stuff—hats and sweatshirts and water bottles with NYC written on them. There was a middle-aged woman wearing a yellow vest behind the cash register. She took a step back, removed her glasses, and rubbed her eyes, staring at us with her mouth hanging open.

I glanced around. There was no one else in the store.

I bent down and picked up the postcards, putting

them back on the stand that Romy was repositioning as if we hadn't just appeared out of nowhere. "You did it, Cia," she whispered. I stared at the postcard of the Statue of Liberty I'd just picked up. I didn't want to look at Romy or think about what she was suggesting. I hadn't done *anything*. It was just the magnet we'd used! It must have been a super powerful one that didn't require a wand; that was the only possible explanation. I placed the postcard back on the stand. Beside me John was gently adjusting Mom's position on his shoulder. She was muttering and her eyelids were flickering. I noticed that John's bruise had bloomed into a full black eye. He looked terrible.

"Excuse me, are we in the Empire State Building?" I asked the woman behind the counter.

"This is the gift shop," said the woman, looking at us warily. "We're not even open. . . . How'd you guys do that . . . just appear like that?"

"With one of those," said Romy, grinning and pointing at a tray of small fridge magnets—identical to the one we had just used—on the counter in front of the woman.

"What the—" began the woman.

"Let's go," I said, glancing at Romy and John and

heading for the door. Once the gift shop lady recovered from the shock of seeing us materialize out of nowhere, she'd call security.

Outside, I inhaled the smell of exhaust fumes and pretzels and caramelized nuts and just a hint of garbage. New York City had never smelled so good. Yellow taxicabs went whizzing by, and I felt a jolt of happiness. We were just a car ride away from home.

"Where am I? I have to get back to the forest!"

John carefully loosened his hold on Mom. She looked pale and scared. Her long hair was plastered against her face. He helped her to stand on the sidewalk and guided her toward a bench. I sat down beside her.

It was early morning, and there were a few people out with their dogs and others walking purposefully toward the subway, clutching coffees in one hand and phones in the other. No one gave us a second look, even though Romy and I were wearing ripped, sweat-stained party dresses (and I was missing a shoe—I'd left it at the tapestry, I realized). One of the pant legs of John's tuxedo was ripped to shreds as if he'd just had a close encounter with a vicious dog, and Mom looked like she was on her way home from a Renaissance-themed costume party.

"Mom," I said, taking both her hands in mine. What was it Miss Pesky had told us? What had Mom said to her to get her to leave her fairy tale? "Mom, the forest and the prince . . . that's not where you belong."

Opposite us a man was opening his hot dog stand, pulling down the shutters. Mom watched him, mesmerized, as he arranged bottles of mustard and relish on the counter.

A look of pain crossed Mom's face. She put her hand up and touched her forehead as if she had a headache.

"Look around you, Mom," I said. "You're not in the forest anymore."

She shook her head and turned her gaze upward, craning her neck back as she looked up at the buildings.

"It's New York, Mom," I said gently. "You brought me and Riley here last week to go to a show. You and me, we loved it, but Riley said there was too much singing. . . ."

Mom's eyes veered back toward me. She had a confused, searching expression on her face. She lifted both her hands and covered her mouth and nose. She gasped and then, over the tips of her fingers, her eyes smiled at me.

"Cia!"

She grabbed me into a hug. I felt myself go limp with relief, and happiness flooded through me. Over Mom's shoulder I saw Romy and John smiling at me. Romy bounded over and threw her arms around me and Mom. John stuck his hands in his pockets and looked at the ground. I pulled away from the hug.

"Mom, this is John Lee."

"Nice to meet you, Mrs. Anderson," said John, extending his hand toward Mom. "Big, big"—he gulped and blushed—"fan of your work."

"Thank you?" replied Mom, giving John a questioning look. I saw that her wrinkles had come back and that her hair was shot with gray. It made me feel ridiculously happy.

Mom's face fell; she stared at John and touched the top of his cheek. "Are you hurt?"

"Nah," he said, dipping his head down and pushing his hair over his forehead. "This is nothing."

"What about you two?" said Mom, giving me and

Romy a concerned look as she took in our stained, ripped dresses.

"We're fine, Mom," I said, smoothing down my hair and straightening out my dress. One of the buttons popped off, and a sleeve tore away from the shoulder seam.

"How did you all get to the tapestry?" asked Mom, sounding amazed. She squeezed my hand. "How did you even know about it?"

"We—" I stopped. I didn't want to talk about me and Romy and John. I didn't want to talk at all.

"Mom, how did *you* get to the tapestry?"

Mom stared at me for a moment, then at John and Romy, her eyes focusing on John's bruise and Romy's ripped dress. Then she looked ahead, as if she were trying to make up her mind about something.

She stood up.

"There's a place one block from here," she said. "Come on, let's go."

Mom led us to a nail salon called Posh and Polished. It wasn't open for business yet, and Mom was just lifting her hand to knock on the door when it was flung open by a tall man with dyed blue hair.

"What an honor," he said, looking at Mom with a mixture of admiration and delight. He then looked at me, Romy, and John, took a step to the side, and bowed low like a knight in a fairy tale, which was probably what he'd once been. Mom never, ever got her nails done. If she knew this man, it must have been because she'd rescued him from a story.

"Hello, René," said Mom, gesturing at me, John, and Romy. "This is my daughter and her friends. We're just looking for a quiet place for a bit."

"Come in, fair ladies and sir," said René, leading us to a table at the back of the salon. "So humbled that you would grace my establishment with your presence."

The four of us sat down. Me and Mom on one side, Romy and John on the other.

"René was a cupbearer in a French fairy tale," said Mom as René walked away, still talking about how honored he was. "The tale of Prince Darling. He's much happier now," she said, smiling to herself. "Though he acts like he's still in a royal court." She turned to me, frowning. "Do you think his manners might be a bit over-the-top for the customers?"

"No, they're kind of nice," I said. Mom was asking for my opinion on how a fairy-tale character was adapting to life outside his fairy tale? My heart swelled with surprise and relief.

"So, you want to know how I got to the tapestry," said Mom, picking up the conversation we'd begun when we were outside. She glanced at me, then looked at Romy and John. "I'll start from the beginning," said Mom. "Or as far back as I can remember. . . . In the days when wishing was still of some use, a king's son was enchanted by an old witch and shut up in an iron stove in a forest."

Romy gasped.

"So, that's your fairy tale, Mom?" I asked. "We just read it!" I tilted my head at Romy, who was looking at Mom excitedly.

"The princess in that is awesome, Mrs. Anderson. She rescues the prince, climbs mountains . . . that was you! That's so cool."

"No," said Mom, giving Romy a small, sad smile. "I wasn't the princess. And yes, you're right, she has a cool

story. But that wasn't me. I was the miller's daughter."
She looked down, pulled at the rough brown material of
her dress, and raised her eyebrows. "They'd never dress a
princess in this."

"So, the miller's daughter," I said. I wanted Mom
to keep going, even though talking about her fairy tale
seemed to be making her sad. She was finally being honest with me, and I didn't want her to stop.

"Well, you know how that story goes . . . the bewitched
prince is trapped in an iron stove in the forest. Three girls
try to rescue him. A miller's daughter. A swineherd's
daughter. And then a king's daughter. The miller's daughter tries to rescue him first . . . that was me . . . but when the
prince realizes that she's not royalty, he sends her away."

Mom took a deep breath.

"Not what you'd call"—she looked at each of us and
gave a sad smile—"a starring role. I never even had a
name. Just 'miller's daughter.' And I served no purpose in
that story. All I got to do was scrape away at an iron stove
for twenty-four hours and say seven words." She paused,
inclined her head at an angle, and cupped her ear with
her palm. "'I fancy I hear my father's mill.' And then the

trapped prince would shout, 'You are a miller's daughter!'" Mom mimicked a booming, deep-throated voice. "'Go away at once and let a king's daughter come!'"

"So, you never got the guy," noted Romy.

"Never even got to *see* the guy," clarified Mom, giving Romy a serious look.

"But you got out," said John, frowning.

"I did," said Mom. Her face broke into a huge smile, and she put her arm around my shoulder and looked at me with such love that I felt embarrassed that Romy and John were seeing it. "And then my life really began."

"But how did you break out, Mom?" I asked, wanting to steer the conversation away from the emotional turn I was worried it was taking. The sides of my eyes were starting to tingle, and Romy was getting that goofy look she got when she watched sad inspirational movies. John had grabbed a bottle of purple nail polish off the middle of the table and was looking at the label like it was the most fascinating thing he'd ever seen.

"I started paying attention to other things in the forest. I heard voices, just snatches of conversation, and I found footprints and candy wrappers. Then one day I was going back to the mill, and I came across a campsite. I hid and I saw people and then I knew. . . . I started to remember. And once you start to remember, you can walk away."

"Remember?" said John, putting down the nail polish. "Remember what?"

"Remember that I had been someone before I was the miller's daughter."

"What do you mean?" I asked, my heart thudding in my chest. "That you were 'someone before you were the miller's daughter'?"

"Well, before they took me, I was someone else," Mom said matter-of-factly. "Before they put me in the fairy tale."

"They took you?" shrieked Romy. "What do you mean, they took you?"

"I thought you guys had figured that bit out," said Mom, looking at me, Romy, and John. "Carabosse and the others. They take people and put them in their stories."

"No," whimpered John. "I never thought that." He looked at me.

I shook my head. I'd never thought that either.

"That's horrible," said Romy, putting her hands over her face. "That's absolutely horrible."

Mom wasn't swiping characters out of their stories. She was rescuing people.

"You mean Belle and the Beast—they were, like, regular people before they became fairy-tale characters?" asked John.

"Snow White, Rapunzel, Cinderella, the Sea Witch?" muttered Romy, talking over John.

"Yes," said Mom, nodding. "They were all someone else before they became fairy-tale characters. But I think a lot of them signed up for it. Some people are happy to get a starring role. They think it's better than the real life they're living, and there's also immortality. That can be hard to say no to."

"Immortality?" repeated John. "You live forever if you're in a fairy tale?"

"Yes. You live forever and never get a day older than the day you enter it," said Mom thoughtfully. "Some think that's a really good deal."

Like the Evil Queen. She'd definitely have signed up for that.

"So, you walked out of your fairy tale, and then what happened?" asked Romy.

"Just figured things out. Met Cia's dad, went to college. Cut my hair—" She grabbed a handful of her hair. It was back to its usual color but not style. It was still down to her waist. "That's the first thing I'm doing as soon as we get home. Chopping this off." She paused and smiled at me. "Anyway, I couldn't stop thinking about all the characters who were trapped like I'd been, playing pointless roles that made no difference to what happened in the story with no chance at all at getting their own happily ever afters. So, I learned everything I could about fairy tales. Even got a PhD in it. Then I started looking for the stories that no one told anymore."

"Abandoned adventures," I said remembering what Miss Pesky had called her tale.

"That's right," said Mom. "And when stories aren't told, they fade away into the depths of the forests or the caves or the ruins of the cities where they were once told. That's where I'd go, and I'd tell them that there was a world outside their tale, and some would listen and some would not." A look of sadness crossed Mom's face.

"But what about Belle and the Beast?" asked John excitedly. "They're living in Paris. We met them." He looked eagerly at me and Romy. We nodded, and he continued, "Can't you just go and lead them out?"

"Their story is not abandoned," said Mom. "It lives. You've all heard of it. Everyone knows the story of 'Beauty and the Beast.' The force that keeps them in their story is much too strong for me. They can't be led out of their tale."

"But Hildee did it!" said John. "She's Cinderella's stepsister, and she married a guy—we were all at the wedding—" He grabbed the lapel of his jacket like it was proof that there really had been a wedding. "And they flew off together in a helicopter. . . ."

"Carabosse and the others will never let her go," said Mom. "Cinderella is one of the hallowed stories. Those characters can't walk away."

"But Madame Fredepia," I said. I couldn't stand the thought of Hildee going back to a life where she felt like she wasn't good enough and had to live with an awful mother who didn't love her. She'd been so happy when she married Hugo. Hildee deserved to be happy. "Madame Fredepia's the one who made sure Hildee could get away after the wedding—"

"Madame Fredepia's magic isn't powerful enough to keep Hildee out of her tale," said Mom firmly, narrowing her eyes at me.

"Well, what about Anansi?" I suggested. Hildee couldn't go back to being Cinderella's overlooked, unloved, and undervalued stepsister. "He helped us to find you when we were at the tapestry. Maybe he and Madame Fredepia could work together to—"

"Anansi?" said Mom wearily. "He's the one who took me from Paris to the tapestry."

She stared at me, Romy, and John.

"So, I went to Paris to stop the queen from carrying out her plan." She turned to me. "I already knew all about it. That night when I was packing, and you came into my room. I wasn't really packing for Istanbul; I was packing for Paris."

"Why couldn't you have just told me that?" I asked, starting to feel the same hurt and confusion I'd felt that night. But now, I felt something else too. Shame. It gripped my heart and tightened around it. Mom could have told me, but I could have listened to her too. If I'd done what she'd asked, just gone to school and trusted her, then

Gavin and the others would have been fine, and she'd never have been taken to the tapestry. "But I dragged John and Romy to Paris," I said, my voice breaking a bit, "and you mean we didn't have to go?"

"Yeah, you kind of dragged me there," said John softly. "But I had an awesome time. Well, maybe not the Groac'h stuff and the getting cursed. And stealing the *Mona Lisa . . .*"

"And getting stuck in a web," added Romy, shuddering at the memory.

"But the private jet—that was so cool," John said, grinning at Romy. "And the Rolls-Royce and those magnets." His eyes widened. "Finding out about Miss Pesky, seeing that tapestry . . ."

"And the wedding, before Carabosse showed up," said Romy, smoothing down her dress. "I got to be a brides-maid—"

"And Hildee wouldn't have met that duke guy if you hadn't made us go to Paris, Cia," said John, smiling at me as he said "made us go."

"Yeah!" said Romy. "That wedding would never have happened without you."

This was the longest conversation I'd ever heard Romy and John have without fighting with each other, and the way they were talking and grinning at me made me feel like I'd won the lottery or scored the winning shot in a basketball game or been voted class president. But there was still a tightness in my chest.

"But there's something else," I blurted out. "Mom, it's my fault you ended up at the tapestry." I spoke fast. I wanted to get the words out quickly. "I told the queen—I mean, I didn't mean to tell her—but because of what I said, she figured out what you were doing and then—"

"It's okay, Cia," said Mom. "It wasn't your fault. You didn't say anything the queen didn't already know."

"You mean . . . ?" I said. "She knew about your"—I stopped, thinking about what word to use—"your work?"

Mom nodded.

"But the way the queen looked . . . ," said Romy, leaning her elbows on the table. "When Cia said that thing about contacts on your phone. She looked all superior and evil, like she'd just worked something out." Romy sat back in her chair, flared her nostrils, and pulled her mouth into a half smile. It was a pretty good imitation of what the queen had looked like.

"What you saw," said Mom, looking at Romy, "was the queen figuring out that Cia didn't know that I'd once been in a fairy tale and that now I spend my time pulling people out of them. She realized that Cia didn't know anything about her own mother. I'm sure she thought she could use that information against me at some point."

Mom put her hand on mine.

"I'm sorry, Cia," she said, turning to me. Her eyes were full of concern. "I'm sorry I never told you the truth about fairy tales. All I wanted to do was protect you."

The tightness in my chest disappeared, but I got a lump in my throat.

I stared at the table, not wanting to look at Mom. She looked so miserable, it made my heart hurt.

"It's okay, Mom," I said.

It was okay. I could see why Mom hadn't wanted to tell me anything. For her, fairy tales meant imprisonment and suffering; of course she'd wanted me to stay away from them.

Fairy tales are dangerous.

Whenever Mom had said that, I'd felt angry and hurt. Angry because she had refused to tell me *why* they were dangerous. Hurt because I'd believed that she thought I wasn't smart enough and brave enough to be told. Now, I knew that she'd been right: fairy tales were dangerous, and—

"I was wrong, Cia," said Mom. "I didn't need to protect you; I needed to prepare you. And even though I didn't, you still"—she took a deep breath and exhaled loudly—"figured out so much. You were the one protecting me." She laughed softly. "You rescued me."

"I had a lot of help," I said, smiling at Romy and John.

"Yeah, you so did," said Romy, nudging John. She raised her arm and gave John a fist bump.

For a moment, no one said anything. Then Romy spoke.

"How did you stop the Evil Queen from carrying out her plan? From taking Gavin's bravery and the other kids' talents?"

"I made a trade with her," said Mom. "She promised to call off her plan if I gave her something she wanted."

"What did you give her?" I asked.

"A pair of shoes," said Mom matter-of-factly.

"A pair of shoes?" said John, looking confused.

"The iron shoes!" shouted Romy. She slammed her hand on the table.

Mom laughed and nodded.

"The iron shoes!" continued Romy, turning to John. "At the end of the 'Snow White' story, the queen is forced to wear a pair of hot iron shoes, and she dances until she drops dead." She gave me a big grin. She looked really proud of herself. "I told you, Cia, those shoes were the answer to everything!"

René gave us money for the subway back to Brooklyn. None of us made it to school that day—we were too tired—but John went to football practice. He told me and Romy about it over lunch the next day.

"After the globe-trotter warm-up, we did side shuffle drills—" he said, stopping to take a bite of his burger. Romy's eyes had glazed over, but I was trying to pay attention because even though I couldn't care less about what happened at football practices, John did. And he'd helped me rescue my mom, so I could listen to him talk about football.

Miss Pesky walked by our table, caught my eye, and smiled. When we'd gotten home yesterday, I'd asked Mom if Miss Pesky and Captain Argus and René and all the other people who'd been rescued from fairy tales were safe. Wouldn't the fairy godmothers find them and stitch them back into the tapestry? And what if they came looking for Mom again? Mom said they wouldn't. According to her, the Tapestry of Tales would now have to be moved, a project that took up to a hundred years—which wasn't a massive amount of time if you were immortal like a fairy godmother, but if you weren't, it was a lifetime—so, the fairy godmothers would be busy with that for a very long time, not hunting down missing fairy-tale characters.

I looked around the cafeteria, wondering where Gavin was. I'd seen him just before first period, and he'd told me all about his trip to Paris and meeting Elvira Queen. I'd listened to him, the knot in my stomach getting tighter and the lump in my throat getting bigger with every word he said. I'd met Elvira Queen just before he had. I'd jetted off to Paris to stop him getting hurt, and I didn't say one word about it. I felt like I'd lied to Gavin. I'd been feeling bad about it all morning.

"I've been thinking about something," I said. I put an elbow on the table and leaned my chin on the palm of my hand.

"What?" said Romy, narrowing her eyes. "You look super serious."

"I am," I said. I took a deep breath. "There's something I want to do, but I can only do it if you two are okay with it."

"What?" said John, putting down his burger.

"I want to tell Gavin what happened." I lowered my voice. "You know, about everything. Everything that happened to us in Paris—"

"Yeah, I get it," said Romy, nodding. "We wouldn't have gone if it hadn't been for Gavin winning the competition—"

"No," I said. "Well, maybe that's a bit of it, but . . . it's because . . . I want to tell him because he's my friend and he doesn't know about this amazing, wild thing that happened to me and"—I pointed at Romy and John—"you guys too."

I took a sip of water.

"I just don't know if you can be friends with someone

and not tell them something this huge about yourself." I'd been thinking about it all morning, wondering how I could sit beside Gavin in science class for the rest of eighth grade and never tell him about what had happened. Every time he mentioned his trip to Paris, I'd be cringing inside. I'd feel like a fraud.

"Gavin's cool," said John, looking thoughtful. "You can tell him stuff and he won't tell other people." He nodded. "I say we do it."

"Okay," I said, my heart swelling with happiness. I couldn't wait to tell Gavin.

"So, are you thinking the four of us could be some kind of a club?" asked Romy as she poured milk into a glass. "Like, after school? Maybe a book club. We could read all the fairy tales, and—"

"What about a travel club?" said John excitedly. "I've been thinking." He dropped his voice to a whisper. "If we could borrow magnets from Madame Fredepia, there's a lot of places we could visit, like—" He took a deep breath. "The Library of Alexandria and the Temple of Artemis—"

"We've got other stuff to take care of before we do that," said Romy, leaning in closer to John. She held out her palm and tapped two fingers on it as if she were about to go through a list of action items. "We need to make sure Hildee's okay. Let's stake out her stepmother's place, and if we don't see Hildee there, then we'll know she hasn't been stuck back in her fairy tale. And we have to check that the *Mona Lisa* is back in the Louvre, and if it's not, then we need to make an anonymous call to the French police." Anonymous was a good idea, even though the three of us now thought that French police had never actually been looking for us. On our way home on the subway yesterday, John had pointed out that the piece of paper Madame Fredepia was waving when she showed up at the tapestry looked exactly like the piece of paper we'd seen in the police officer's hands when he'd showed up at her apartment. It had probably been the notice to shut down her business and not a warrant for our arrests. (So, did that mean that the police officers were actually fairy godmothers pretending to be the police? That was another thing we needed to discuss.)

"And we need to get to a zoo so we can get rid of Carabosse's curses," added John. "I need to talk to a kangaroo."

"We've got until our sixteenth birthdays to do that," said Romy. "Loads of time."

I sat back in my chair, looking at Romy and John chatting about fairy tales and about our adventures, as if talking about them was no big deal. I felt so happy. I saw Gavin walking toward our table, holding out a tray. I waved at him.

He sat down beside me.

I turned to face him.

"Hey, Gavin—what are you doing after school?"

Acknowledgments

I owe a huge debt to my agent, Claire Anderson Wheeler, for your brilliant insights, hard work, and dedication to this book. Your suggestions on an early draft of *The Tapestry of Tales* led me to take it in a different, and so much better, direction.

I am so grateful for my wise and wonderful editor, Jessica Smith, at Simon & Schuster, Aladdin. Your feedback and guidance have made me a better writer, and this book is richer, funnier, and more creative because of you.

To the rest of the team at Simon & Schuster, Aladdin. You did it again! Thank you to Karin Paprocki and Sara Mensinga for the spectacular cover. Mike Rosamilia, the interior designer, for making the pages of this book beautiful. Christina Solazzo, managing editor. Sara Berko, production manager. Nicole Valdez, publicist. Nicole Tai, copyeditor, and Sarah Mondello and Kathleen Smith, proofreaders extraordinaire, who spotted—and fixed—my many errors and made this book shine.

I also want to thank:

The wonderful middle schoolers who read an early draft of *The Tapestry of Tales*: Riley Andrews, Blake Dennison, and Vanessa Hong.

My niece, Molly Lalor.

Cathy Andrews, Carrie Gentry, Rachel Garcia, Virginia Gorelick, Leshia Hoot, Jackie Keating, Alicia Reffett, Rosanna Martinez, Jennifer Newbill, and Alicia Reffett—book club friends for almost two decades—who have cheered me on (and cheered me up) on every step of the book writing/publishing journey.

My parents, Mary and Brendan O'Neill, and my in-laws, Krishna and Mohinder Kadyan.

My sisters, Ellie and Niamh, and bonus sister, Ulyanna.

My brother, Shane.

My daughters.

My husband.